BLOODLINE

MIKE BARON

WOLFPACK
PUBLISHING
— EST 2010 —

**WOLFPACK
PUBLISHING**
— EST 2013 —

Published in the United States by Wolfpack Publishing, Las Vegas

Wolfpack Publishing
6032 Wheat Penny Avenue
Las Vegas, NV 89122

wolfpackpublishing.com

Paperback ISBN 978-1-64119-840-0
eBook 978-1-64119-841-7

Library of Congress Control Number: 2019948564

BLOODLINE

WENDIGO

Zeke's was a ramshackle roadhouse out Highway 126 near Roxbury, not far from the river. Schlitz and Old Milwaukee glowed neon orange in the window. The parking lot glittered with broken glass, filled with pick-ups, cars, and a dozen motorcycles. It was nine-thirty July 31, faint orange glow peeking over the Baraboo Hills. Inside smelled of beer and peanuts, shells on the floor. Two Vermin out of Minneapolis took turns at the pool table in the back. Truckers killed a few hours with beer and darts before going home.

Josh Pratt kept an eye on the crowd from his perch at the bar nursing a Pepsi-Cola. Josh had been working the door for a week, making the rounds during the day seeking investigative work among Southern Wisconsin's ambulance chasers. Josh was five eleven with a buzz cut and tribal tats creeping down from his shirt sleeves. It had been a quiet week with only one falling-down drunk whom his old lady dragged home.

Josh didn't need the money, but a man can't just sit around.

It was Friday night and Zeke's interior volume rose precipitously. Half the crowd watched the Brewers vs. the Red Sox while the other half shouted to be heard over the old-fashioned juke box blasting Thorogood's "One Bourbon One Scotch One Beer".

Josh looked down the bar at the blonde perched on a stool staring into her cell phone, then up at the door. She'd been there since seven-thirty expertly swatting down one come-on after another, like a vaudeville performer with a tennis racket. A sasquatch in pegged jeans and a black leather vest with Vermin colors drifted over and leaned on the bar. His colors showed a deranged Ed Roth-style monster puffing an enormous spliff on a chopper. Josh watched him say something, the blonde looked up with a weak smile and shook her head.

Sasquatch leaned closer.

Every guy in the bar had clocked her as soon as she'd walked in like Glenda the Good Witch entering a cave of trolls. She was a diamond in a coal bin, a light that cured leprosy. She lugged a North Face backpack instead of a purse, giving her a down-to-earth quality. She didn't belong there, and every man knew it. That didn't stop them from hitting on her. They started thick and ended thin. Until Sasquatch, it had been twenty minutes since the last attempt.

The blonde was five two, long blonde hair hanging down

to her ass, a perfect heart-shaped face, green eyes that glinted fire, wearing a sleeveless white sun dress. Josh wondered if her over-the-shoulder purse contained a pistol. She appeared fearless.

Sasquatch had one hand on the bar and one on the angel's shoulder, oblivious to the fact that she was leaning back to escape his breath. Zeke behind the bar caught Josh's eye, nodded toward Sasquatch. Josh got up off his stool and slowly made his way down the bar. Half the patrons watched surreptitiously the other half oblivious. Up close the sasquatch was six four and would not have looked out of place on *Duck Dynasty*. His patch identified him as Wendigo. Josh squared up in his personal space. Wendigo looked at him with close-set eyes.

"Fuck you want?"

"The lady would like you to leave her alone." Wendigo opened his wet little fur-lined mouth. "She ain't said that."

"Please go away," the lady said.

"Wendigo knows when to go," Josh said.

Wendigo drilled a sausage-like finger into Josh's chest. Josh grabbed the finger with his left hand, inverted it and bent it backward toward its owner. Wendigo's mouth went 'O!' as Josh steered him like a motorized dolly toward the door. The Vermin in back put down their cues and followed. As they passed the bar, Zeke called out.

"Hey! I just called the county."

A cadaverous Vermin whose patch said Pete squared off

across the bar. "You want some?"

Zeke held his cell phone. "They'll be here in five minutes."

Josh walked Wendigo out with a wrist lock through the front door into the warm, humid evening. A car filled with kids turned into the lot, windows open. You could hear them laughing, loud rap booming from the trunk.

Josh walked Wendigo away from the entrance and let go. Wendigo threw a ponderous roundhouse which Josh ducked, slamming a knee into Wendigo's gut. The big man whoofed and bent over.

Pete and a friend ran out the front door, the guy in back whipping off his metal studded belt to use as a flail. Josh skipped toward Pete and side-kicked him hard in the sternum with the outer edge of his foot. Pete collapsed writhing in pain. The third Vermin circled Josh, grinning, whipping his one pound buckle like a bolo. A Columbia County cruiser crunched into the lot and hit the lights and siren, releasing one abruptly cut-off whoop. Bolo boy looked over, grinned and put his belt back in his pants.

"This your lucky day, boy!" he exalted, running his finger beneath his nose and snorking loudly.

A jumbo-sized deputy in a tan outfit got out of the cruiser and approached with a hand on his holster. "Everybody, calm down," he said in a stentorian voice fixing each in his glare. He turned toward Josh.

"What's going on, Josh?"

Josh had introduced himself to Deputy Carter when

he took the job a week ago. He always did that. He didn't like to bounce, but the dearth of investigative work made it necessary. He didn't have to work. But a man couldn't just sit around.

"Officer there will be no further trouble if these gentlemen will leave."

Carter glared at the three Vermin who stood in a triangle.

"Let's see some ID."

The bikers truculently produced their licenses. "Wait here a minute," Carter said, returning to his vehicle. Josh back-pedaled. The deputy took his time, returning ten minutes later.

"Jerome Curtis, you have an outstanding warrant in Hennepin County in Minnesota. Normally I'd take you in and notify our friends across the river, but it's late and I'm tired. So if you boys will just take yourselves out of my county, I'm willing to cut you a little slack. How 'bout it?"

Wendigo flipped Josh the bird. "This ain't finished, motherfucker."

Carter gave him the stink eye. Muttering, the Vermin went to their chops and popped up and down like mustelids. Their engines roared to life without baffles, a big fat finger to the squares. Loud pipes save lives. They rode down the road with a cacophony that caused glass to dance on the asphalt. Josh and Carter listened until the noise had diminished to a faint howl.

"What happened?" Carter said.

"Wendigo there was bothering a patron. Zeke asked me to remove him. Know anything about those guys? The Vermin," Josh snorted.

Carter stared down the road where the bikers had disappeared. "Third rate morons."

"Well huh. Truth in advertising."

"Glad to see there's nothing serious. Anybody dealing in there? I don't care about weed."

"Sir, I would not know. If they're doing it, I can't see it."

"Okay. Stay on the straight and narrow, Pratt. You're doing good."

"Thank you, sir."

"You may have to watch your back for a while."

"I'm aware of that."

CHAPTER 2

AN OFFER

Josh returned to the bar. New players seized the pool table, Melissa Etheridge was on the juke and life went on. He took his usual seat at the end of the bar close to the door and picked up his Pepsi. The parfait blonde got up from her stool, glided down the bar and sat next to him. She wore a flowery scent that made him want to rip her clothes off.

"Thank you for interceding on my behalf," she said. "May I buy you a drink?"

Josh held up his Pepsi. "Thank you, ma'am, I've got this. You waiting for someone?"

"Is it that obvious?"

Zeke followed her down the bar and handed her her drink.

"Thanks." She turned to Pratt. "What's your name?"

"Josh Pratt."

She offered cool fingers with pink polish. "Jane Franklin."

She was in her mid-twenties, pale blue eyes, long blonde hair. She had a red heart tatted on her bicep.

"Who you waiting for?"

Jane rested her chin on the back of her hand. "Boyfriend. He was supposed to meet me here at eight."

"Is he reliable?"

"He has been. If not tonight, tomorrow."

"Didn't he specify the day?"

"Not really," she said taking a sip of her drink. "I think I'll call it a night. Will you be here tomorrow?"

"Tonight and every night until I find a real job."

"What do you do, Josh?"

"I'm a private investigator when I can find work."

She looked him up and down. "Not what I would have guessed." She stood. "Well so long."

"Let me walk you to your car," Josh said.

"That's not necessary."

Josh stood, held the door for her and watched as she walked across the parking lot, her black heels making a crunching sound, to a blue Prius which beeped and flashed at her approach. He watched her drive off in the opposite direction of the Vermin and went back inside the bar.

Zeke came over. "You ridin'?"

"Of course."

"You might want to borrow my pick-up, those sunsabitches don't try to run you off the road."

"'Preciate that, Zeke, but I'll be okay. I'll take the back way out of here. I'll be home before those dumb bastards realize life has passed them by."

Zeke shook his head. "They ain't never gonna figure that one." Zeke was an ex-biker and Vietnam veteran who'd opened the roadhouse ten years ago. It was a favorite not only of bikers, but bicyclists riding the nearby River Trail. Zeke featured live music on Saturdays. A poster tacked to the bulletin board just inside the entrance advertised the James Eisele Blues Band.

The baseball game went into extra innings. There were no more incidents and Zeke shooed the last customer out at one. He and Josh were the last ones out. Zeke shut off the lights and stood on the stoop gazing up and down the highway. Aside from the lights of a few farmhouses gleaming in the distance all was quiet.

Zeke bopped Josh in the shoulder. "You gonna be all right?"

"See you tomorrow," Josh said and headed for his 2001 Road King Classic. After he got out of the joint, he reinstalled the baffles. He'd changed in prison. Most of it was due to reflection, but Chaplain Frank Dorgan had also had a profound effect on him. Before prison Josh had been angry all the time. A psychiatrist would have a field day with his tangled psyche. In fact, psychiatrists had. He'd seen several in the joint. Abandoned by his father when he was fifteen at a Bosselman's Truck Stop, Josh had made his way through life as a sociopath. No one taught him so he learned by observing.

The things his father taught he'd tried to forget.

Josh inserted his key and thumbed the big bike alive. He backed up and rolled slowly around to the rear, tires crunching on glass dust. It was a clear night, the fields lit by a half moon and splash of stars. Behind the green dumpster lay a cornfield. A rutted dirt road lay between the cornfield and the adjacent sorghum field and it was down this trail Josh carefully rode his bike. Soon he was surrounded by the gorse and locust that grew in the grooves between fields. Night scents of corn and clover overwhelmed him. He paused in the middle of the field to inhale.

Fifteen minutes later he emerged on Brewster Road, a snaky stretch that cut through coulee country. He rode Brewster slow, pausing to watch a doe and her fawn cross the road in front of him. Eventually he emerged on County Rd. AB which he rode south until it joined up with State Highway 12.

He got home around two in the morning, keyed opened his garage, wheeled the bike in, shut the garage and went into the house. His German shepherd mix Fig greeted him with lavish and slavish approval, leaping and licking. Josh crouched to ruffle the big dog's fur and murmur sweet nothings in her ear.

He took a shower and fixed a glass of hot chocolate. He sat in his barren living room with Fig's head in his lap, put his feet up on the scarred wood coffee table next to a disassembled panhead and opened his phone. Someone had left a message.

"Josh? Phil Bass here. We met at Dave Lowry's party.

Like to get together with you when you have time. Please give me a call."

Sighing, Josh deleted the call. He knew what they wanted. They wanted to buy him out.

OFFER

Josh bought the house in 2007 with money from an insurance settlement. Little old lady T-boned him at an intersection. She was driving a 1968 Dodge with a 383. Josh admired the car as he flew ass-over-teakettle. Somehow, he escaped serious injury, but he'd had the presence of mind to retain criminal defense attorney Daniel L. Bloom and was able to finance most of the house.

A modest three-bedroom ranch style with attached garage.

Then the developers began surrounding him with million dollar mini-mansions. Josh's lawn was less than perfect. Until recently, a '68 Camaro had rested on cinder blocks in the front yard. Josh made a point of greeting new neighbors with a six pack of IPA. Some found him disconcerting.

Two years prior he got in a beef with three Insane Assholes who confronted him at home and were shot to death by Madison police. Since then, neighborhood disapproval was palpable, and he had been waiting for their opening move.

After the MPD shot up his house he had it repainted and installed a fence around the backyard for Fig. He'd tamed his lawn. He sold the Camaro. Wasn't that enough?

Only Dave Lowry, who lived across the street and whose schnauzers he'd saved from a dog fighting ring, was in his corner. Now they were talking neighborhood association. Josh was there first, damn it. They would have sued him for bringing down property values if they weren't afraid of him.

Josh and Fig went to bed. Before getting in, Josh knelt, his head bowed in prayer.

"Dear Lord, I have spoken to you before about the trials of the Harley-Davidson Company. Please, Lord, I know you're busy, but the Harley holds a special place in our hearts. If you could find some way to help them rediscover their mojo, millions would be grateful. Amen."

Fig whined in sympathy and jumped on the bed.

The trouble with Harley was that they were now marketing a lifestyle instead of a motorcycle. Sure, the new eight valve was terrif, but an aging demographic had absorbed all the 700 lb. bikes it could, and now Indian was eating Harley's lunch thanks to the Scout, the most innovative cruiser in decades. Josh planned on getting one.

He fell asleep thinking about that new Scout.

Josh woke at seven, made coffee, chewed on Duck Dynasty Hickory Smoked Bacon Jerky and some bread, put on his sweats and went for a run, Fig loping easily at his side. The scarred asphalt had been replaced with velvet blacktop. The woods had been terraformed into perfect emerald lawns. Profligate sprinklers tossed water in his face. It felt good. So did the pounding through his legs. He ran two and a half miles, waving as a car passed, really pouring it on the last half mile. He turned around and ran home. He'd been doing it so long it had become a habit.

When he got home, a big buff guy in golf shorts, sandals and a knit pale-yellow golf shirt was just turning away from his front door. Josh walked up to him and smiled.

"Hello!"

The man stuck out his hand. He had a ruddy face and had probably played college football. He appeared to be about fifty. He stooped and petted the dog. "Nice doggie! Phil Bass, Mr. Pratt. I phoned yesterday."

"Oh sure," Josh said going in through his unlocked front door. He recognized Bass from TV interviews with his neighbors following the shoot-out. Bass had expressed his dismay and disgust. "Come on in. You want a cup of coffee?"

Bass followed him. "That would be great. You want to take a shower or something? I could come back. I live right up the street."

Josh went into the kitchen. "No prob. I like to cool off first or I just keep sweating."

Bass went into the kitchen. "How far do you do?"

"About five miles." Josh poured him coffee in an Indian mug, took out a bottle of milk. "There's sugar on the table." He poured himself a glass of water from the faucet and glugged it down.

Josh pulled out a kitchen chair and gestured for Bass to do the same. "Have a seat. What's on your mind?"

Bass sat and looked out the bay window at the seedy backyard, a covered hot tub on a concrete apron next to an overgrown lawn that ended twenty feet back with the last surviving stand of forest in the neighborhood. He sipped.

"Good coffee." He looked at the mug. He looked at the framed poster on the wall showing a scantily-clad young lady thrusting her butt while soaping down a chopper. "So you're a biker."

"Yup," Josh said fixing himself a cup with milk and sugar. He sat opposite Bass.

"I used to have a Yamaha 650 in college," Bass said. "Man, I loved that thing. Rode it to class every day, used it to pick up chicks."

"You don't ride anymore?"

"No," Bass said. "I lost control while cornering too hard in the rain and broke my wrist. Haven't been on a bike since."

Josh mentally tallied how often he'd crashed and broken things. "That's too bad."

"I miss it," Bass said. "I've even been thinking of getting back in the game, but my wife wouldn't allow it. I've got two girls in college. Maybe after they graduate. What do you ride?"

"Modified Road King," Josh said. "I've got a hard-tail in the garage I'm working on."

Bass nodded appreciatively. "You go to Sturgis?"

"Many times." Josh was patient.

"This land is worth a lot of money," Bass said.

Here it comes.

"We're prepared to offer you a half million for your place." Bass didn't blink or blush when he said it.

Josh set his cup down. "That's a lot of money." Josh had paid 250 ten years ago and had seen his assessment rise every year. The property was now valued at 350. His property taxes had risen accordingly. "Why do you want it?"

"We are looking into creating a neighborhood association. You know, an overview board that would be responsible for garbage pick-up, plowing. This is an ideal location for a clubhouse."

"Nobody contacted me about a neighborhood association," Josh said.

Bass colored. "Right now. it's just a handful of us. I hope I'm not out of line."

"Not at all. In fact. I admire you for having the guts to come ask. We both know what this is about. My house is an eye sore and I'm a menace."

"I didn't say that," Bass said.

Class differences went unmentioned. "Does Lowry know about this?"

"Dave is not involved in the discussions."

"Let me think about it, Phil. Leave your card if you've got one."

Bass reached for his wallet. "You bet. You have any questions just give me a call."

CHAPTER 4

SATURDAY NIGHT

Dan Bloom's death at the hands of the maniac Eugene Moon had cast Josh's incipient investigative career into temporary limbo. He'd lost two clients, but lucked out on the last, the Sioux blues singer Buffalo Hump, whom Elliott Geddings had hired him to protect. That had been last fall. Hump had survived that weekend, but Geddings hadn't.

Jobs were slow. Hence his current employment. Josh had since hooked up with criminal defense attorney Steve Fleiss who fed him summons to deliver and the occasional investigative job.

Fleiss was unavailable so Josh left a message. It was late afternoon by the time Fleiss phoned back.

"Sorry for the delay, I was golfing. What's up?"

Josh told him about Bass' offer. "What do I do, Steve?"

"What do you want to do?"

"I'm in no hurry to sell."

"Then don't. They're low-balling you. If you don't mind moving and wonder if they're serious, ask for a mil."

"That's what I figured."

"Hey what are you doing these days? I might have a job for you."

Josh told him.

"Okay," Fleiss said. "Just hang in there through the weekend. I expect to have something for you next week."

"Another summons?" Josh said.

"Can't speak about it 'til it happens. Talk to ya."

"Thanks, Steve."

Josh had dinner in Middleton before heading back to the club at seven. It was early August and in the eighties and Josh rode in a black tank top that showed elements of the dragon tat wrapped around his torso.

He didn't worry about the Vermin on the way to work. Josh cut toward Lodi on the Old Lodi Road, turned off on 113. At four in the afternoon, a half dozen choppers lined up outside the club along with a couple pick-ups and a Subaru with a bumper sticker: SPELUNKERS DO IT DEEPER.

As he backed his bike to the curb the white Prius slunk in and parked next to him, the crunch of glass beneath its tires the only sound it made. It had a VOTE GREEN PARTY! bumper sticker. Jane Franklin got out wearing a black and white shift that fell to just above the knees, black mules, black cats-eye shades and carrying a Coach computer pack that swung at her side.

"Josh!" she said. "How are you?"

"Good. Maybe he'll show tonight."

She shot him a hint of hurt that evaporated when she smiled. "I hope so. There's only so much baseball I can watch." She hefted the computer case. "I brought work."

Josh held the door for her. "What work?"

"I'm going for a masters in Cellular and Molecular Plant Biology at the UW."

They entered the cool, pungent room. It took a sec for their eyes to adjust to the light. There were a dozen people, half at the bar, four in two booths, and two on the pool table. James Eisele fiddled with his amp on the small stage toward the back. All eyes turned to Jane, then turned reluctantly away.

Josh nodded to Zeke. "What do you want to do?" he said to Jane.

"Produce more food. I spent a couple years with the Peace Corps in Paraguay, and I saw how they struggled to put food on the table. A lot of it was bad agriculture but a lot of it was seed stock as well. Imagine if we could double our corn or grain yield in the same amount of space through selective breeding." She took her usual perch.

Zeke came over with a can of Pepsi. "Anything happen?"

"Yeah," Josh said, popping the tab and glugging. "My neighbors want to buy me out." Josh explained while Zeke tutted.

"You knew that was coming," Zeke said. "You a menace to society, bwah!"

The front door opened, and four Road Warriors entered

bringing with them the scent of dust, motor oil and body odor. They took a booth. Zeke's bartender Julie came out from behind the bar to take their orders. The Brewers battled the Red Sox on the tube. James Eisele twanged his guitar and shouted to the sound man. As far as baseball and Josh were concerned every day was Groundhog Day. He didn't "get" baseball. He'd never played it as a kid. He hadn't played any sports. He got in a lot of fights.

The club quickly filled, sports fans positioning themselves where they could see one of the five flat screens hanging from the ceiling. The din approached that of a 747 taxiing for take-off. Every stool was taken.

Around nine Zeke came over. "The Road Warriors are snorting meth off the tabletop."

Josh ambled over. They all looked up, one hurriedly shoving some works inside his vest pocket. The closest Road Warrior had a ginger mane and beard, a big rawboned look and a pug nose. His patch said "Sylvester".

Josh leaned in, hands on the table. "Gentlemen, the management kindly requests that you do not imbibe controlled substances in the establishment as it could very well lead to the loss of his livelihood."

Sylvester blinked a couple times. "Sorry about that, bro. We won't do it again."

Josh thanked them and returned to his seat.

Electric blues filled the room.

Shortly after ten two pool players came to blows. Without warning one shoved the other who fell to the ground pulling down a center-stand table along with two glasses of beer and some condiments. He came up swinging his pool stick. James Eisele, an aging longhair in a vest, duck-walked to the edge of the stage and flung power chords at the combatants. Josh raced to the back of the bar, slipping and sliding sideways among the crowd. Pool cue's first swing missed as his target leaned back and Josh caught the swinger in a Nelson. Josh let go the Nelson, ducked when Pool Cue swung on him and smacked him hard with the flat of his hand on the side of his head.

The swinger staggered, prepared to rush.

"Wait a minute!" Josh snapped. "Time out!" He made the T-sign with his hands.

"What?" Pool Cue said.

Josh pointed to the door. "Out. Both of you."

They looked at each other. They looked at Josh. Pool Cue was a big, buff farm boy with a shaved head and a silver earring. The other guy was a roundish Latino with long eyelashes and a mustache.

"Come on, man," said the Latino. "Let's go."

Pool Cue looked around for support, found none, tossed his cue on the table. "Fuck you, man," he said, head down, heading for the exit.

"Gee!" someone said. "I hope they're not driving!"

Everyone laughed.

Jane left at eleven. Josh followed her into the parking lot until she had pulled out onto the highway. A Columbia County sheriff's car lurked in the shadows at the edge of the road. Josh waved and went back in.

Zeke closed the bar at one without further incident. Josh took the farm trail running between fields to Brewster Road. He'd gone perhaps five miles on County AB when headlights appeared behind him.

ROAD ANGEL

Three bikes, lights on high. Josh did not like riding fast at night. He rolled around a gentle curve in the road and a pick-up truck barred his way. On one side was a steep ditch and a barbed wire fence. On the other, a fallow field. God knew what lay in it. Josh didn't want to take the chance. If he went into the field route the pick-up would just run him down.

Josh stood on the brakes and brought the big Harley to a halt by the side of the road. He set the kickstand and got off, hand going to the five-inch balisong in his pocket. He wanted a gun, but ex-cons weren't supposed to have guns.

Josh backed into the field as Wendigo got out of the truck grinning, slapping a tire iron into his palm.

"Hey there, Yogi Bear!" Wendigo boomed. The other three Vermin pulled up behind Josh, parking their bikes in a line by the side of the road. The four formed a semi-circle backing Josh into the field. He could run for it. He was pretty sure he could outrun and out jump these jive-ass motherfuckers, but they would almost certainly destroy his bike. He looked around for a weapon, a club, something to keep them at bay.

The guy on the left had a shaved skull and a gut that preceded him, highlighted by the bulge of his white T-shirt, over which he wore a denim vest. Gut, tall guy, short guy, Wendigo. More than enough to stomp Josh into jelly. Gut twirled a tractor chain. Tall guy smacked brass knuckles into one hand. Short guy clutched something Josh couldn't see. And Wendigo had a tire iron.

"You shouldn't have FUCKED with us, boy!" Wendigo boomed.

"Now we're gonna fuck you up," Gut said.

Josh backed up, one foot crunching an aluminum can. There weren't any decent rocks in the field. Soon he would have his back to barbed wire, unless he leaped the fence and jack rabbited. He would take Gut first. They wouldn't expect him to rush them.

"Think you're tough?" the short guy said.

"We gonna make an object lesson," Wendigo said.

Gut twirled his chain so that it whistled. "S'matter, tough guy? Cat got your tongue?"

At first Josh was unaware of the sound, just another insect chirping in the dark. It turned into the rumble of a V-twin. Everybody froze. There wasn't time to move the truck out of the way. A rider appeared around the bend from the west, slowed as he approached the roadblock, finally coming to a complete stop. There was enough ambient star and moonlight to see that he was big. He stopped in the middle of the road and kicked out. There was a moment of silence.

Wendigo gestured for him to go around the truck. "Keep moving."

The big man kicked out and got off.

"Get the fuck outta here!" Wendigo bellowed. "What are you, stupid?"

The big man walked to the edge of the road at a slight elevation to the field, put his hands on his hips and looked down. He wore black leather pants that covered hand-tooled snakeskin boots and a black leather vest over a Bruno Mars T-shirt. His black head was shaved. Four gold rings dangled from one ear and there was a gold chain around his neck

"Fuck's goin' on, fellas?" he said in a conversational baritone.

The gut turned around twirling his chain. "Get the fuck outta here, Jimbo. This ain't your business."

"Jimbo?" the big man said. "Is that like some kind of racial slur?"

"What part of get the fuck outta here don't you understand?" Wendigo said.

The intruder looked at Josh. "What about you, holmes? Four against one—what's that all about?"

"A minor misunderstanding," Josh said.

"You need any help?" the big man said.

"I wouldn't turn it down."

"Well alrighty then," the big man said, striding down the embankment straight at Gut, who spread his feet and twirled the chain faster. It was like staring down a freight train. The big black guy strode right up to Gut as he lashed out with his chain. Big guy caught it at the half swing, let it twine around his arm as he kicked Gut in the gut with a size fourteen boot. All air left Gut who sat down hard on his ass. The big man tossed the chain and turned as the others rounded on him, lashing out backwards with his right foot like a mule, smashing Gut in the head.

The little guy threw his rock. The big man caught it like a softball in his right hand and tossed it with deadly accuracy right back at the littlest Vermin, catching him square in the forehead with a sound like an ax hitting meat. The little guy went down. The two remaining Rustlers looked at each other. Every instinct told them to flee but they couldn't just abandon their brothers.

"Tell you what," the big man said as if he were ordering a hamburger. "We'll help you load this horse meat in your truck and then you can leave. How's that sound?"

Josh picked up Gut's chain and held it loosely in his hand facing Wendigo, who tossed his tire iron in the ditch. "Fuck it," he said in defeat.

Wendigo and tall guy loaded the little guy in the back of the truck. The big man stooped and hoisted Gut, who must have weighed 250 lbs. as easily as a sack of rice and unceremoniously dumped him in the back of the pick-up, which groaned in protest. Only then could Josh see the big man's colors. The patch on the front read, Vice President, Jugan M/C.

The Jugan MC. Their symbol was the flat, placid face of a Mongol in an 11th century helmet. The bottom rocker said Dodgeville.

Leaving their chops by the side of the road, Wendigo and tall guy got in the pick-up, did a Y-turn and booked. The big man and Josh stood on the patchy tarmac until the truck's taillights disappeared around a bend.

Josh stuck his hand out. "Josh Pratt."

The big man did the clasp, the shake, the bump and the slide. "Bobby Hines."

"Thanks, bro. Why'd you stop?"

"I didn't like the odds."

"You won't believe this," Josh said, "but this is the second time this has happened to me."

CHAPTER
6

ASSIGNMENT

Josh explained about the Rustlers.

"A jive-ass crew, a rum lot," Bobby observed dryly. "You have a good day now."

"I will thanks to you, Bobby," Josh said. They rode together to the Sauk City crossing where Bobby headed west, and Josh headed south.

Sunday morning Josh ran, showered, and attended the ten o'clock service at Bethel Baptist Church, a small country parish west of town. Pastor John was a good, simple man like Chaplain Frank Dorgan, and he rode a 2004 Bonneville. Pastor John would be the first to tell you that the bike was an extravagance and false pride, but he was otherwise doing his best.

Josh went home, fed Fig, played ball with her in the back yard and worked on the Basket Case Harley in his garage until it was time to go to the club. The Rustlers' bikes were gone by the time he rode past the site of last night's imbroglio. He hoped they'd got the message. It was seven-thirty when he arrived at the club. There were already a half-dozen chops, several pick-ups and a shiny new Cadillac CTS in the lot. No white Prius.

Inside, the joint was hopping, Carrie Underwood on the juke. Zeke waved from the far end of the bar where he poured whiskey. No green-eyed girl. In her place sat a buff middle-aged man with short silver hair wearing a light gray sport jacket over a plain black T. Zeke said something and pointed at Josh. The man got up and came down the bar.

"Lew Franklin," he said.

Josh took his hand. He could see the resemblance in the bone structure and the eyes. "Josh Pratt."

"You know my daughter Jane?" Franklin said.

"I've met her."

"She's disappeared. I understand you're a private investigator. I'd like you to find her."

"She was here yesterday, Mr. Franklin. How could she disappear?"

"According to her neighbor she never returned to her apartment. My ex-wife and I are very concerned."

"How old is Jane?"

"She's twenty-six. She just got back from two years in the Peace Corps in Paraguay. She's dangerously naive."

"She's an adult. She was waiting for her boyfriend. I suggest you give her a day or two and if she's still missing in 48 hours you should go to the police."

Franklin pinned him with arctic blue eyes. He could have starred in some soap like *Dallas* or *The Good Wife*. "Are you a private investigator?"

"Yes, I am, sir. I'm speaking from experience. She told me she was waiting for her boyfriend. Likely he came."

"Zeke told me how you interceded on Jane's behalf."

"How did you know to come here?"

"I called her neighbor. Thank you for helping her."

"Just doing my job."

"Her boyfriend is a dangerous thug. He's an ex-con and a motorcycle hoodlum. I am very concerned he's going to get her hooked on drugs. He's behind her erratic behavior. She was never like this before. She needs to be deprogrammed. I have friends who speak highly of you. I will pay you generous compensation."

"To do what?"

"I told you. Find her."

"And that's all?"

"Yes. I need to know if she's all right."

"What friends?"

"Lud Newton, Heinz Calloway."

Josh met Charlotte "Fig" Newton when she hired him to look into her brother's death. A UW senior with an NFL tryout, Stan had been found naked and drowned in Lake Mendota following a night of late-night drinking. Josh eventually traced his murder to a federal judge who had concocted a scheme to kill white college athletes at random in retaliation for "white privilege". The judge had resigned and was currently under investigation for sex crimes.

Fig, the only truly great woman Josh had ever known, died at the hands of the maniac Jesuit. Josh beat himself up about it every night.

"I would be happy to locate her for you if you like. I get 200.00 a day plus expenses."

"Let's make it 300," Franklin said, reaching for his wallet. He peeled out six hundred-dollar bills and handed them to Josh. "Here's a two-day advance. I require a report every evening around six if it's convenient." He took a little spiral notepad from inside his jacket pocket and jotted notes. Keeping track of expenses.

Josh took the money and stuck it in his wallet. "I need pictures, a list of her known associates, and all the information you can give me on this boyfriend."

"Give me your e-mail address," Franklin said. Josh pulled a card from his wallet and handed it to Franklin who gave Josh one of his.

Franklin Farms, Dodgeville, WI/World's Best Breeder Service/President and CEO Lewis M. Franklin

Josh took out a small spiral pad and a pen. "Tell me about the boyfriend."

"Carl Kuhn. Calls himself Orlok. He's the Big Poo-bah of the Jugan biker club, a bunch of degenerates and drug addicts."

"Have you met him?"

Franklin reached inside his jacket and withdrew a white envelope. He took out a photo and handed it to Josh. It was a black and white police booking photo of a man with a head like an artillery shell, no neck, a G.I. Joe beard and eyebrows criss-crossed with scar tissue. Kuhn's name was written on the back.

"I got that off the internet."

"Do you know how Jane met him?"

"I think it was an online chat room. God knows what those two have in common."

"How do you know Calloway?" Josh said.

"An employee of mine died in Madison two weeks ago. He was struck by a hit and run driver and died instantly. Detective Calloway is investigating. My daughter does not have the best choice in men. I don't know how or why she started corresponding with this creature while he was still locked up, but apparently he has some kind of hold on her."

"Did you say he was a Jugan?"

"I did. Calloway told me that. He recommended you because you're a biker and are familiar with the gangs."

"That's true."

"He told me you are an ex-con and that you found Jesus in prison. Is that true?"

"Yes."

"I got no problem with that. I did a little digging and discovered that Kuhn is a decorated Marine, a twenty-year man. You can understand my concern."

"Yes, sir, I certainly do."

"Then I leave you to it. Let me know as soon as you find her."

Franklin laid a twenty on the countertop and left.

CHAPTER 7

WHITE BOY

The internet had revolutionized investigations. A savvy tech could accomplish more out of his mother's basement in Belarus than the type of gumshoe personified by Humphrey Bogart and the Continental Op. Josh had taken several investigative seminars at the university and knew how to acquire criminal records without leaving his home. Beyond that he relied on Aaron Kofsky, co-founder of Dovetail Inc., a search engine company that worked for the Defense Department, and Randall Kleiser, former "Anonymous," now a Dovetail employee.

Josh knew his strengths and weaknesses. He was honest, indefatigable and had a forceful personality when necessary. He was plodding and thorough and always performed due diligence. But in the new age of electronic data and the internet he was a fossil. He could disassemble a Harley engine and put it back together blindfolded but when it came to finding stuff on the internet he was as lost as your grand-mother.

There had been no incidents on the ride last night and he'd slept well. After his run and shower he sat at his monitor in his office and dug. Carl Kuhn had formed the Jugan four years ago upon his discharge, precipitated by his assault on a superior officer. No charges were filed.

Kuhn's criminal record began at age eighteen in West Allis, a Milwaukee suburb. Young Carl liked to joy ride. A judge had given him a choice: the Marines or prison.

Kuhn thrived under Marine discipline and applied to Instructor school at Camp Pendleton where he taught hand-to-hand combat. He was a devotee of Okinawan karate. Josh found a video of Kuhn breaking a wine bottle cleanly with a *shuto* strike to the neck.

Kuhn served a total of eight years ten months overseas, most of it in Afghanistan. His military records were beyond Josh's meager abilities. Maybe Kleiser could help.

Kuhn just got out after serving two years for manslaughter. Bar fight.

All Josh had to do was find the girl. It shouldn't be that hard.

Jane had recently returned from a two-year stint in the Peace Corps and her FB album contained numerous photos, with or without Jane, of Paraguayan markets, jungles and people. She was "in a serious relationship". Her last entry was three days ago. Josh sent her a friend request.

Josh searched Iowa County plat records and tax rolls to

learn the exact location of the Jugan property. He used Google Earth to look straight down on the unspoiled patch of earth, seventy per cent wooded with a pond, several springs, and spectacular rock formations.

Like most MC clubs the Jugan had a website. The main page featured their colors with the helmeted Mongol, bio, credo, and mail-order ginseng.

Credo: Brothers bonded in blood, united by God, family and country, dedicated to the pursuit of the open road. If you ain't ridin', you ain't livin'.

Award-winning ginseng: Grand Prize for Most Trusted Company and #1 in American Brand Power recognition in the American Health Food industry, Jugan Ginseng is consistently rated a top brand in health food categories. Winner of the Grand Prize in Health Food category in the American Brand Power Index. Winner of the Grand Prize in the Most Trusted Company Award.

There was no way to identify individual members. The only pictures were of their bikes, nicely modified bobs and choppers, mostly Harley, one Honda 750 hard tail, and some crazy ass sixties-era Triumphs that somehow still ran.

The Jugan weren't on the National Gang Center's database. Their page described them as a group of mostly ex-military who enjoyed riding, socializing and good works. Every year they sponsored a Children's Toy Ride and BACA, Bikers Against Child Abuse. Josh could relate. The group photos could have been anyone. The only differences between the Jugan and other one per centers was their mixed races and shaved or close-cropped skulls. Their page featured a statement of support for the military.

"We are serious fun-loving men who like to ride and grow ginseng."

Bobby Hines had a Facebook page. Josh sent him a request and noted a picture of Bobby partying with his fellow Jugans in a bar beneath a poster that said, "When you're out of Point you're out of town." The Stevens Point Brewery brewed Point Beer, which for years was a local secret. In the eighties, the success of the *Badger* comic book increased Point's profile so that by the turn of the century they were shipping their beer to all 48 contiguous states. Josh went through Bobby's picture file and came to a pic of the boys lounging around their choppers in front of Chief Konapacki's Bar and Grill, a cedar and shingle roadhouse with a cigar store Indian by the front door. Chief Konapacki's was located on County II in Monroe County, a stone's throw from the Jugan compound.

Bobby accepted Josh's friend request.   Josh messaged him.

Josh: *Hey.*

Hines: *How you doing, white boy?*

Fine, thanks to you. Can I buy you a drink?

You know where Chief Konapacki's is?

No.

Go west past Spring Green. Go south on 130 til you come to Spring Valley. West on Spring Valley til you come to II. South on II three miles. Can't miss it. It's on the west side of the road.

Look for the cigar store Indian. Come around six tomorrow.

C U then.

Josh felt an electric jolt travel up his spine in slo-mo. Here we go. He'd been a drifter and a troublemaker for most of his life. Thanks to the grace of God and Chaplain Frank Dorgan, he'd undergone a profound change in prison, a rigorous, twisting inside-out of the soul. Pride in honest work came with it. Finally, he was off the bouncer beat, helping people and getting paid for it.

Thank you, Lord.

Ex-military would be savvy internet users. Josh had nothing to hide. He'd gained a degree of notoriety two years ago because of the Eugene Moon massacre. The maniac killed a half dozen people before being killed by his adopted son, the animal child. It was the type of grotesquerie Wisconsin relished in the tradition of Ed Gein and Jeffrey Dahmer, soon replaced by new sensations.

Then the shoot-out with the Insane Assholes. For a couple weeks the media pursued Josh like some kind of one man murder magnet. They made much of the fact that he'd had two girlfriends killed, both tangential to cases he was working.

His client Polly Furst died at the hands of a crazed jihadist. Three women died from being close to him.

Josh hated the spotlight and refused to cooperate. Eventually they went away.

He broke at six, rode into Middleton and ate at the Hubbard Street Diner. He read last week's *Isthmus* which featured a "courageous and transformational" blind, para-plegic lesbian of color who made dolphin sculptures out of broken glass. The meatloaf was excellent.

"What's in this meatloaf?" he asked the waitress.

"Bacon."

He rode home and sat on his front deck wearing skeeter cheaters on both wrists reading the latest *Motor Cyclist*. An electric motorcycle had set a new record for the Pike's Peak Hill Climb. What next? Honest politicians?

At dusk a lone cyclist motored through, his straight pipes reverberating off the trees and houses. The cyclist slowed down in front of Josh and glanced his way.

Well fuck.

The Rustlers were still on his ass. Was it possible they hadn't heard about what happened to the Insane Assholes?

Josh phoned the police and explained the situation. They assured him they would increase patrols in his area. The fat burghers of Josh's neighborhood had little patience for riff-raff. The Vermin had to be bone-stupid to think they could ride through a neighborhood like this without penalty.

Josh laughed. Danny told him it was always smart to buy the cheapest house in a good neighborhood. Of course, Josh was there first.

Josh curled up on the sofa in the living room with Fig, and turned on the TV. A woman who looked like Honey Boo Boo's mother said, "I got hit by a car and the insurance company only wanted to give me two thousand dollars. So, I went to Steve Fleiss and he got me $350,000!"

Fleiss appeared with a determined expression. "Of course, I can't guarantee you $350,000, but if you've been in an auto accident and the insurance companies are refusing to pay up, come see me. Steve Fleiss, the Hammer!"

Josh tossed ball with Fig, read *Crime and Punishment* and went to bed, where he bowed his head and put his palms together.

"Dear Lord, let Jane be all right. I hope I find her."

Fig, sitting next to him, woofed.

"Fuck an A!" Josh said, getting into bed.

CHIEF KONAPACKI'S

Monday.

Josh rose at six and ran five. Campaign signs had sprouted on his neighbor's lawns, many of them supporting Sheila Livermore-Epstein for state rep. After a shower and breakfast, Josh went online. Franklin had e-mailed him pictures of Jane and a list of her known associates. Nobody jumped out but Josh dutifully set about contacting each one with little success. Most of the phone numbers Franklin sent were no longer working. Josh used Jane's Facebook page to locate several. Nobody knew nothin'.

He scrolled through her pictures, most taken in Paraguay. Jane with local friends standing on an improbably clean flagstone road between gleaming white-walled stucco. Jane in the field with fog and hazy mountains in the background. Jane in the market.

He called her cell phone and went straight to message.

"Jane, this is Josh Pratt the bouncer at Zeke's. Please call me. Thank you."

Josh emailed Franklin asking if he knew the domain name of the chat room in which Jane had met Kuhn. He called Calloway who called back. They arranged to meet for lunch at the Memorial Union overlooking Lake Mendota.

Jane had an apartment in the isthmus not far from Orton Park. Josh rode downtown and parked on the dead-end street butting up against Lake Monona. Jane lived in a three-story wood-frame house, a once splendid dowager chopped into student housing. Jane's unit was on the second floor. On the friendly East Side there was no lock on the building's front door.

Josh climbed the stairs on the balls of his feet next to the wall making no noise and used a credit card to slip the laughable lock on Jane's door. Her neighbor had a Sheila Livermore-Epstein campaign poster taped to her front door along with a COEXIST bumper sticker and a picture of the Monsanto logo with a red bar through it.

As soon as Josh entered, a gray tabby appeared twining between his legs and purring. Its food and water bowls were full. So was its odorous cat box, emanating from the bathroom off the kitchen. Who kept the bowls filled? A ten-speed man's bike leaned against the living room wall.

Jane lived simply and ate a lot of Ramen noodles. Josh found her passport in her top dresser drawer along with a small hardbound volume, *Transformational Protocols* by Heinrich Hochrein. He opened to the introduction.

*... To pretend otherwise is sophistry. The somewhat bal-
kanized intellectual construction of the process itself created another set of problems. ... Chapter 10 Integrated
assessment of climate change. Chapter 11 An economic
assessment of policy changes -. Main Point 8 ...*

His eyes glazed over. He closed the book and put it back.
On the wall were posters of Charlton Heston defending the
Second Amendment, Angelina Jolie in *Malificent*, and a shot
of the interior of the Capitol when it was being occupied
by union protesters following Governor Walker's legislative
victory over the teachers' unions above the legend, "Annual
Meeting of the Young Communist League."

Josh opened the passport. She'd visited Paraguay, Columbia, and Mexico in recent months. He checked the bathroom. She had more make-up than Walgreen's. There was
no home computer. Josh searched thoroughly and found no
weapons or drugs. As he slipped out her front door the door
across the hall opened and a short woman with a near buzz
cut, wearing steel-rimmed glasses looked out.

"Are you the boyfriend?" she said.

"No, ma'am. I'm a private investigator. Josh Pratt."

"Isn't that breaking and entering?"

"Yes, ma'am, technically it is. But these are unusual circumstances."

"What circumstances?"

"Jane is off the radar. Her father hired me to locate her."

"Are you the bouncer?"

"Yes ma'am."

She offered a man-like grip. "Peggy Albright. Haven't seen her since yesterday morning. Is something wrong?"

"No, ma'am. Her father is merely concerned that she has made herself unavailable."

Peggy snorted. "He's a fucking pig, her dad. It's a miracle she turned out as well as she did."

"How do you mean?"

"Lew Franklin makes his living off genetically modified organisms. He's fucking with the fate of the world. He is also heavily invested in Israeli robotics and domestic fracking. If Franklin had his way, we'd all be drinking poison water. You vote?"

"Yes ma'am." His voting rights had been restored upon his pardon.

"Listen. You vote for Sheila. She'll introduce a bill stopping this genetically modified bulldozer from giving us all cancer. Hang on a sec."

Peggy returned with a pamphlet, listing Livermore-Epstein's achievements, her beliefs and goals.

A *vote for Livermore-Epstein is a vote for sustainability*.

Josh put it in his hip pocket. "Have you met her boyfriend?"

"Never seen him but from what Jane says he's a right-on dude. Punched out his senior officer and now he devotes his time to green causes."

"Are you taking care of the cat?"

"Yes."

"Would you clean the litter?"

"Yeah, okay."

Josh gave her his card and thanked her. "Please call me if she appears."

Josh rode to the Memorial Union and kicked out in a striped area in the Union's tiny parking lot. The front entrance was lined with a collection of advocacy groups including Students For Justice in Palestine, Greenpeace, and Sustainable Protocols. Josh walked up to the folding card table from which hung the Sustainable Protocols banner and picked up a pamphlet. The surly kid behind the table, glasses, billy-goat beard, was too absorbed in his iPad to look up. Josh went through the lobby, past the Babcock Hall ice cream dispensary, through the cafeteria out to the patio where he secured a table under a green umbrella. On summer days the Memorial Terrace was a Monet painting with 21st century hipsters. Many of the same faces appeared year after year, aging academics who'd come for a degree and never left. Retired professors who rode the bike trail from their homes on the near west side. Laughing exchange students and doting parents.

Calloway arrived a quarter after, a tall black man with a shaved skull and a rogue eye which he used to devastating effect in interrogations.

Josh marked their table with his backpack and a cap and joined Calloway in line at the outdoor bar and grill. They returned to the table with brats and beers.

"To what do I owe the honor?" Calloway said.

"Jane Franklin is missing. Franklin thinks she ran off with a marine ex-con named Carl Kuhn."

Calloway ate half his brat, chewing slowly and quaffing beer. He set down his empty cup.

"Carl Kuhn."

"Marine, two tours of duty in Iraq, now heads the Jugan, a motorcycle club dedicated to good works and ginseng."

Calloway removed a small spiral notepad from his light gray cotton suit. "How do you spell that?"

Josh told him, adding what little he knew about the club.

Calloway, who was the Madison gangs expert, said, "No sir. Never heard of them."

"Franklin said you were investigating a hit and run involving one of his employees."

"Pat Murphy was a breeding technician who worked for Franklin Farms. He was killed on the eighteenth near Warner Park. We got one witness says he saw an old pick-up fleeing the scene."

"What's your impression of Franklin?" Josh said.

"What bearing does that have on your case?"

"Come on, Heinz. I'm working for the guy."

"I got nothing against Franklin. Made a fortune selling bull jizz."

"What about the Jugan?"

"I will take a look. By the way. Did you sleep well last night?"

"What happened?"

Calloway finished his brat withdrawing his finger with a smack. "Around one-thirty here they come—a half dozen Vermin down Rosa Road. We busted them for noise, found three invalid licenses, enough meth to power a Saturn booster and a shitload of outstanding warrants. They are currently estivating at the city's expense."

Josh put his face in his hands. He'd just dodged a bullet. His neighbors were already eager to see him go after the shoot-out. On the other hand, if they thought Josh was attracting bad elements maybe they'd increase their offer.

"Wow, that's great, Heinz. I really appreciate it. Know anybody in the Iowa County's Sheriff's Department?"

"No.eniz"

"I'm heading out there this afternoon to hang with the Jugan."

"What is a Jugan?"

"I looked it up," said Josh. "It was a hundred-man unit in Genghis Khan's army."

"Now there was a Khan," Calloway said. "Not like these wimpy little Khans today."

Josh left home at five riding west through rolling farm hills on secondary roads. Like most bikers he would rather travel twice the distance on back roads than go fast on the interstate. Riding was olfactory as much as anything and the air was rich with honeysuckle, pine, mint and cow manure, which Josh liked in small doses.

He passed a farmhouse whose front yard was filled with rustic metal sculpture — birds and dinosaurs welded together from cast-off farm implements, wheels, scrap metal. He passed a herd of grazing llamas. He paused to let four wild turkeys cross the road in a dignified shuffle.

Josh would have recognized Chief Konapacki's by the choppers lined up out front. As he backed his chop to the curb, he heard a two-handed piano player popping Horace Silver's "Nica's Dream". Among other things, Chaplain Dorgan had turned him onto jazz, particularly the mid-sixties Blue Note catalog. How strange to find it on a jukebox in SW Wisconsin.

When Josh entered the chill interior, he paused to let his eyes adjust to the gloom through his shades. Three bikers in a booth at the front scoped him out. It wasn't a jukebox. Bobby Hines sat at an upright piano against the wall hunched over and groovin' high.

Josh took a seat at the bar and ordered a Point. The bartender was a Daisy Duke type in a man's plaid shirt tied across her taut belly, brown hair in a ponytail, wearing a badge that said Brandy. Behind her the hand-carved bar was circled with Western and Indian paraphernalia: horseshoes, postcards, pictures of Indians, a tomahawk, a ten-gallon hat, neon cacti, branding irons.

Bobby finished the song and held the chord to fade, got up, walked to the bar, slapped Josh on the shoulder and fitted his bulk precariously on the round padded seat.

Bobby signaled for Brandy. "Give my friend another." Turned to Josh. "So you found the place."

"Hard to miss," Josh said, clinking bottles with the big man. "Man you play some mean piano."

"Comes naturally. Earl Hines was a great, great uncle of mine."

"Who?"

"I see we got to do some woodsheddin'. Any more trouble with our friends?"

"No. They tried to buzz me last night, but the Madison PD hauled 'em in."

"You don't need that shit after what happened to you."

"Does everybody know about that?"

Hines pulled his head back. "Of course, everybody knows! It's part of your biker lore!"

Josh sighed. He craved nothing more than anonymity and to be left alone. With instant media bombarding people with the latest news about the Kardashians, he had slipped form the public consciousness.

But not among bikers.

Josh raised his shades and worked the mirror behind the bar. There was no one in the bar that matched Kuhn's photo. "I live in an upscale neighborhood. My house is trash. If it had wheels, it would be a trailer. I bought it before the neighborhood grew up around me but because I'm surrounded by lawyers, doctors, and fund raisers we get first class service. They don't like the music of the pipes."

"You want to meet the boys?"

"Sure."

They walked to the booth. The three men in the booth looked ex-military with buzz cuts and tats.

"This here's Pratt," Hines said, "the dude I told you about. Marcus, Feral, Panda." They shook hands. Panda, the biggest of the bunch, slid to the wall.

"Have a seat."

Josh sat. Bobby snagged a chair and sat at the end.

"Yeah we heard about your little set-to," Panda said. He was bald, six five, and wore round glasses.

Feral slouched against the wall with a curled lip. He had red hair, was long and rangy with whipcord forearms covered in blue ink, an Adam's apple like the gearshift knob on a '64 GTO and one-inch grommets in his ears. "You the one killed Moon?"

"I didn't kill him. The person he abused for fifteen years killed him."

"But you caused his death," Feral sneered.

"Moon was a mass murderer," Josh said.

"He was a legend," Feral said. "He was ten times the man you'll ever be."

"Did you know him?" Josh said.

Feral was done talking. He stared daggers at Josh.

"Feral didn't know him," Bobby said. "You hear these stories and you think the guy is something he wasn't."

"Don't mind him," Marcus said. "Feral's had a stick up his ass since he was busted for jerking off at *The Lego Movie*."

Feral held out his left fist fingers up and rotated an imaginary crank with his right hand. His middle finger slowly rose.

"No love for Vermin," Panda said. "Buncha drug addicts and degenerates."

"Thing is," Bobby said, "we just suffered a death in the family which leaves the Jugan one short. You lookin' to pledge?"

"Sure," Josh said.

Feral rolled his eyes.

CHAPTER 9

KISS THIS LAND GOODBYE

They drank until it was dark. A tourist couple entered around nine, took one look and left. At ten the window-panes rattled, and glasses danced across tables at the rumble of V-twins pulling into the lot. Bob Seger was on the juke as the door punched in and a man the size and shape of an Abrams tank popped through followed by two Jugan.

Orlok bopped fists with Bobby before taking a seat at the bar flanked by his lieutenants. He had a close-cropped military haircut, an Old Testament beard, and both arms were covered with tribal tats. Bobby waited until the newcomers had drinks. He clapped Josh on the shoulder.

"Come on. He wants to meet you."

Feeling a buzz Josh got to his feet and followed Bobby to the bar. Josh was not a big drinker, but he didn't mind a couple beers. Orlok rotated like a tank turret on his stool as they approached and proffered his fist. He had no knuckles.

Where the knuckles should have been was a solid, massive ridge of scar tissue. His head was carved from granite with a broad, sloping forehead.

"Bobby tells me you had a spot of bother."

"If Bobby hadn't stopped, I would just be a grease mark in the road."

Orlok quaffed beer. "The fuckin' Vermin, man. The collective IQ of a goat. Reason I asked you out, I understand you did my old lady a solid."

"Just doing my job."

"Yeah, well the Jugan needs men like you. Hang with us why don'tcha."

"Thanks. I will."

"You still bouncing?"

"No. That was temporary. I got my private investigator's license and now I got a job."

"What's the job?" Orlok said.

"Confidential," Josh said.

Orlok drained his glass. "I can dig it. Most of us got day jobs. Bobby plays piano at the Edgewater. Panda manages the 'seng operation."

"'Seng?" Josh said.

"Ginseng," Bobby rumbled. "The chinks go crazy for that shit. It's highly profitable, perfectly legit and the feds can't do shit. Apparently, there's some element to our good Wisconsin soil that produces first rate 'seng."

The door opened admitting two sirens. A long tall black girl with a seventies 'fro wearing hip-huggers and a gold halter top swayed to the bar and draped her hands over Bobby's neck. A short, stacked redhead in black leather pants plopped on Marcus' lap.

Bobby introduced his girlfriend as Ashton. She shook Josh's hand firmly.

"Hey how are ya?"

Ashton and Robin were dancers at Ho Chunk Casino in Tomah. The boys in the booth laid out some lines on Robin's purse mirror and snorted blow. Orlok, Bobby and Josh stuck to beer and whiskey. Ashton and Robin danced with each other to Temptations and Gretchen Wilson.

Josh sat at the bar, fixated on Orlok's knuckles. There was only one knuckle, a solid mass of scar tissue four inches long and an inch wide. The side of his hand was like that too. Orlok caught Josh staring in the mirror and grinned, flexing his hand.

"You like that? That's what comes from hitting makiwara day after day."

"Show him the bottle break," Bobby said.

Orlok rolled his shoulders. "Aw, no, man. I don't want to make a mess."

Brandy said, "I'll clean it up!"

Bobby pumped his fist. "Bottle break!"

Other Jugan took up the cry.

"BOTTLE BREAK! BOTTLE BREAK! BOTTLE BREAK!"

Grinning and sighing, Orlok got off his stool and removed three bracelets and four rings from his right hand, setting them on the bar. One of the rings held a nine-karat diamond.

The bartender set an empty Johnny Walker Black bottle on the bar. Orlok settled back into a horse stance, breathing deeply. Josh remembered watching a space shot from Cape Kennedy, the missile hissing steam just preparatory to the launch. Legs at right angles, Orlok breathed in, sucking all the air out of the room. He exhaled, putting it all back. The Jugan gathered in a semi-circle, holding drinks and women.

Orlok placed his massive, wedge-like right hand against the neck of the bottle, brought it back over his head, and slowly lowered it again. He did this three times. On the fourth time, he erupted like a depth charge, a guttural, industrial clang as of two massive iron gates slamming shut, body pivoting, right hand snapping asp-like and withdrawing. There was a clink and the bottle neck flew across the room and smashed into the wall.

It had been a clean break. Two pieces.

People clapped and cheered and slapped Orlok on the back, and Orlok bought the house drinks. The Stray Cats' "Rock This Town" blasted from the juke.

At midnight, Orlok got up. "You wanna follow us back to the club?"

Josh didn't want to ride back to Madison. Fig had plenty of food and water and a doggie door to the fenced-in yard. In his present condition Josh wondered if he could even keep the damn bike upright. "Sure."

"How 'bout a line for the road?"

"Sure."

A line of blow would clamp his head down for the ride. Josh had done a shitload of blow back in the day but since getting out of the joint he rarely drank. He blew a little reefer. He didn't like the after-blow feeling but it was better than veering off the road in the middle of the night and cracking his skull on a rock.

Orlok motioned Josh and Bobby to follow him to a back booth where Ashley produced a mirror. Orlok pulled out a tiny zip-loc and wrangled four lines.

Eight bikes weaved through the night followed by Ashton and Robin in Ashton's F-150. Josh willed himself to relax, stay centered and follow the taillights. Twenty minutes later, they came to a locked aluminum gate off a twisting forest road. Feral got off, unlocked the gate and pushed it open. They filed through. Feral waited until the girls had passed before locking the gate behind them. Two hundred yards in the trees opened up on a pristine valley with an old three-story brick farmhouse and a red barn. A yard light on a pole cast blue light.

Orlock set his stand and got off on the paved apron in front of the house. "Bobby, show Josh where he can sleep."

Josh followed Bobby up the steps to the wrap-around porch.

"House got nine bedrooms," Bobby said over his shoulder. "They had big families back then."

Bobby showed Josh a small plain room off the kitchen on the first floor, with an adjacent half bath. Inside a futon lay on the floor. "Here's your digs. See you in the a.m."

It took a long time for Josh to fall asleep. He kept getting up and peeing as was his wont when he mixed booze and blow. He drifted off as the light turned gray in the east. He woke to clattering pots and pans and the smell of coffee. Emerging bleary-eyed he found an impossibly cheerful Ashton frying bacon on a six-burner gas stove.

"There's a shower and towels in the basement," she said, handing him a steaming mug. Wordlessly Josh added milk and sugar and followed her hand down the steps into the large stone basement, a single room punctuated by steel girders jutting from the concrete floor to the beams holding up the first floor. A big green furnace lurked in a corner next to the water heater. Dozens of cardboard boxes were stacked against one wall and there was a smattering of odd furniture — kitchen chairs, an end table, an old sofa. The shower head jutted from a corner of the concrete floor which had a drain in it. Josh felt better after a hot shower. When he returned to the kitchen Marcus and Bobby were chowing down on pancakes and bacon.

Josh took a seat as Ashton served up a plate. Nothing but the sound of eating. Marcus and Feral drifted in as Josh finished and went to check his bike. Bobby followed him out. They looked at the modified Road King.

"What's it got?" Bobby said.

"Engine: 88 with oil cooler. Changed the cams to S&S gear drives with .510 lift.

Took out the fuel injection and replaced it with an S&S

Super E, Yost Power Tube, S&S manifold and Pingle High Flow petcock. S&S Tear Drop air cleaner cover with a K&N filter. Screaming Eagle Hi Performance ignition unit with a 6200 rpm rev limiter. Accell Super Coil, Fire Wire plug wires and spiral wound metal core wires. Accell Platinum tip plugs. Five speed tranny with Barnett kevlar clutch, self-adjusting hydraulic chain tensioner. Screaming Eagle dualies. Progressive springs in front with higher viscosity, Progressives in back. Changed the rear swing arm bushings to "STA BOW" nylon high density. SBS semi-metallic disc brake pads and the brake lines are stainless steel braids. Went to tubeless wheels."

"You took out the fuel injection?"

"I'm old school. Fuck it."

Bobby pointed to a modified V-Max. "That's mine. I call her the Freedom Train."

"Mods?"

"Chipped intake exhaust—Vance & Hines CSOne. ECU Retune from Tim Nash at Gurued Gear. Modified intake; restrictions removed. 240 series tire kit; new rim and wide tire that's at the max the swing arm can handle. Double D clutch spring kit. It's the funnest bike I've ever owned. Exceptionally twitchy throttle response...instant on violent acceleration—you have to be paying attention or you'll be paying the emergency room. Hit a bump, twitch the throttle, launch forward with scary thrust."

Marcus came out on the porch bare-chested, scratching an armpit. He had a small Marine tat on his right bicep. His cut body was tanned and strong. "Boss says show Josh the back forty."

"Oh yeah," Bobby said. "Let me put some shoes on and I'll give you the grand tour."

Josh sat in a swing chair on the porch and watched the morning light strike the trees. He called Louise Lowry and asked her to check on Fig.

In daylight the red barn was perfect, a Disney barn. A green and yellow tractor thrust its snout through the entrance. Bobby returned wearing baggy camo trou, jungle boots and an XXXL Sturgis T-shirt showing a wolf-maned Indian riding an Indian.

They walked past the barn. "We don't use that tractor much. Orlok thought we should have one."

A couple pick-ups and a yellow '68 Stingray were parked in back on gravel. The Stingray was blackened at both ends and looked like an old banana. The dirt road led into a pasture that stretched two hundred yards before ending at the foot of a bizarre sandstone structure that might have come from Southern Utah.

No Prius.

"Lotta weird rocks around here," Bobby said. "The Indians thought it was a holy place. They kept up the ginseng. We got a couple fresh springs and an effigy mound. Don't tell anybody about what you see. State finds out we got an effigy mound you can kiss this land goodbye."

CHAPTER 10

EFFIGY MOUND

Following the natural contour of the valley brought them into a depression ringed with gorse, locust and birch trees out of sight of the farmhouse. A mourning dove sounded from the trees and the air smelled of honeysuckle with a faint whiff of cow manure and marijuana.

They passed a depression that ended in a man-made berm behind a wood frame holding the remnants of paper targets all shot to hell. Josh looked down. Brass littered the ground.

"Is Jane Franklin here?" Josh said.

"I don't know. She might be. Says you came to her rescue."

"Just doing my job."

They followed a trail out of the depression into an oak and elm forest. At a shaded clearing in the center of the copse Bobby pointed to a series of broad-leafed groundcover with red berries. " 'Seng."

The big man knelt, carefully examined a plant, pulled out a jumbo toad sticker and worked it around the base. He pulled loose the fat, turnip-like root which resembled a troll. "This one's ready to harvest. We try to stagger 'em so they don't all come ripe at once. They're not like an annual crop. Takes nine years for a crop to mature. It's a long game, 'seng."

"Who buys this shit?"

"The Chinks. They can't get enough. They're flying me and Orlok over in October! We had 'em out in June. They were very excited but cautious. Inscrutable and shit, but you could tell. They're all talking to each other behind their hands—that's to hide their bad teeth 'cause I don't lip-read Mandarin. Lotta smiles and bowing. Orlok eats that shit up. Thinks he's Genghis Khan. That's what an orlok is, by the way. It was a Mongolian general."

"Funny," Josh said. "He doesn't look Mongolian."

"Nahh. Some kinda Viking. Me, I'm an all-American mutt of Negroid ancestry including but not limited to Native American, Latvian Jew, and Maine coon cat."

"So you sell all this shit to the Chinese?"

Bobby folded his knife and stuck it in his trou. "Some. We also sell a shitload to domestic health food nuts including the Willy St. Co-op. We got a distribution deal with Sprouts, an upscale grocery chain outta Denver. Come on—we got a lot of ground to cover."

They hiked to the top of the ridge from where Josh saw a half acre of brilliant green waving in the morning breeze.

The wind shifted and he got a contact high. He bee-lined toward the marijuana patch. The plants were waist high and stretched in geometric lines twenty yards to a wind break. Josh did math and calculated over 200 plants.

"Now you're talking!"

"Orlok thinks Wisconsin's gonna legalize pot as soon as a Democrat wins the governorship. And when that happens, we'll be ready to roll."

"The state ain't gonna sanction a pot farm for an ex-con."

Bobby held up a brat-sized finger. "Well that's the beauty of the brotherhood, see? We're not a criminal organization. They got no papers on us. I myself will serve as CEO of this operation. We're gonna call it Cannabis Khan."

Josh smiled.

"That's Feral's baby and he knows his shit. He used to smoke marijuana for the government. You should ask him about it."

"I don't think he likes me."

"That's just his act. Feral may seem like a violent, anti-social sociopath, but deep down inside he's actually a violent, anti-social sociopath. He's been splicin' and dicin' the reefer gene for years, says his new strain Harley Gold comes in at 22% pure THC by weight. I smoked it, brah. Ripped my skull inside out. Sucked my eyes out my asshole."

"Great!"

"Give it another sixty days it'll be good to go. We got some cured back at the house we started inside in February. We'll check it out when we get back to the house."

"Yeah, man."

Bobby led downhill to a copse around a pond. Dappled shade covering his broad back like a mantle, he crouched by the pond and pointed to a stream of bubbles rising through limpid water. "Check this shit—one of two natural springs on the property. We could bottle this shit and sell it as pure Kettle Moraine spring water. The hippies would go crazy. You can drink it. Go ahead."

Lasers of sun peeking through the trees brought a mystical quality to the isolated spring. Josh crouched and stared mesmerized at the mirror-perfect surface. A stream of bubbles rippled up from the bottom like a string of tiny, perfect pearls. Josh leaned over and cupped water in his hands, bringing it to his mouth. It was icy cold and delicious. He leaned down and cupped water to his mouth. A frog leaped away, startling him.

"We got deer, pheasant, wild turkey, maybe a bobcat and a couple coyote."

Josh stood. "You hunt?"

"Bow and arrow. Come on. I've saved the best for last."

Josh followed Bobby out of the depression to a ridge from which they could see all the way to the Blue Hills of Baraboo. "Injuns considered this sacred land. It was held in trust by the Ojibwa Tribal Council. We picked it up relatively cheap. They were already into 'seng."

"Yeah," Josh said. It was a hot day and his shirt clung to the small of his back. "How'd he do that?"

"Orlok saved the life of an Ojibwa name of Arlen Lovejoy up in the Kandahar Mountains. The ragheads had him pinned down. Orlok came up behind them with an M-50 and sent a shitload to Allah. We formed the Jugan in Afghanistan."

"You all former military?"

"Mostly. The Jugan's one hundred men. We got chapters in Florida, Colorado and South Dakota. Marcus never served. He's an ex-con, like you."

Josh looked up.

Bobby grinned. "I know how to use a computer. I've heard of Moon. He was some kind of bad motherfucker, huh?"

"He was the most frightening human being I've ever known."

Bobby led the way along a rock ridge with a sheer hundred-foot rise into a shaded grove through which ran a stream, stepping with rare grace for a man his size. They followed the ridge into the forest, followed a winding game trail through mingled birch, oak, elm and sycamore before emerging in a clearing the size of a basketball court. In the middle of the clearing was a smooth earth formation, bulging three feet above the plain, with thick peninsula jutting over the prairie.

Bobby led the way through thigh-high grass. The ground around the effigy mound had been trampled flat. With a grunt Bobby planted a boot on one of its appendages and heaved himself up. Josh followed. They stood in the middle of the oval-shaped knob, which was about ten feet head to tail. It had four stubby legs extending from the center and shapeless blob of a head.

"What is it?" Josh said.

"We think it's a turtle."

"Maybe it's a badger," Josh said.

Bobby stared down rubbing his chin. "Possibly."

The effigy mound was green and fuzzy as a Chia pet. A series of stones had been laid up its spine ending with a sandstone triangle that pointed forward like a neck tat.

"Mike—he's Ojibwa. You ain't met him. Says this is a sacred place honoring their spirit brother."

"Turtle or badger."

"Yeah." Bobby looked at his watch. "Let's head back. I got to be in Madison by noon. Tuesday brunch crowd."

When they got to the clubhouse, Orlok greeted Josh with a stapled document. "I don't usually do this, but these are unusual circumstances. These are rules for prospects. Be sure you know them."

CHAPTER 11

JOB OFFER

Josh and Bobby rode to town together, Josh pulling off on the west side to head for Ptarmigan Rd., Bobby heading downtown. Josh pulled into his driveway around noon. Weeds grew through cracks in the cement. Setting the stand Josh went in through the front door where Fig sat, tongue lolling, tail wagging.

He took a shower, made a pot of coffee, sat in the living room with his feet up on the coffee table and phoned Franklin.

He went straight to voice mail.

"Mr. Franklin, this is Josh Pratt. Please call me at your convenience."

The lawn needed mowing. He opened the overhead garage door, wheeled out the Honda and went to work. He was trimming the last patch as his cross-the-street neighbor, David Lowry, came out the front door of his prairie-style mini-mansion to retrieve the Sunday *State Journal* from his velveteen drive. He waved.

Josh shut off the mower and loped across the street. Lowry waited for him at the top of his incline.

"Dave!"

They shook hands.

"What's up?" the fundraiser said.

"Could you or Louise feed Fig tonight? I won't be home."

"Sure," Lowry said. "I've got your key."

"Do you know about this deal Phil Bass put together to buy me out?"

Lowry looked pained. He was a middle-aged former athlete with a silky comb over and a modest gut. "Yeah he called me and said I had no interest. They think you're a menace and a threat to property values."

"I could always tear it down and move into a double-wide."

Lowry smiled. "Serve 'em right, wouldn't it? Here's the deal—they can always petition the county commissioner to condemn your property."

"You're shitting me," Josh said.

"Nope. I've seen it done. Not around here, in Indiana. But given the political climate it could happen. Just a head's up. I'm on your side. Hell, I wish you'd bring that Camaro back."

Josh turned and looked at his house. It was a simple seven room pale yellow ranch house, common as field mice, found in any blue-collar suburban neighborhood.

And that was the problem.

Josh heard George and Gracie, the schnauzers he'd saved from a dog fighting ring, yapping from inside the 5500 square foot house. The door opened and Lowry's wife Louise slipped out with a practiced maneuver and shaded her eyes with her hand.

"Hi, Josh! Dave, Nancy's on Skype."

"Gotta go," Lowry said. "We'll talk later."

"We'll have you over!" Louise said.

Josh crossed the street, finished the lawn and put the mower away.

He sat in a folding lawn chair on his front stoop and popped a can of Capital lager. His phone chimed.

"Josh Pratt."

"Franklin. Did you find her?"

"Maybe. I found Kuhn, spent the night at their clubhouse. It's in Iowa County. She may have been there, but I didn't see her, and I didn't see her car."

"How did you spend the night at their clubhouse?"

"It's a long story, sir, but they're trying to recruit me."

"Can you come over? I've got another problem."

"Sure."

Franklin gave him directions to his place in Pine Perch, an upscale community on a butte off Highway M on the southwest side. It was a ten-minute ride. Josh followed the winding blacktop to a butte west of town, million-dollar houses on secluded lots, past several under construction, to Franklin's.

Josh kicked out the stand on the red brick apron in front of Franklin's Bauhaus box. The garage door was open revealing the back ends of Franklin's Cadillac and a Boxster convertible. Before Josh could ring the bell, Franklin came around the side of the house wearing plaid Bermuda shorts and a purple and green Hawaiian shirt.

They shook hands.

"Thanks for coming. We'll go to my office."

Josh followed past the open garage, catching a glimpse of Franklin's neighbor through the woods dragging a hose. Out back was a wide patio, green and yellow lawn furniture and a rectangular swimming pool. Franklin opened a sliding glass door into an airy glass cubicle outfitted in Danish modern. He beckoned Josh to a wood-framed Barcelona chair and took a seat in a beach wood Sitzmaschine that cost more than Josh's Harley. Persian rugs dotted the blond wood floor. A glass coffee table held copies of *Barron's*, *American Cattleman*, and *The Wall Street Journal*. Behind him, a wall of books marched to the ceiling. At least a foot was devoted to legal-sized spiral notepads lined up like soldiers. One lay open on his desk.

"You met Kuhn?"

"Yes sir. They're grooming me as a pledge. Kuhn seems highly intelligent. Apparently, they make a living growing ginseng."

"But you didn't see Jane."

"No, sir. She may well have been there. I'm going back tonight. I will keep at it until I find her."

"And then will you bring her to me?"

"All I can do is ascertain if she's in danger. If she is, of course I'll try to get her out, but if she's seeing Kuhn of her own free will I don't see where I can do anything other than report. Have you phoned her?"

Franklin glared. "Of course, I phoned! She's not responding. She's punishing me for my GMOs."

"You don't get along?"

"We love each other, but we always seem to be fighting. She was always a rebellious child. I was against that Peace Corps thing. Not that I don't believe in the Peace Corps, but Jesus Christ, I was paying fifty large a year for her to get an education!

"She alternates between me and her mother in Chicago. She doesn't approve of me. She doesn't like that I support our first black President. She'd rather live among thugs and drug addicts than in her own private suite. This Orlok guy is like Manson."

"I did stop by her place downtown and met her neighbor."

"More than I've done. I begged her not to get her own place."

Josh smiled.

"If my neighbors knew my true beliefs, they'd lynch me. Some blithering idiot stopped by here last night, wanted to plant a sign in my lawn for that fascist prick Hightower. I told her to try the Rethugs across the street. Makes me sick."

"I noticed the sign," Josh said.

The door opened revealing a svelte brunette in her late thirties in a jogging outfit. "Oh hi! I didn't know you had company. I'm Marian."

Josh stood and stuck out his hand. "Josh Pratt."

"Josh is helping me in a business matter, Marian."

"Well I won't bother you boys. Would you like a glass of lemonade, Josh?"

"Yes, thank you."

She left. Josh looked at Franklin who shrugged his shoulders. "Six months and counting. Who knows? I met her at the Madison Club."

"You said you had another matter about which you wished to ask me."

Franklin reached inside a drawer on the free-form walnut slab that served as his desk, withdrew a brochure and skated it across the top. It sailed off the end where Josh snatched it one handed. It was vertical, in color, and showed a lone bull standing on a hill, a herd of contented cattle in the foreground.

FRANKLIN FARMS
WORLD'S BEST BREEDER SERVICE
DODGEVILLE, WISCONSIN

The interior contained a series of pictures of various bulls, charts and graphs relating to beef production and a map of countries in which Franklin sold its product.

"One straw sells for $100. I'm missing over ten-grand in

inventory."

"What is a straw?"

"It's a unit of bull semen preserved in albumen and frozen in liquid nitrogen. Beef production is an intensely competitive international business. We lead the world in genetically-modified beef reproduction. We have a 20-straw minimum. A bell, or unit of 20 straws is about the size of an insulated picnic jug, like an Igloo. It is completely self-contained and with proper care will maintain viability for seventy-six hours. We have had six missing bells over the past three months, total value, $12,000."

"Sir, would I be right in assuming that Jane opposes your business?"

"Of course. But not for what you think. She's perfectly fine with GMOs, it's the fact that I'm trading with countries like Russia, the Ukraine, and Poland. She thinks they're all sinkholes of commie corruption. At first, I blamed it on youthful rebellion but ever since she went to Paraguay, she came back somewhere to the right of Attila the Hun."

Marian returned with two tall plastic glasses of lemonade on a tin Coca-Cola plate which she set on Franklin's desk.

"Thank you, ma'am," Josh said.

"Thank you dear."

Marian smiled and left, closing the door behind her.

"Do you think this might have something to do with Pat Murphy?"

"It crossed my mind."

"You want me to look into this?" Josh said.

Franklin picked up his glass and slugged half, Adam's apple bobbing, setting it back in the tin with a clang. "I do."

"Why me? I mean I can see hiring me to find your daughter. I have expertise in that area. But I'm just a sole proprietor. There are much bigger firms in town with impressive track records."

Franklin steepled his hands, peering at Josh with steely blue eyes. "I'm a pretty good judge of character. I've done my research. The Farm is six miles from this Jugan club house."

"Were you aware of their proximity before I reported?"

"No. I knew the land was private and that we would see the occasional biker, but I had no idea. We employ wranglers. Do you have any experience with bulls or beef cattle?"

"No."

"That's all right. We'll teach you."

CHAPTER

12

THE DOCUMENT

Josh fed Fig, flipped through the news, turned off the TV, lay down on the sofa with Fig between his legs and pulled out Orlok's document.

> *From time to time there is found to be some confusion about the reason for prospecting, and, what prospecting is supposed to accomplish. In some cases, this "purpose" may not even be clear to the Prospect himself.*
>
> *This text was therefore put together to give you a clearer understanding of where you stand in the eyes of the Club and what will be expected of you. It will also give you a sense of the level of commitment that will be required for you to earn and keep your patch.*
>
> *Once you understand the scope of the task you are undertaking you should examine your feelings and question your motivations for wanting to become a part of this Brother-*

hood. Be certain that you're both willing and able to commit yourself to the level that will be required. Be certain that your family understands the demands that the Club will make on your time. And, that those demands will continue to an even greater extent once you become a Patch holder. There are many veterans' organizations, touring clubs and motorcycle associations that expect, and receive, only casual participation. This club is not one of them.

If after reading these remaining pages you have any doubt about being able to meet the responsibilities outlined, it would be better not to consider moving forward at this time. Instead, continue your association with the Club in your present status until you feel you are ready and are confident of your success. Such a decision would be respected and would be to your credit.

The intention of this section is to give you an overview of the structure and philosophy of the traditional motorcycle club (M/C.) In some cases, this does not necessarily describe the Jugan M/C, as all motorcycle clubs differ on some points. It will be left to your sponsor to explain those particular differences where they may apply to our Club. It is important that you understand the perspectives of some of the other clubs that you will be associating with from time to time.

If your lifestyle is influenced by motorcycles, you are part of the motorcycle community. Of all the types of organizations found with that community, the motorcycle club stands apart and ranks highest in stature. A serious M/C commands respect for one, or both, of two reasons:

1. Those who are informed recognize the deep level of personal commitment and self-discipline that a man has to demonstrate and sustain in order to wear a Patch. So much so that it is akin to being a full time profession for the individual. They realize that a Club's Colors are closely guarded, and the membership process is long and difficult. All else put aside, you have to respect the man for what he has accomplished by being able to earn and keep the Patch he wears.

2. Those who are less informed see only the surface of things. They see the vigilance of mutual support. The potential danger of invoking a response from a well- organized unit that travels in numbers and are always prepared for confrontation. They know that no one can provoke one club member without being answerable to the entire club. And that such an answer is a point of honor that must come, to the last man. The type of respect that this generates is one that is born of fear.

The serious motorcycle club will conduct itself publicly in a highly professional manner. They will not go out of their way to cause trouble or to present themselves as an intimidating force, without purpose or provocation. Their respect is gained from both of the items cited above.

There are many lesser clubs whose membership is made up of equally lesser individuals. These clubs, without a continual show of strength, would have no respect at all. The majority of these types of clubs are short lived, however.

The general public does not draw a distinction between different club colors. If one club causes a problem that touches the public sector, the offending club's identity is either confused or ignored, and heat comes to suppress all.

There is also a natural hierarchy that is recognized between motorcycle clubs themselves. The strongest and most established club will assume charge of the particular State in which they ride. This dominant club will, for reasons that are beneficial to all, authorize the establishment of new clubs within the state; will disband clubs that cause continual problems; will act as mediators to resolve problems between existing clubs; will step in and enforce their own solution if the feuding clubs cannot come to terms on their own; will provide communication links and coordinate interclub events; will call on the clubs within a state for additional support if needed when dealing with a threatening external force.

If it were not for the major club of a State taking this leadership position, clubs would not enjoy the luxury of putting their time and resources to the benefit of their individual brotherhoods. Nor would we enjoy the agility and freedom of movement that comes with peace and order.

Within the motorcycle club itself, officers are elected to the traditional posts of President, Vice President, Secretary, Treasurer, Road Captain, Sergeant of Arms, Enforcer, and War Lord. The Road Captain is responsible for the logistics of effectively moving the club from point A to B. The Enforcer answers only to the President and sees that the

President's orders are carried out. He will also be the one who travels if a problem has to be addressed at a distance. The War Lord is in charge of tactics and strategies in time of stress. In some instances, he is also responsible for the club's security issues. In most clubs, the positions of War Lord and Enforcer are combined.

Given this limited background information, let us now turn our attention to the individual Patch Holder and how he views his club.

In most cases, the Pacth Holder was a Hang Around for at least a year. Before that he was a long-standing acquaintance and his attitude and overall conduct were well known. He then Prospected for the club from one to two years before he was awarded his Patch.

Of all the things in this man's life, his loyalty and commitment to the well-being of his club comes first. Above family, friends, job, personal possessions and personal safety. There is never, ever, any doubt or time spent on even considering which comes first. The only thing that approaches his commitment to the club, is his commitment to his brothers. But even here, the interests of the club always come before that of the individual. His family can walk out on him without a second's notice. He can lose his overnight, and even good, close friends come and go with time. But his club and his brothers will always be there for him. It is one of the few, if not the only thing, that can be counted on. He knows this because he, himself, is committed to always being there for them.

To be certain that this ethic and standard of attitude is carried by new members, he participates in conditioning, educating, and at times testing, the club's Prospect. The term Prospect comes from "prospective member." As such, before he allows another man to wear his Colors, as a symbol of their mutual commitment, he will feel certain that the new member brings with the same loyalty and dedication that he himself displays.

He understands that he is a Patch Holder 24 hours a day. If he is wearing his colors or not is of no consequence. The day that he accepted his patch he surrendered the luxury of having a personal public opinion. Everything that he does and says in public is taken to be the entire club's position or attitude. He can no longer settle personal differences without involving his club. Regardless of his personal feelings, he will agree with and fully support his brothers' actions and words in public. If a hand is raised to his brother, he is committed to participating in neutralizing the threat without delay, even if the odds are ten to one, or one to ten. He accepts the fact that wearing a patch carries responsibilities that affect the lives of a lot of people in and outside the club.

Wearing a patch is more than getting together for good times. It is also getting together in bad times. It constitutes a lot of work. It is committing yourself to a lifestyle in which you do not look for how your brothers might help you, but for ways in which you can be of help to your brothers. You always look to give, but never to receive.

CHAPTER 13

THE JOB

Franklin Farms occupied sixty-five acres in Dodge County not far from Chief Konapacki's. Barbed wire enclosed the grazing land while hurricane fencing topped with concertina wire surrounded administration and breeding facilities. In the center sat an enormous twelve-sided barn from which wings and corrals extended like propeller blades.

Josh announced himself at a steel box mounted to the gate beneath a camera. The gate clicked and rolled silently open. Josh snicked into first and drove up the fresh tarmac to the administration building, a long, low steel-frame construction extending from the hub that gave no indication of its function save for the company logo on the glass door.

Josh left his bike in a spot marked VISITORS and entered the foyer, a rectangular room with a faux marble floor, a pair of sofas, framed portraits of select sires, a massive chart showing various breeding stock, and a map of the world marked wherever Franklin stock sold. A middle-aged woman with silver hair swept in a wave looked up from her computer and smiled.

"Good morning! You must be Mr. Pratt. I will notify Mr. Franklin that you are here. Would you like a cup of coffee?"

"I'm good, thanks," Josh said sitting on the sofa and looking at the magazines on the low table in front of him. *American Cattleman, Progressive Cattleman, Cattle Breeding and Reproduction, the Brahmin Journal, Wisconsin Cattleman, Time, People, The New Republic,* and *Men's Health.*

He picked up a Franklin Farms pamphlet and read a short, sanitized biography.

Born in 1966, Lewis Franklin was the sixth of nine children born to Wallace and Joan Franklin of rural Wauwatosa. Wallace raised dairy cattle and was the first farmer in Wauwatosa County to use artificial insemination on his cows. Lewis attended the University of Wisconsin where he was a Big Ten NCAA heavyweight wrestling contender and studied animal husbandry at the Babcock Institute. He graduated in 1990 with a Masters in Animal Husbandry and a Minor in Business. He married Samantha Barnes in 1989 and has one daughter.

Franklin founded Franklin Farms in 1995 with an initial investment of two and a half mil. His partners remained silent and invisible. For the first five years of operation Franklin had no home other than the farm and lived on-site.

A minute later Franklin appeared wearing worn blue

jeans, work boots and a blue work shirt. Josh stood and they shook hands.

"Come on, I'll show you around."

Franklin led the way down an antiseptic, institutional corridor with doors on both sides opening into office suites. "This is administration—sales, billing, maintenance, all the boring shit."

He went straight back and out the door at the rear which led to a dim corridor between sloping concrete walls, as in a stadium. They emerged in the center of the hub, a hexagonal corral approximately two hundred feet in diameter with a series of catwalks anchored in the center by steel cables rising to the top hub, suspended by four graceful arcing girders. Slices of bleachers stretched back behind concrete abutments.

Josh looked up.

"We use this place to show off our lines, sometimes we have a little radio. The Arabs love that. Most of our R&D takes place in here. It goes without saying that ranchers want maximum yield for the buck, and they want top grade beef, so our goal is to develop strains that propagate easily and result in high quality beef."

"What do I do?"

"We're hiring you part-time as a wrangler to help with the bulls. Willoughby will show you the ropes. Later, Ellie will get your particulars and put you on the payroll. Job pays 15.50 an hour."

Josh looked around. Individual enclosures, gates made of

timber and pieces of old tires, lay between the corridors. Behind them, dark shapes snorted, shuffled and rapped against their boundaries like bass drums.

A hulking figure in coveralls scooped hay into one of the enclosures with a pitchfork.

"That's Axel," Franklin said. "Hey, Axel!"

Axel straightened and returned his wave. He was seven feet tall with sloping shoulders. His hands were the size of catcher's mitts.

"He's a little slow, but Dionysus loves him. He's got a way with the bulls.

We have two of the country's top producers in here, Sir Max Granfield, Angus, and Sir Boscobel Rosenschweig, Hereford."

"So the Queen knighted them?"

Franklin chuckled, heading toward an enclosure made of six-by-eights, padded with tire segments and furniture blankets. "Cattle has its royalty. The American Cattleman's Association bestows these titles during three days of judging. Every year it's in a different place. Last year it was in Sioux City. We're pushing to host it in Milwaukee."

"I looked over your notes. The six bells came from four sires, but you only identified three of them."

"We're a little uncertain who the missing sire is. We've been unable to find Murphy's notes. Guidelines require that he file each bell as he loads it, and that it be properly identified on the casing."

"Do you think his death has anything to do with the

missing straws?"

Franklin put his arms on a chest high enclosure. Josh stood next to him and peered into the darkness.

"Yes. We want to handle this without the police. This is Sir Gunther." A sign on the gate identified him as a Limousin, weight: 2556 lbs.

An enormous red bull with soulful eyes stared at them, tail twitching. Franklin reached down and grabbed a handful of silage from a bin affixed to the fence and held it out. The bull ambled over and gently took it from his hand, chewing thoughtfully with a sound like wet oatmeal between wood blocks.

Franklin conducted a counter-clockwise tour, identifying each bull by name, sometimes feeding and talking to them. He led the way down a corridor to a back door that opened on a pie-shaped fenced-in pasture with holding gates such as those found at a rodeo, and a black bull munching in the distance.

"We have to keep the bulls separate. We have twenty-six enclosures and twenty-four bulls, so we rotate them. Some pastures are always fallow to allow regeneration. We use border collies and cowboys to control them. I'd like you to start tomorrow, get here at eight. Willoughby will show you the procedures and your responsibilities."

"How do you get the semen you don't mind my asking?"

Franklin chuckled. "Probably our most asked question. There are several methods, but we use a steer affixed with a prophylactic sleeve. A pheromone excites the bull and a technician guides him into the slot."

"Is that my job?"

"You may be asked to assist, yes."

"Great," Josh said.

They went inside and he filled out the paperwork. As Josh left the facility, he passed a steel pole barn with eight bays, three of them open. Axel appeared in the nearest bay carrying a V8 engine block like a six pack.

CHAPTER 14

FITTING IN

When Josh pulled up to the Jugan gate there was a tall kid inside sitting in a lawn chair with a can of beer, feet up on the seat of a cafe racer based on a Yamaha 500 single.

"I'm Pratt," Josh said from his bike facing the aluminum gate. "I'm a pledge."

The kid heaved himself up out of his chair and opened the gate.

"Yeah me too. I'm Fast Eddie."

They bumped fists.

"They always have someone at the gate?"

"No but there's some shit about the Vermin lookin' to tag you and Bobby."

Josh barked. "As if! Where'd you hear that?"

Fast Eddie shook out a Marlboro from a sleeve pack, held the pack out. Josh shook his head. "Friend in lock-up. The Vermin bailed out today. Our friend said they were calling up reinforcements to deal with the problem."

"My ass," Josh said.

"That's what I think."

Josh snicked into gear and slowly rolled past the gate. Fast Eddie shut the gate behind him.

"I don't know what it's like where they come from but these county mounties have zero tolerance for outlaws You all got the right idea—keep a low profile and show respect."

Fast Eddie closed the gate. "Yeah. They'd have to be stupid."

Josh looked at the cafe racer. "Sweet."

"Thanks. Built it myself."

Josh motored onto the farmhouse. It was six-thirty and the sun still hung, the temp in the low eighties. There were four chops in front of the house including Orlok's and Bobby's. No sign of the Prius or Ashton's F-150.

Orlok, Marcus and Bobby sat on the veranda in Adirondack chairs drinking Sheep Shagger Scotch ales in bottles, feet on the rail. Orlok had a blue tooth plugged into one ear and was talking. As Josh came up the steps Marcus reached into a cooler at his feet and tossed him a cold bottle.

Josh twisted off the cap and sat in an empty chair next to Orlok.

"How'd you join up?" Josh said.

"I was kickin' around after I got out of Marquette. Played nose tackle, had a try-out with the Falcons, but they passed. One day I'm hangin' out in this bar and we're drinking. Wondering what the fuck I'm doing. I look up. There's the

Vice-President greeting a bunch of flag-draped coffins at Kennedy. I put down my beer, went outside. The Marine recruiting office was two doors down."

"Wow."

"You ever play football?"

Josh gazed at the trees. "No, man. I never played anything."

"No baseball, no soccer?"

"My old man was a petty thief and a grifter. Half the time I wasn't even in school. He abandoned me when I was fifteen."

"That's cold."

"I got my GED in prison."

Orlok touched his ear and turned to Josh. "You know how to clean guns?"

"I've cleaned a few," Josh said.

"Well, have we got a surprise for you."

Marcus stood and motioned for Josh to follow him into the house into the living/dining room, a large space with a hardwood floor, leather furniture and a big round oak table set about eighteen inches off the ground in the center of the room. Square cushions surrounded the table. On top of the table lay twelve weapons: two AR-15s, four AK 47s, three automatics and three revolvers. There was a heap of rags, brushes, rods, and a bottle of Hoppe's. Marcus picked up a remote and turned on the big flat screen against the back wall.

"Get busy. You watching *Sons*? We got it on DVD."

In the very center of the table was a big wooden bowl filled with brass. The guns had been recently used and were lined with with carbon. There were several boxes of ammo. Josh picked up a fat white plastic cylinder containing 100 rounds 9 mm made in Belarus. He got to work, expertly stripping the AKs first. He finished his beer and switched to the news channel.

American TV was closing its doors after a sixty-year run. The Dane County Coliseum wanted to add more parking. Sheila Livermore-Epstein appeared. Josh turned it up.

"For too long we have looked the other way. there's a reason Wisconsin motorcycle fatality rates dwarf those in Nebraska, New York, and California. Those states have helmet laws. If I'm elected, I will push for re-institution of the helmet laws. We must protect those who are too young or too foolish to protect themselves."

Fleiss appeared before the scales of justice. "Have you been the victim of an automobile accident and unable to gain satisfaction from insurance companies? One million, two million, three million! Those are some of the settlements I've recently procured on behalf of my clients. Now I'm not saying your claim is worth three million, but if you're tired of butting your head against the wall of insurance call me, the Hammer. Steve Fleiss." There was a number.

Josh switched to the Home Shopping Network where two women of a certain age gushed over *faux* ruby bracelets. Josh had a Colt .45 auto stripped and laid out on an old towel when Feral stormed in trailing a pong of cig smoke and body odor. He pulled up short and did an exaggerated double-take.

"Well fuck me runnin'! Look at the prospect. You'd better be gentle with that one, boy. That's mine."

Josh ran a cloth through the barrel. "Fine gun."

"Fuckin' A, it's a fine gun. Used it to pop two Al Qaeda motherfuckers who were looking to fry my ass. You're an ex-con so you wouldn't know about serving your country. I don't know what the fuck Orlok was thinking, inviting you out. You think you're better than me, don't you?" Josh didn't know what to say. Feral was jacked. He could feel Feral pumping himself up to explode and thought the best course was to lay low and act meek. "No, sir."

"What? You look at me when I'm talkin' to you, boy!"

Josh looked up into Feral's mean little deep-set eyes. Feral was six feet, raw-boned and rangy with the squinty eyes and the big knuckles of a hillbilly brawler.

"I do not think I'm better than you, Feral."

Feral essayed his death stare. It was pretty good. Josh could see the Jugan was higher than William Seymour Hoffman, possibly on meth or blow, with pinprick pupils, meth stench, and twitchy. Josh started clicking the '45 together. Feral reached down and wrenched it from Josh's grasp.

"Fuck it. I don't want you touchin' my shit."

Feral snicked it back, grabbed a magazine, jammed in six cartridges, shoved it home, jacked one into the chamber and turned the barrel on Josh. "Now what, motherfucker?" he grinned.

Josh knew Feral wasn't crazy enough to shoot him in the clubhouse. But this was a biker gang. It wasn't a meeting of the Young Socialists Club. Looking down as if ignoring the threat Josh grasped the aluminum cleaning rod with his left hand and drove the rod as hard as he could into Feral's groin.

Feral's eyes bulged as Josh rose up, twisted the pistol upside down in a two-hand grip, slamming his right elbow down Feral's face. Feral jerked back, forehead cut. Tossing the gun, Josh caught him by the back of his head and pulled him into a knee to the stomach. Josh stepped back and let Feral collapse groaning to the floor where he curled in fetal position.

Orlok and Bobby ran into the room and stopped short, mouths open.

"Ho-ly fuck," Orlok said.

"I told you not to front him," Bobby said.

CHAPTER

15

CONSEQUENCES

Feral curled like a shrimp. "You *motherfucker*...(GASP)... you're DEAD motherfucker!...(GASP)...oooooohhh..."

Orlok snapped his fingers at Josh and pointed to the front porch. Josh went out followed by Bobby.

"What the fuck happened?" Bobby said.

Josh told him. "Can't have a guy pointing a gun at me."

"Dumb fuck. I told him not to give you shit. He's always been like that. Always got to find someone to grind on. In the sand it was always the new guy. He drove three prospects out of here. If he hadn't been with Orlok in Kandahar, we would have kicked him out long ago. *Semper fi* and all that shit. Now we got a situation. You stay out here and chill while I talk to Orlok."

Sighing, Josh collapsed into one of the chairs and put his feet up on the rail. A quarter moon poked above the tree line. It was quiet out here except for the crickets and cicadas and the muted voices coming from within. Feral was loud and adamant, Orlok a barely discernible rumble. Josh had seen no women since arriving and didn't think Jane was there. The house gave off a male vibe.

After a while Orlok came out and lowered himself into one of the chairs. They sat in silence for a few minutes.

"Feral says you sucker-punched him."

"He pointed a gun at me."

"Says you should have known it was a joke."

"Don't care if it was a joke. I can't have people pointing guns at me."

"'I won't be wronged. I won't be insulted. I won't be laid a hand on. I don't do these things to other people, and I require the same from them.'"

"Pretty much sums it up."

"Understood," Orlok rumbled. "I apologize for Feral's behavior. However, since Feral is a charter member, he has certain rights. He demanded we give you the boot. I said that wasn't acceptable. You hadn't violated any rules and in fact have behaved in an exemplary manner. We wouldn't even be having this conversation if you hadn't pulled that loser off Jane."

"I was just doing my job."

"All too rare these days. But here's the thing. Feral's demanding a trial by combat."

Josh gazed over the tree line at the emerging stars. "What happens if I lose?"

"You're out."

"What happens if I win?"

"You stay. So does Feral. He'll just to live with it."

"Will I have to watch my back?"

"Feral might be missing one or two key elements but he knows that if you win, and he tries something sneaky he'll be betraying a brother and that we cannot allow."

"When?"

"Tomorrow."

"I have a day job," Josh said. "It will have to be in the evening."

The heady aroma of marijuana drifted out through the screen door.

"What's the job?" Orlok said.

"Wrangling bulls over at Franklin Farms."

"No shit. That's Jane's father's gig. He ships bull sperm all over the world. She help you with that?"

"No, sir."

"Huh," Orlok said. "Well good for you. It's a bare-knuckle fight. No groin shots, biting, or eye gouges."

"How many years did you pound a brick to make your hand like that?"

Orlok extended his right hand, fingers spread, made a fist and looked at it. "I started training in Okinawan karate when I was ten. My father encouraged me. I was an Army brat."

"He still alive?"

"No, he died in the Gulf War. My mother's still alive. Don't talk to her much. She disapproves of my lifestyle. She wanted me to preach the gospel. I've been an atheist since I was twelve. You got family?"

"My father abandoned me at a truck stop when I was fifteen," Josh said. "I bounced around from home to home 'til I discovered the Bedouins. They're the closest I have to family."

"But you're not affiliated."

"That was a condition of my release."

"Ahhh," Orlok said. "What happens if we give you colors?"

"Won't know 'til it happens."

Orlok slapped Josh on the thigh. "Good attitude."

Orlok got up and went inside. Josh phoned Louise Lowry to check up on Fig. She was doing fine.

Josh set an old kitchen chair against the doorknob of his room that night and pulled Fig close.

CHAPTER 16

IT'S A JOB

Thursday.

Josh woke at six-thirty, stopped at his house, played with Fig, stuffed some things in his tank bag and reported for work at eight a.m. The receptionist, the same silver-haired woman from yesterday, stood and greeted him warmly. "Mr. Pratt! Welcome to Franklin Farms. I'm Ellie Rossiter. If you'll just have a seat, I'll call Willy. He's our head wrangler. Would you like some coffee?"

Josh looked at the coffeemaker on the sideboard.

"No need to trouble yourself, ma'am. I'll get it." He downloaded a cup and dumped in three half and halfs and four packets of sugar. Seconds later a small, wiry middle-aged man with a fringe of gray hair, wearing carpenter's pants, T-shirt tucked tight around his hardball belly entered the room. Josh set his coffee down and shook hands.

"G'day, mate!" Willy said. "Welcome to the funny farm.

Come on. Let's get you squared away. We've got a lot of ground to cover."

Willoughby turned into a combo board/meeting/storage room, went to a wall of metal shelving holding box after box of equipment, rummaged around and tossed Josh a pair of leather gauntlets. "You'll need those." The wrangler looked at Josh's black motorcycle boots.

"You sure you want to wear those? This job is hell on footgear."

"No prob. They're old and beat-up."

Willoughby turned a rheostat and the room brightened. He pointed to a jumbo bulletin board on which color pictures of bulls were arranged by breed with charts and descriptions of their characteristics.

"Twenty-four bulls. You need to familiarize yourself with each one. They have different personalities and can be easy or difficult depending. Clem Kadiddlehopper, our prize Angus at the moment, is a real sweetheart. Some you can lead around with food or nose ring. We also have four Australian shepherds, very sharp, will respond to dozens of voice and hand commands. We use the dogs primarily to move the bulls around in open spaces but of course when it's time to milk, no dogs."

Willoughby sat at a computer station, brought up some files and pushed buttons. The printer chugged and hummed.

"While that's printin' out, let me show you around the barn."

They circled the room clockwise, Willoughby greeting

each bull by name and describing his characteristics. Josh didn't mention that he'd gone that route the day before. "Barney loves carrots, don't you big chazzer?" Willoughby introduced Josh to fourteen bulls. Some were personable, most were not. The two men moved outside where a geometric of white-painted fences described a dozen enclosures, most occupied.

"The Farm comprises sixty-five acres. We rotate the pastures to allow us to grow hay and alfalfa for feed." Willoughby gestured at a wind break. "We got twenty acres on the other side of those trees and there's a guardhouse over there." He pointed to miniscule cameras mounted on light poles and in some cases, in trees. "Cattle rustling is big business. There's a four-man security patrol on duty at all times."

Willoughby led Josh toward an enclosure inside which an Australian sheep dog worked in tandem with a cowboy to lasso a Texas Longhorn. "Regular buckaroos. You ride a horse?"

Josh grinned. "Not me, Willy! They're big stupid animals. I ride a motorcycle."

"Tried herding them with ATV at first," Willoughby said. "Bull didn't like it. Flattened the ATV against the side of the barn and damn near gored me!"

"How long have you been here?"

"Ten years. I was raised on a sheep station in Queensland, so I grew up riding. But you don't have to ride. Mr. Franklin wants you in the slot with the bull when we milk. We all got our faves. 'Cept Dionysus. Nobody likes Dionysus."

"Who's Dionysus?"

Willoughby headed back to the barn. "Dionysus is our A number one money maker, an American beefalo. You won't see Dionysus in the sales brochures or on the web site, no no. Dionysus is *sub-rosa*! Very hush hush. Dionysus is the Rolls Royce of bulls."

"Can I see Dionysus?"

"Not now. We've got to milk Sir Reginald Thune, Esq. Rush order from Dubai. You'll like Sir Reginald. Wear those gloves at all times. Do not stand directly in front of Sir Reginald or behind him. Don't turn your back on 'em."

They entered the barn, which smelled pleasantly of hay and manure. "They raise beef in Dubai?"

Willoughby shrugged. "You can get anything you want in Dubai. It may just be a front organization for growers in South Africa or Brazil who don't want us to know where it's going."

Josh followed Willoughby to a fenced enclosure with a steel roll-up door to the outside. The door was up, and they could see an enormous liver-colored bull walking toward them followed by a dog and a cowboy.

"I made a mess of this town," the cowboy sang.

Sir Reginald entered the enclosure. Willoughby pushed a button on the fence and the door rumbled down shutting off the sun. The barn was dimly lit by a series of hooded lamps hanging from the ceiling. The enclosure was double-wide, so the bull had room to turn around. The floor was covered with hay. Each enclosure had a slot entrance, too narrow for any bull, through which a man could slip in a second.

With gloves on, Willoughby squeezed into the enclosure talking to the bull, running his hand over its hump. "Good Sir Reginald, nice Sir Reginald, 'ow'd you like to getcher rocks off?"

He turned to Josh. "Go on! Give it a burl!"

Josh slipped into the enclosure staying next to the wall, a few feet from where Willoughby stood. Sir Reginald's horns had been cut to an inch so that he resembled a bovine Hellboy. A buzzer sounded and a yellow light on the wall flashed.

"Careful now, here comes Sir Reggie's date, the lovely and accomplished Miss Delilah Monsoon."

The metal door rumbled into the ceiling and a steer entered with the dog at its heels. As soon as the steer was inside the dog backed off and the door rolled down. Willoughby took a rubber apparatus that resembled a pipe fitting and affixed it to the steer's hindquarters with a series of elastic velcro straps that stretched around each rear leg and up and over the back.

"Now's the fun part, mate! You get to guide Sir Reginald into the landing slot."

Josh's grin froze. "How the fuck do I do that?"

Willoughby reached into a pocket and tossed Josh a tube of KY. "With your hands, mate! You can use his nose ring to maneuver him into position. Once I blast the pheromone, look out. Fair suck of the sav! You've got to be fast and accurate—you only get one shot and if you blow it, that's $250 wasted."

Josh stared at the tube of lubricant. "Fuck, fuck, fuck."

Willoughby made a few adjustments to the device. The rubbery black portal under the steer's ass was the size of a kosher salami. Willoughby produced a small aerosol bottle from one of his many pockets.

"Are you ready? Stay to the side there, once Sir Reg is off his front legs you can guide him in. Miss Delilah won't be kicking anyone."

Willoughby stood on one side of the cage and spritzed the aerosol in front of Sir Reggie, who immediately started shifting from leg to leg, jockeying for position. And then he was up, his erect member the size of a pork loin as he jabbed at the steer's hindquarters. With a glob of KY in his mitt Josh seized the bull's member and guided it into the black tube, whose outer entrance resembled one of those squeezable plastic pocket change pouches. Josh stepped back until he hit the fence, sweat popping on his forehead.

Sir Reginald's gyrations could be felt through the floor, like a level three earthquake. It was over in an instant. The enclosure smelled of hay and cattle. Sir Reggie hung there for a minute panting then eased out of the steer and dropped his forelegs to the ground.

"Hang on," Willoughby said, unstrapping the device and lifting it clear of the enclosure. "Hug the wall." He hit a button, the door rolled up into the roof, Sir Reginald and his paramour ambled out into the sun.

CHAPTER 17

PRODIGAL DAUGHTER

Josh assisted with six more bulls. By the time he was through he felt like he'd been run over by a truck. Brookline Massachusetts, a Guernsey with truncated horns, hip-checked Josh into the wall, painfully smashing his left shoulder. Sir Dusseldorf, a limousin, head-butted the same shoulder. Josh hoped he didn't have a torn rotator cuff.

At the end of the day he was covered with hay pollen, sweat and dust and his boots were caked with bullshit. His shoulder was purple. Willoughby directed him to the sports facility-like men's room which featured two shower stalls. As Josh dried himself off, he saw that Willoughby had left a stack of new T-shirts on the bench. Josh put one on and looked at himself in the mirror. The shirt was a portrait of a handsome bull over "Franklin Farms—the Finest in Select Sires" in gold cursive.

Josh found several jars of Tiger Balm by the sink, rubbed

it into his aching shoulder. Punching out his timecard he exited through the front office and stopped cold. Perched on Ellie Rossiter's desk happily gabbing was a familiar blonde.

"Jane!" Josh said.

She looked up surprised, her fresh face lighting up. "Josh! What are you doing here?"

"Your father gave me a job. Two jobs actually."

"Do you want to get a coffee?" Jane asked.

They went into the break room. Jane went to the sideboard. "Why are you limping?"

"Sir Dusseldorf stepped on my foot. Brookline Massachusetts side-checked me."

She laughed, pouring him a coffee. "How do you like it?"

"The coffee? Or my foot?"

"Coffee."

"Plenty of milk and sugar. The first job was to find you. Your father is very worried. Have you called him?"

Jane rolled her eyes and stared at the ceiling. "I'm fine. Tell Daddy I'm fine. I do not wish to speak with him because all he's gonna do is badmouth Orlok."

"What are you doing here?"

"I used to work here in high school and college. Doing books. That was before I realized daddy was helping prop up dictators. I have a lot of friends here—I just stopped by to say hello to Ellie."

"Are you staying at the club house?" Josh said.

"Who's asking? My friend Josh or Josh the PI?"

"Both."

"So now you're a Jugan."

"Not yet." He didn't mention the evening's entertainment.

Franklin appeared in the doorway red as a beet. "Jane!"

Jane flipped her hair. "Hello, Daddy."

"I've been worried sick about you! Why haven't you answered my phone calls?"

"I don't want to hear you rail about Orlok. I'm a grown woman and I can choose my friends, thank you very much."

Franklin rounded on Josh. "And you! Why didn't you tell me you'd found her?"

"Sir, I was going to report in a minute. I only laid eyes on her five minutes ago." Someone must have tipped off Franklin. Ellie, probably. She was his employee.

Franklin shut the lounge door and turned to his daughter. "I want you to move back into the house. You have your own suite and a separate entrance. These fucking environmental whackos are gearing up to destroy my business and they could conceivably target you."

Jane flicked the air. "I'm moving in with Orlok. No one will know I'm there and I'll be safer than if I were in the White House. Besides, Daddy. You know how I feel about your trade with fascist regimes!"

"You didn't object when I put you through grad school!"

"Oh Daddy," she said witheringly. "I intend to pay you back."

"From what? One of your stupid non-profits?"

"No, Daddy. Orlok is hiring me as business manager for his ginseng operation. I believe we can increase our market by at least five hundred per cent within two years. There's a reason I minored in business."

Franklin turned to Josh as if he were a referee. "She wanted to major in European history. Can you imagine?"

"What's wrong with it? And I switched after two semesters. Just a chip off the old block."

Franklin looked as if he were considering man-handling his daughter out of the building. Josh tensed up, Franklin caught it and relaxed. "Look. I've been getting death threats from these nuts. It's possible they're going to try and drag you into it."

"No, they're not! Everybody knows I support the anti-GMO protesters! It's only as a courtesy to you, as your daughter, I don't join them on the picket line!"

She seized her purse, shot out of her chair and headed for the exits. Franklin balled his fists and looked as if he were going to explode but didn't try to stop her. He made a physical effort to calm himself, went to the counter and made himself a cup of coffee. He leaned against the counter and took a sip.

"Well?"

"Sir, as to the first job, there she is, although I had nothing to do with it. Just like I said, I saw her five minutes before you arrived. As to the second, I'm just getting the hang of things. I haven't had an opportunity to go through the personnel files you gave me, but I plan to do that over the weekend. I have yet to meet all the personnel. I need to talk to your chief geneticist. He's the guy who oversees the jiz op, right?"

"Dr. Gruber is in charge of breeding. He's aware of the missing product. He should be back tomorrow. You can see him then."

"I'll be able to keep an eye out for Jane since I'm staying at the Jugan compound."

Franklin's horizontal eyes narrowed. "How is that?"

"I thought the best way to learn about Orlok was to join the club."

Franklin sucked in his lips. "Do you think there's any connection between the Jugan and my missing product?"

"I don't know. They haven't said boo about bull sperm. Far's I know they operate a legitimate ginseng operation and most of those guys have regular jobs. What's the deal on Dionysus?"

Franklin looked startled. "Dionysus? He's a beefalo. Why?"

"Willy says he's your number one rainmaker but he's not listed in any of the catalogs. Why the secrecy?"

"Right now, we are conducting studies with a select number of customers who have all signed a non-disclosure agreement. Come to think of it, I'm going to have to ask you to sign one as well."

"How come all the greenies are freaked out about your bulls? What's the danger?"

Franklin threw his hands in the air. "There is no danger! Those people are nuts. We've been eating genetically modi-fied foods for decades. Jesus! Haven't these people heard of corn hybrids? What they think is, the devil spawn of these crimes against nature will turn us all impotent or cause our navels to disappear and reappear on the back of our necks."

He rose. "Stop by Ellie and sign the non-disclosure agreement before you leave. Bill me for hours on Jane."

CHAPTER 18

TRIAL BY COMBAT

A half dozen rag-tag protesters stood outside the front gate chanting and carrying signs.

"Hey, hey, ho, ho—GMOs have got to go!

One of the placards depicted a two-headed calf. The man holding it had granny glasses, a long white beard, and was wearing what appeared to be a wizard's robe. They respect-fully backed off as Josh motored through, closing again in his wake and taking up the chant.

Josh headed northwest.

When he arrived at the compound, Jane's Prius sat next to Bobby's V-Max and three other bikes including Orlok's new Indian. Feral's hard-tail was not among them. Ash-ton's F-150 sat on the dirt on the side. Josh went inside the big farmhouse and smelled something delicious emanating from the kitchen. Jane, Ashton and Robin buzzed around like electrons setting the table, baking and cooking.

"Hi!" Jane said. "The boys are back in the barn sorting seng. Dinner in a half hour."

Josh went through the house out the back door to the barn. Inside, on a rough wood floor, Orlok, Bobby and Marcus gathered around a big table containing dozens of rectangular plastic compartments. A couple of plastic bins on the ground held the harvest. Several motorcycles huddled in a corner next to a workbench. In back, tarps covered vehicular shapes. They looked up as Josh approached. Bobby hugged him, Orlok and Marcus exchanged fist daps.

"When's the fight?" Josh said.

"Whenever Feral gets here."

"'Cause dinner is in a half hour and I'm hungry."

Orlok headed for the house. "Well let's eat."

"Good," Josh said catching up with him. "I hate to fight on an empty stomach."

Dinner was salad, meatloaf and mashed potatoes. It was seven by the time they finished, and Josh began to hope that Feral had rethought his challenge and was laying low. No such luck.

After dinner the boys took their bourbon out on the porch and settled into the chairs. Josh heard the rumble coming up the road and seconds later Feral arrived on his hard-tail, kicked out and hopped off with a jagged edge. Josh saw chemical craziness in Feral's eyes as the outlaw took the three porch stairs in a leap. He stank of b.o. from four feet.

He turned to Josh with pinprick pupils. "How 'bout it,

motherfucker? You wanna try me when I'm ready?"

With a massive sigh Josh heaved himself out of his chair, went down the three steps to his bike and took something out of the tank bag. "I'll be with you in a minute."

Feral took a step toward him. "What the fuck is it?"

Josh held up a Thai steel cup he'd got from Nelson Ferreira of the Zhong Yi Kung Fu Association and went into the house. He emerged shirtless and shoeless to find everyone outside on the lawn, chairs hauled up, six bikers he didn't know drinking beer and passing a joint, Feral warming up with stretches hopping around like a jitterbug. An unknown Jugan with a scraggly beard stood in his corner working his shoulders and speaking in his ear.

Orlok stood in the center of the lawn, hands on hips, wearing voluminous camo trou and a black tank top that showed blue ink on ham-like arms. Bobby stood in Josh's corner with a towel and a bag of ice.

Marcus aimed a video cam. Josh did a few limbering up exercises, but he was pretty much stretched out after daily sessions. A couple more Jugan whom he hadn't met joined the crowd on the lawn. Orlok raised his hands.

"No crotch shots, eye-gouging or fishhooks. You do and I'll land on you like a meteor. The fight goes until someone gives or is no longer able to continue. Are you gentlemen ready?" He pointed to Feral.

"Ready."

He pointed to Josh.

"Ready."

Orlok held his hand in the air. "Then let's do it." He chopped the air.

Feral charged across the lawn like a bull to take Josh down. Josh was ready and sprawled with his hands on Feral's shoulders and for a moment they danced around like an awkward piece of furniture. Feral backed off and struck a fighter's stance. He was a couple inches taller than Josh and came in behind his jab pumping like a piston. Josh circled away and when he got a little space described a head-high crescent with his right foot. It was an abort move, designed to stop any kicks cold, and it worked.

Feral moved in circling and throwing that jab. Josh timed the jab and held up his left elbow so Feral connected with the point and stepped back, flexing his hand.

"Go Feral," the scraggly beard said. "Waste that fucker!"

"Go Josh!" Jane shouted, drawing looks and whistles.

Using his superior height and bulk Feral closed with massive body hooks. Josh pulled his elbows in tight and threw an uppercut as Feral connected with a left that bent Josh's ribs and radiated shock through his body. Josh hunched over and leaned into the hooks with his elbow tight to his rib cage, grabbed Feral by the back of the neck, leaped up and slammed his knee into Feral's midsection. Josh's arm screamed where the bull had jammed him. As Feral shook himself free Josh slammed his right shin into Feral's thigh. Josh saw pain in Feral's eyes and followed it up with a right roundhouse kick to the head which Feral barely blocked, staggering sideways.

They circled each other heaving while bikers placed bets. Josh's ribs were on fire.

"Bouncer's tough," someone said.

"Feral's tougher."

Feral tried a Superman punch. Josh turned into it, grabbing Feral's arm and went for a hip throw but Feral slammed his elbow into the back of Josh's head and he lost it. Feral twisted in, got his right foot behind Josh's leg and tripped him. They fell to the ground twisting and grappling, both getting up with their hands on each other. They broke.

Feral skittered forward with a blow to Josh's gut and when Josh automatically dropped his guard Feral went high and tagged with a stinging jab on his right cheekbone. Josh oozed blood. They clanged together, Josh using both elbows to deflect Feral's blows, scoring with a swooping overhand right that staggered Feral for an instant.

Josh rushed in, ducked low and grabbed Feral around the midsection, heaving him up, twisting, and throwing him to the ground. Josh fell, slamming into Feral with his full weight, grabbing Feral's right wrist in both hands. Feral fought back like a cornered alley cat, kicking and scratching, trying for an eye gouge with Orlok unable to see, vision blocked by Josh.

Josh slammed the crown of his skull into Feral's nose and felt the cartilage snap as blood exploded all over his face. Josh got his right arm beneath Feral's head, gripped Feral's right wrist and snaked his left hand beneath Feral's bicep, using both arms to lever Feral's right arm up in an unnatural direction. Josh torqued it and heard the shoulder snap.

Planting his knee on Feral's gut Josh stood up, sweating and panting. He was splattered with blood and long red grooves down his chest where Feral had raked him. Feral sat up sucking air, cradling his arm and cursing.

Orlok raised his arms. "Josh stays."

"Yayyyy!" Jane said.

CHAPTER

19

PAT

Thursday night and Friday morning.

Feral couldn't ride so Josh left. He didn't want to be around until things calmed down. It was inevitable he would make enemies. Feral had a lot more friends in the club than Josh, who got home around ten-thirty, put the bike in the garage and took his second shower of the day, pausing to admire the purple marks overlaying the ink on his torso. He looked like a tortoise shell. It hurt every time he moved. In a couple hours he would be too sore to ride.

Josh took four ibuprofen and went to work. No point trying to sleep. He sat in his living room with a legal pad on his knee and wrote, "Jane stealing bull jizz?"

It was far-fetched, but then so was his life. Jane was the common denominator between the farm and the Jugan, but there was nothing in Orlok's background that indicated any interest whatsoever in cattle breeding, much less the international contacts to make it worthwhile.

Sure he'd been in Afghanistan and Iraq. Not exactly cow country. On the other hand, dealing ginseng to China showed a certain amount of business savvy. The Chinese ate beef, didn't they? Josh researched Chinese cattle operations online.

> *Before reform and opening up, cattle were always treated as servant instead of meat. Chinese government actively encouraged peasants to feed cattle on straws not until the early 1990s in order to decrease straw waste and to promote the cyclic utilization of straws. As a result, the costs of feeding cattle declined, and the passion of cattle farmers was stimulated. All of these promoted the rapid development of beef cattle industry and the development of beef cattle slaughtering industry and beef processing industry in China. In 2012, the output volume of beef totaled 6.623 million tons in China, increasing by 2.3% YOY.*

Due to lack of grasslands Chinese beef production was few and far between. They imported mostly dairy cows from Australia, New Zealand and Paraguay.

Josh couldn't stand Chinese food. Made him want to gag. He'd been trying it for twenty years on his friends' say-so and he still didn't like it.

But that didn't mean the Chinese weren't interested in steaks and burgers.

Or Jane might have nothing to do with the thefts.

Pat Murphy was a mystery man. His personnel file offered the bare bones: he was thirty-six, unmarried, no siblings, no living parents, a man without a family. Born in Viroqua, he graduated from the UW with a Masters in Veterinary Genetics and went to work at twenty-six for Franklin Farms. He had no virtual profile and had lived quietly in a rented cottage in Verona. The cops had searched his place and found zipco.

Josh went through the personnel files. Dr. Gruber was conspicuous by his absence, but the head geneticist was probably not the thief.

Finally, around two a.m. Josh crashed on the sofa under a Harley blanket. He woke with Fig nuzzling and a slight hangover which he ran off, returning red-eyed and exhausted to shower. Again.

Murphy's house off Highway 69 in Verona was a small white cottage with green trim, what had once been an in-law house on a large farm. The foot-high lawn was rife with dandelion and creeping Charlie, the wood staircase sagged and dust covered the living room window. Murphy hadn't been much of a housecleaner. Josh walked around to the back and found the kitchen door open.

A cold cast iron pan rimmed with grease sat on the electric oven. There were mouse turds on the curled linoleum floor and insects buzzing around the open garbage can beneath the sink. Using a paper towel Josh snagged the garbage can, took it outside and put it in a sealed aluminum trash can.

Empty bottles of Konig Pilsners and Jagermeister on the dirty linoleum kitchen table. The tiny living room was furnished with student cast-off, an ancient cathode-ray television hooked up to a VHS player with a scattering of cass-ettes on the shelves below: Arnold Schwarzenegger and Sylvester Stallone movies, and a modern X-Box with its own flat screen and control yoke. Games lay around: *Call of Duty, Dominion, Red Dead Redemption, Grand Theft Auto*. The sole wall decoration was a cheaply framed poster of Scarlett Johansson as The Black Widow.

In the bedroom Murphy's single was made with military precision. Bedside reading material consisted of *American Cattleman* and *Beef Magazine*. In the bed-stand drawer Josh found copies of *Hustler* and a jar of Vaseline. Research.

In the closet Josh found neon orange hunting duds and a box of twelve gauge shells. No doubt the cops had taken the gun.

Murphy's hard drive was also missing.

Where were his next of kin? Had no one catalogued the dead man's belongings? Josh phoned Calloway and went straight to voice mail.

"Call me."

Josh arrived at the farm at nine and punched in. This time he had brought a pair of Timberland boots and cover-alls. Willoughby was waiting for him when he entered the barn.

"Josh! Oi'm glad you're here. Oi need to draw some blood and you're gonna help."

Josh clapped his hands together. "Can't wait."

Using the dog Monty they brought in a Hereford named Dabny. While Willoughby extracted blood and handed the vials to Josh, a tall man with iron gray hair and military bearing, wearing a white lab coat came over to the enclosure, head and shoulders visible over the fence.

"Good morning, Willy," he said with a slight Slavic accent.

"Dr. Gruber. This is Josh Pratt the new wrangler."

"Very pleased to meet you, Josh. Perhaps later we could have a beer together." His voice was like molasses, low and slow. "Boys, I hate to ask but Axel's home sick and I need a sample from Dionysus."

"Dionysus the beefalo?" Josh said.

"Dot's right," Gruber said.

"Well," Willoughby said drawing blood, "you have to meet him sooner or later. We'll get on it as soon as we're done."

"Thank you."

As Gruber walked across the barn, Willoughby put a hand up and said *soto voce*, "*Jawohl, mein obersturmbanfuhrer!*"

"He's funny," Josh said.

"Ve are breeding za perfect bull!"

"What's the story on Dionysus?"

"He's a right bastard. Put two wranglers in hospital and crippled one guy for life but has yet to get the best of me." Willoughby pointed to his temple. "That's because O'im smarter than he is. Usually we leave him to Axel."

"Why Axel?"

"'Cause he's almost as big as the fookin' bull. And he's got a way with 'em. Almost like he can talk to them."

"Like Badger," Josh said.

"'Ooh?"

"Badger. Wisconsin's very own comic book superhero."

"Oi don't read comic books."

Willoughby approached a red Toyota pick-up, opened the door and whistled. Monty the Aussie shepherd leaped in with a grin.

"You drive," Willoughby said. "I'll saddle up and meet you in Pasture Z."

CHAPTER

20

DIONYSUS

Josh and Monty, snout in the wind, jounced along a dirt road that ran between pastures through the wind break to a field not visible from the research complex. A slot entrance stood next to the steel and aluminum gate. The fence surrounded a ten by twenty box just inside the main gate with its own gate, which was open. There was a steel water trough inside the enclosure.

A minute later Willoughby arrived on a big sorrel.

"Get the gate," Willoughby said.

Josh got out, unlatched the gate, swung it inward, waited for Willoughby to ride through, walked in with the dog and closed it again.

"What's the plan?"

"See that enclosure? We'll herd him in there and you'll feed him carrots while I take blood."

"What am I supposed to do while you and Monty are

herding?"

"Wait." He paused. "Used to be Murphy's job. You 'eard about Murphy?"

"Yes. Am I his replacement?"

"I doubt anybody could replace him, no offense. Axel's the only other guy Dionysus will obey and he's not here. Right now, we're just trying to figure out how to get Dionysus to cooperate. Let's give it a burl. Monty! Let's go." The dog trotted happily after Willoughby, wagging its tail.

Josh boosted himself up and sat on the fence as Willoughby and Monty went after Dionysus, fifty yards away. Willoughby's commands were unintelligible to him, but the dog reacted with military precision, taking a stance on the far side of the beefalo, lowered himself into the weeds and rose barking. Willoughby jockeyed up so that he was at Dionysus' ten, Monty at two.

At first Dionysus paid no heed but as Monty and Willoughby got closer, he whipped his head from side to side and trotted in a circle away from the enclosure. Willoughby and Monty adjusted, always maintaining the ten and two position. Dionysus stopped, looked from one to the other and pawed the ground. Willoughby's horse skittered sideways as Monty dashed in barking, drawing the buff's attention.

Dionysus turned on the dog and lunged forward with a bellow but Monty neatly sidestepped and ran off, circling behind Willoughby and the horse. Willoughby yelled something loud and came forward.

Dionysus turned toward the horse and charged. The horse reared in panic, tossing Willoughby on his ass and snapping its front leg in a gopher hole with a noise like a rifle shot. The horse collapsed bleating as Dionysus bore down like a runaway locomotive.

Willoughby was up and running for the nearest fence. Dionysus plowed into the horse with the sound of a sledge-hammer hitting a side of beef. The horse screamed and exploded as the beefalo sank its horn and ripped upward. Gore arced through the sun. The horse's death cries frayed Josh's nerves with a dull knife.

Willoughby went down. One second he was running, the next he flopped to the ground like a closing trap door. Josh threw open the gate and ran for the truck. He got in the seat and watched as Dionysus ripped and tore at the remains of the horse until there was nothing but bone, gobbets and blood, an exploded meat bomb.

Josh started the engine and put it in first gear. It was a light Toyota pick-up and couldn't have weighed more than 2900 lbs, slightly more than Dionysus. Josh couldn't see Willoughby who lay flat so as not to attract the buff's attention. Dionysus looked around snorting explosively. The bull stared at Josh but was too far away to read facial expressions—at least Josh hoped. The bull danced in a circle bowing to the four winds. The bull pawed the ground.

Josh felt a bolus of dread congeal in his gut. He leaned on the horn, floored it and up-shifted into second, the little truck jouncing and hopping over the pasture. The bull rotated toward him like a gun turret. As soon as it turned its back, Willoughby sprinted for the sidelines.

The bull launched itself at the truck. Josh barely had time to react, turning the wheel when Dionysus was twenty yards away hurtling toward him like a black hammer thrown by a vengeful god. The truck jounced and wavered going up on two wheels as Josh turned sharp, the black beef adjusting for angle.

Why hadn't they trimmed its horns?

Josh circled around toward the entry gate hoping to stop the truck in the gap preventing the bull from escaping the pasture. He glanced fearfully in the rear view as the black asteroid bore down on him.

The bull rammed the back of the truck, tossing it up so that the tailgate pointed at the sky. For an instant the truck balanced precariously on its grill, Josh holding himself off the wheel with arms extended. He'd never fastened the seat belt.

The bull turned in a tight circle and rammed the underside sending the truck ass over teakettle to land on its roof in the middle of the gate. Josh smashed his chin on the wheel, threw open the door and slithered out, shoulder screaming. Dionysus snorted, pawed the ground, turned and ambled off to the center of the pasture where he stopped and cropped grass.

Willoughby, clothes smeared with grass stains with a purple bruise on his forehead, twisted through the slot gate in the adjoining pasture through which he'd walked back to the entrance.

"So much for Plan A," he said.

CHAPTER

21

INITIATION

The truck had landed so that they were just able to shut the
gate. A Jeep Rubicon in green and yellow Franklin Farms
livery raced up the dirt lane and stopped, sending a cloud of
dust washing over them. A young man in dungarees and a
green FF shirt that said Brett on the breast pocket got out.

"Jesus Christ! Are you all right?"

Willoughby brushed himself off. "Fuck I'm good! Just
ask me."

"Fine," Josh said. He realized he was in a state of shock,
went to the fence and sat down with his back against it.

"I told Dr. Gruber. He's on his way."

A Porsche Boxster rolled up top down and Gruber got
out carrying a black leather satchel. "What happened?"
he said staring over the fence at the beefalo which grazed
peacefully.

Willoughby told him.

"*Gott verdammt nochmal in die Hölle!*" Gruber said. "Dionysus—is he all right?"

"No worries, but he tore Elsa up like a wet Kleenex."

"We can get more horses," Gruber said, "but there's only one Dionysus. Brett, call a towing company and get this truck out of here."

"Yes, sir." Brett pulled out his cell.

"You boys can harvest another bull. Look at the schedule."

Leaving Gruber and Brett, Willoughby and Josh walked back toward the compound, Monty at their heels.

"Why didn't you trim Dionysus like the other bulls?" Josh said.

"You'd have to ask Herr Gruber. It's like Samson's hair I gather."

"Pat Murphy. What was he like?"

"He was a fair dinkum bloke. Not much of a talker, quiet sort. Liked to play those video games, fancied himself a real hellion. Went over there once but I ain't one for sittin' in front of a screen. I never was. He liked *Call of Duty.*"

"No family, next of kin?"

"No, that's the sad part, i'nt it? Struck me as lonely. Franklin was his whole life. He loved that buff. Woulda took it home with him if he could."

They spent the rest of the afternoon milking four bulls. Josh punched out at six-thirty and rode to the Jugan. Jane's Prius sat in front of the house, Jane and Orlok on the veranda drinking gin and tonics. No sign of Feral or his chopper.

The report of gunfire echoed through the trees.

"Hello, Josh," Jane said. "Would you like a gin and tonic?"

Josh went up the steps and sank down in an empty Adirondack. "Sure."

Jane went in the house.

"We got a little shootin' range out back," Orlok said. "The boys like to stay sharp. Maybe we'll go back in a little while and join 'em. You a shooter?"

"I'm not allowed to have guns," Josh said not mentioning the small arsenal he kept in his safe.

"Yeah, well you can shoot my guns on our land. Ain't no law against that. All Jugan gotta shoot."

"Right now?" Josh said.

Orlok chopped the air. "Tomorrow. I just got back myself. See that you were out at that casino in South Dakota where the state senator got shot."

"I was doing security for Buffalo Hump."

"May, I love Hump. Saw him at Sturgis last year. What's he like?"

"He's a lot like you, Orlok. A thinker. A philosopher. He was always trying to get me to read. Nietzsche, Jung, Frankl, Campbell."

Orlok raised his glass. "Good shit. Weren't for Bobby, I'da gone stupid a long time ago. Until you came alone, he was the only one I could talk to. About philosophy, I mean. I can talk pussy, pills and Porsches all day long and into the night.

"When asked what the first destination on the road to realization was, a Sufi elder replied, 'bewilderment.' The other three are: poverty, unity, and life. All four might be translated as the loss of certainty and identity, non-attachment rather than austerity, connection to one's relations, and finally one's life fully lived as a true human being. Agree or disagree?" Josh raised his glass again. They clinked.

Jane came out of the house with three fresh drinks tinkling on a tin tray which she set on an upended cable spool between Josh and Orlok. They picked up their drinks. Orlok held his to the sky.

"Man is a rope stretched between the animal and the Superman."

They clinked glasses and drank.

"You read Nietzsche?" Orlok said.

"Yes, I read a lot of philosophy in prison. My favorite was Lao Tsu."

"Jane tells me she saw you at the farm."

"Yup."

"You know they're creating genetically modified beef."

"Is that a bad thing?"

"Well it's not natural, you have to grant that. We don't know what effect this may eventually have on children who eat it now. There are a lot of tests showing that today's kids have weaker immune systems than their parents and they think it's because of genetically modified food."

Josh peered through the lemon slice in his glass at the lowering sun. "Or it could be they're overdosed with antibiotics. Nobody knows."

Jane leaned forward with her arms on her knees. "It's corporations. The only way they can make money is to consume a little piece of the earth and spit it out all sucked up or turned to poison! The EU won't permit genetically modified products. Why does the U.S. lag behind the rest of the world? Did you know that coffee you get at Starbuck's, it's all chemically modified? From Monsanto?"

Orlok pinned Josh with guileless blue eyes. "Who does man think he is? How arrogant to think he can improve on nature."

Josh held his hands up. "I need that job."

"Jane and I intend to have kids."

Josh glanced at Jane. Butter wouldn't melt.

"What kind of world are we going to leave them?" she said. "What effect will the chemicals we ingest today have on our children, our grandchildren? Why is autism and asthma on such a huge upswing throughout the world?"

"Not my circus," Josh said.

Orlok chuckled. "Of course. We must lay off my sweet. Josh is but an honest working man."

"I thought you were a detective," Jane said.

"I'm working. Your father hired me to find out who ran over Pat Murphy."

Orlok stood. "Well them steaks won't grill themselves. Grab your drinks and follow me." They went through the house to the deck out back where Orlok opened a gas grill and turned on the propane. A minute later Jane brought out the steaks. There were only three.

"The boys already ate," Orlok said.

Jane kept the gin and tonics coming and brought a salad. For a while, there was only the chirping of the crickets and the call of the birds. After dinner Jane picked up the dishes and didn't return.

Orlok pulled out a leather case containing six fat Cuban cigars and handed Josh a *Montecristo*.

Orlok bit off the end and spat. "You know Fort McCoy?"

"I know where it is," Josh said, rolling the cigar under his nose.

"We're thinking of making a run. Maybe you want to come along."

Josh lit the cigar, rolling it over the flame. He wasn't really a cigar guy, but he didn't want to hurt Orlok's feelings. "Why? Do they have a bar?"

"They got guns. Lots of guns. Guns people want. It's a chance to make some real money."

Josh knew what was coming. "Doing what?"

Orlok blew a perfect smoke ring, then another. "Take the guns, sell 'em to this guy I know."

"You're a veteran. Doesn't it bother you, stealing from the Army?"

Orlok peered at Josh over his cigar and for an instant Josh felt the sheer presence of the man. His density cast its own gravitational field.

"Do you have any idea how much money the Army wastes? Or the Marines?"

"What guy?"

"You don't need to know that."

The trees in the yard blazed emerald in the setting sun.

"What guy?" Josh said.

Orlok took his time. "Jerrel Moore."

Josh took his time. "I know Jerrel. I got my dog from him."

"No shit. What dog?"

Josh pulled out his smart phone and dialed up Fig, passing it to the big guy.

"Noice!" Orlok said. "Been thinking about getting a dog myself. You say Jerrel has dogs?"

"His bitch had a litter. I was just there at the right time. Couple years ago."

"What the fuck were you doing with Jerrel Moore?"

Josh told Orlok the story about how Charlotte, the original Fig, had hired him to find out what happened to her brother, a university athlete who'd been found drowned in Lake Mendota after a night of drinking. The case had wound through a labyrinth of false fronts and strange neighborhoods, including near west side Milwaukee, the most segregated city in the nation.

Josh traced the killings to UW Sociology Professor Jeffrey Wolfe, former radical, former SDS founder, who'd launched a dark net movement to convince minority youth to murder successful young white athletes in the cause of "social justice." They were known as the "Smiley Face Killings," due to the appearance of a graffiti smiley face near each drowning.

"That's fucking incredible," Orlok says. "Respect you all the more, brother! All the more reason you should come in on this."

"Well what are you saying, that we're gonna rob Fort McCoy?"

"Hopefully, we will be burgling them."

Josh sighed. Fort McCoy was a heavily-armed military installation in Monroe County, a training and deployment center, especially for Afghanistan. If Josh wanted to join the Jugan, he couldn't refuse. But he couldn't deny the allure. He'd loved being part of the Bedouin brotherhood. He yearned for that kind of camaraderie.

Maybe it was because he'd always been looking for a father figure. In prison, it had been Chaplain Dorgan. Out here he had no one, until he met Orlok. The dude radiated charisma like a block of dry ice. Part of it was his sheer physical presence.

Dropping out had consequences. He knew things.

"And Jerrel wants all these guns for what?" Josh said.

Orlok opened his hand and released an imaginary butterfly.

"Make war on Whitey?"

Orlok released another butterfly. "I only met him once. You would know better than me."

Jerrel was a canny operator, too canny to align himself with Black Lives Matter or walking around spewing racial nonsense, although he was affiliated with BSPN.

"How much money?" Josh said.

"A hundred thou."

"What's my cut?"

Orlok puffed. "Twenty gees each. Twenty for the kitty."

"Let me think about it," Josh said.

"Or," Orlok said.

OR WHAT

"Or what?"

"You know this Sheila Livermore-Epstein cunt?"

Josh carefully tipped a fat ash over the railing. "I've seen the signs."

"You know she wants to bring back helmet laws?"

Josh tried to blow a smoke ring. "The fight for liberty is never-ending."

"True that. She's also in bed with the GMO boys—Monsanto and that crowd."

Josh watched a flock of starlings zig-zag over the trees in perfect unison. "I thought she was a greenie."

"Oh, she puts up a green front, but she rides around in a Yukon and flits cross-country in a private plane provided by her GMO buddies. She plans to introduce a bill easing restrictions on GMO labeling and giving them tax breaks."

Josh wondered where it was going. "I try not to think

about politics."

"You may not think about politics, but politics thinks about you, know what I'm sayin'?"

"Yup."

"You want to be a Jugan?"

"You bet."

"If you don't want to do the raid, you gots to do one little thang and you're in."

"Tell me."

"Kill that bitch."

Josh blew smoke and let it sink in. "You want me to kill Sheila Livermore-Epstein?"

"That's right."

"I'm not a murderer."

"How bad do you want to be a Jugan? You walk away now, and we have a problem."

Josh suspected that if he tried to walk away, he might never leave the compound.

"I have no intention of walking away. But killing a state senator is suicidal. I'm just a dumb ex-con. A man should know his limitations."

Orlok set his cigar carefully on the arm rest of his Adirondack, the butt not touching the wood. "What do you propose we do about her?"

"Is it personal?"

"No," Orlok said. "It's philosophical. This country was founded on the concept of individual freedom. IN DI VI DUAL. The very concept of the government telling me what or what I can't wear is abhorrent to me. If the Jugan stand for anything, it is the concept of individual liberty as enshrined in our Constitution and Bill of Rights."

"Okay," Josh said. "Let me think."

Several minutes went by punctuated only by bird calls, the distant sound of barking dogs, and crickets.

"What if," Josh said.

"Yeah?"

"What if I could get Sheila Livermore-Epstein to drop this legislation?"

Orlok leaned away and regarded Josh with a sly grin.

"I thought you were just a dumb ex-con."

"Yeah, but what if I could do that? Would I be in?"

Orlok's big hand fell on Josh's shoulder. "You'd be in like Flynn!"

Jane came out of the house with Orlok's fifth. "What's funny?"

"Our boy Josh here is going to convince Sheila Livermore-Epstein to withdraw her helmet bill."

Jane handed Orlok his drink. "Maybe if you had a video of her having sex with a man."

Orlok held up his hand. "High five!"

Jane smacked him. She looked at Josh. "You're gonna do it, right?"

"Yeah, I'll do it."

"That's great, Josh. Just great!"

Orlok reached inside his leather vest and withdrew his works. "You want to do a line?"

Josh stood and stretched. "No thanks. I'm beat up from wrestling bulls. I just want to go to bed."

Orlok nodded toward the six-person spa covered with tan awning. "There's the hot tub. We're goin' into town. Catch you on the flipside."

Orlok heaved himself from the chair and went inside. Josh heard them climb the old wooden steps. Josh stripped, tipped back the awning and stepped into blessed hot water with a faint tincture of chloride. He drifted. Minutes later he heard an engine roar to life and looked up to see Orlok and Jane cruise past in a black Durango trailing Nine Inch Nails. Jane waved through the open window.

Josh waved back. He soaked in the tub for twenty minutes, levered himself out and toweled himself off. He entered the eerily empty house. Where was everybody? He'd heard some bikes roar by earlier and figured the party had moved to Chief Konapacki's. They wouldn't leave the compound unattended. There'd be a guy out by the road.

Josh dressed and was about to head into town and his own bed when he realized he had an opportunity. Orlok's study on the first floor contained an old roll-top desk lovingly restored, many photographs of Orlok with friends and units in Afghanistan and Iraq. Josh identified Feral, Bobby and a few others.

A couple of the photos had no people—scenes of blasted urban areas, a burning personnel carrier, some bones in the desert with hazy mountains in the distance. One black and white photo showed Orlok in a white karate uniform smashing through a cinderblock with his fist.

Built in floor to ceiling bookcase was stacked with Cicero, Epictetus, Lao Tzu, Sun Sao, Nietzsche, Machiavelli, the Durant *History of Civilization*, Winston Churchill, books about Winston Churchill, memoirs of generals. *Encyclopedia Britannica* occupied three feet of gold-lettered leather. A collection of Great Books including *Ivanhoe*, Shakespeare, Dickens, Turgenev, Dostoevsky, Gogol, Hemingway. *The Bible, Book of Mormon* and the *Koran*.

A museum-quality globe rested in a birdbath-shaped plinth.

A Plexiglass case contained a Nazi dagger.

A locked gun cabinet held a Remington 700 with a scope, a Mossbach 12 gauge with a pistol grip and two AKs. On the wall hung Sting, Frodo's sword from *Lord of the Rings*. A CD boom box and a small stack of CDs: The Chi-Lites, Booker T. and the MGs, SOS Band, Earth, Wind and Fire, Etta James, Lavern Baker and Frankie Lymon and the Teenagers.

A flat screen computer perched on a TV table next to the desk. Papers and notepads occupied the pigeon-holes. Josh pulled out a bright rectangle and unfolded. *For Men Only Gentlemen's Club—Your First Drink's On Us!* in the Dells. Some betting stubs from Ho Chunk, receipts for utilities, bills and brass. Several cubbyholes were filled with spent brass: 9 mm, .357 and .45 and a handful of live rounds.

The desk was unlocked. A loaded .357 magnum lay in the top right-hand drawer. The middle drawer contained a smeared mirror, cut up soda straws, pens, post-it notes, paper clips and a staple remover. A gum pack-sized Sony digital recorder. Josh flipped it on. The little light failed to glow.

He put it back and tried the other drawers. The left-hand drawer contained glue, rubber cement, transparent tape, pliers, batteries and flash drives. Josh touched the control button. The computer was off. He was looking for anything that might connect Orlok to the thefts. But how did you even sell stolen bull semen? You had to know the buyers. There was nothing in Orlok's past indicating involvement in commodities or the cattle industry.

Except for Jane.

The bottom left hand drawer held hanging files with hand-written labels: Record, Commendations, Actions, Insurance, Discharge Papers, Pictures. Josh pulled that file and sifted through color photos of mind-numbing destruction and slaughter. The setting was clearly the Middle East— blasted vehicles by the side of a road in a desert, four bodies slumped against a wall, their faces red smears. A blasted skyline with thick black smoke rising from two places.

He put it back, flipped briefly through the rest of the files until he came to the end. He was about to close the drawer when he thought to check beneath the files in case something had fallen down. He reached down behind the final file, his hands closing on a slim square bound book. He drew it out.

Sustainable Protocols by Heinrich Hochrein.

SPREAD THE WORD

Josh gulped four Ibuprofen, packed up and rode to the front gate. Panda lay suspended in a hammock between two trees and didn't wake until Josh blipped the throttle. The hammock nearly touched the ground.

Panda sat up and rubbed his eyes. He reached for his glasses hanging from a twig. "Huh?"

"Goin' home, hoss. See y'all tomorrow."

"Okay." Panda laid back and sawed wood.

Josh got off his bike and opened the gate.

It took ninety minutes riding the back roads watching for deer. Josh counted eight. When he got home, he put the bike away and went to his computer, Fig at his heels. He went to Jane's *Facebook* page, opened up her pictures and went through them slowly one by one. He could tell Paraguay at a glance just from the colors and lighting. Lots of pictures with locals including some stunning girls, grinning kids in Dethrone and Spongebob T-shirts.

Several of the pics appeared to be at some compound deep in the rain forest, a crew of several dozen young people lined up with dazzling grins around a dude in a Nehru jacket.

It took Josh 45 minutes to go through the pictures. He saw no one who might plausibly be Heinrich Hochrein. The dude in the Nehru jacket looked too young. But Josh could be wrong.

He googled Sustainable Protocols and found their homepage, *www.sustainableprotocols.py.*

> *Sustainable Protocols is a non-profit organization dedicated to preserving the Earth for future generations and the benefit of all living things. Sustainable Protocols Fund is nonprofit and tax-exempt to continue the vital work of Sustainable Protocols by increasing public awareness and understanding of environmental issues through research, the media, and other educational programs. Sustainable Protocols Fund also provides grants to support Sustainable Protocol's work around the world for activities that are consistent with its mission.*

No way to contact the organization save donate to their PayPal account or buy the book. Not a word on Hochrein. Josh was no software genius. He had no way knowing where the web page originated, but he had friends who might.

Josh went to bed at midnight, got up at seven and ran

five. It was eight by the time he'd showered.

There was no listing in the phone directory for Peggy Albright, but she was one of Jane's FB friends. Josh sent a friend request and a message: *Tell me about Sheila.* His phone rang five minutes later.

"Hello, Josh?"

"Hi, Peggy. Thanks for getting back to me."

"You bet. What can I tell you about Sheila?"

"I was wondering if we could get together. I'd like to be more politically active."

"Josh, that's great! Great. We need more people like you. I'm working this morning at a white privilege seminar. Perhaps you'd like to join us?"

"Can't. Are you free for lunch?"

"Yeah. I'm down on campus. You just want to meet at the Union? Around one?"

"Sure. I'll see you on the terrace."

"Okay. See you then. I'll bring some reading material."

Orlok had asked Josh to commit murder. As a licensed private investigator, he should report it to the cops. Josh risked his license pursuing this course, but he couldn't stop himself. If his plan worked no one would ever know. He rode to the classic arches McDonald's in Middleton, picked up an Egg McMuffin and an *Isthmus*. In the listings, Bobby Hines at the Rigadoon Room, five to seven.

By one, all the Union terrace tables were taken. Peggy hailed Josh from the second-floor balcony overlooking the patio. They got food from the patio grill and carried it up the lake toward the pier and sat on the steps of the Wisconsin Alumni Association.

Peggy carried a bulging cloth briefcase over the shoulder and when they sat, she removed several brochures and pamphlets and handed them to Josh. "This should answer your questions about Sheila. We're very excited you're willing to do this."

"We?"

"Yes. I told Sheila you were going to help us with outreach to bikers. She is concerned with the safety and well-being of all Wisconsinites. That's the only reason she's in favor of the bill."

"The helmet bill?"

"Of course," Peggy said chomping on her brat.

"Actually, I want to know how she can support expanding tax credits for GMOs."

"Sheila believes it's more important that we feed the world than go into hysterics at the thought of genetically modified corn. We already eat GMOs—they're in our snacks. What's a nectarine but a genetically modified orange?"

"Look," Josh said. "I'm willing to bring her message to thousands of bikers. I'm not kidding. Every Labor Day Harley throws a huge party and I'll be there and so will my buddies. And those guys, most of those guys are registered. And they have families and friends. But first I'd like to meet with Sheila."

Peggy polished off her brat and drained her soda. "Why?"

"To satisfy myself that she is what she says she is."

Peggy nodded. "Fair enough. She's pretty busy but we might be able to find a few minutes if you're willing to tag along on events."

"You must work for the campaign, huh?"

Peggy grinned showing a hint of the pig-tailed tomboy. "How'd you guess?" She reached into her cloth bag and handed him a card. LIVERMORE-EPSTEIN FOR STATE REP/PEGGY ALBRIGHT CONSULTANT.

Josh put it in his vest and gave her one of his.

"She'll be in town tomorrow," Peggy said. "I'll call you."

CHAPTER 24

THE GRAB

Josh rode downtown under an overcast sky. Parking his bike in the King Street Ramp, Josh went to the library and read about Paraguay. The poor but happy natives subsisted primarily through agriculture with some beef production. Seeking info on Heinrich Hochrein, Josh went to the front desk where a bookish young man in glasses had affixed his nose to his laptop.

"Can you help me find something?" Josh said.

"No," the kid said without looking.

"Aren't you the librarian?"

Grudgingly the young man turned his way, dark hair flouncing. "What?"

"I'm trying to find info about a guy named Heinrich Hochrein."

"Have you tried the computers?" the kid said, forcing himself to be polite.

"Yeah, but I'm not very good at that sort of thing. I was thinking this guy's a big social thinker. Maybe you have something by him."

The kid waved around in exasperation. "As you can see, I'm the only one working here. Look—there's an empty computer station. Just google it."

"Yeah okay," Josh said. "Thanks."

There was no Wikileaks entry on Hochrein.

Josh wheeled in front of the Edgewater a little after five, left his bike by the entry and tipped the doorman a twenty. A few guests gave him the stink eye as he walked through the lobby toward the Rigadoon Room overlooking Lake Mendota from whence spilled the tinkle of piano.

The room, with its sweeping view of the lake, white sails flitting, was a third full of weekend crowd. Only a handful of guests sat on the pier as a chill wind whipped up white caps on the gray lake. Josh took a stool at the bar and ordered a Coke. Bobby worked his way through Gershwin, Beatles, Fats, Billy Joel, Art Tatum and Herbie Hancock before breaking. Josh waved to him from the bar. Bobby took a stool.

"What brings you here, my man?" Bobby said.

"I like the way you play. Never was much of a music guy. My old man liked to listen to the Rolling Stones and the Moody Blues. Didn't really start to appreciate music until I was in the can and some brothers put a band together."

"You heading back to the compound?"

"Sure. I'll hang around 'til you're done."

At the end of the break Josh rode over to The Little Red Bookstore on Willy St. and asked the rasta-haired trustafarian behind the counter if they had *Sustainable Protocols*. The dude brightened. He was white, tall and skinny with flawless skin.

"That's a great book but I think we sold out our last copy. Would you like me to order you one?"

"How come I can't just order it off Amazon?"

The kid shrugged. "That's a good question. I believe they made an executive decision to deny Amazon their business because of Amazon's involvement with the government."

Josh picked up a book called *Humans Off Planet*. "What involvement?"

The dude shrugged. "Man, go to *Mother Jones*. They got the whole story."

"You know anything about the dude who wrote it?"

"No not really."

Josh thanked him and returned to the Edgewater. At nine forty-five they pulled up in front of Chief Konapacki's where Marcus, Panda and Feral were playing pool. Feral had a white bandage obscuring his left eye and didn't look up from his shot.

Marcus and Panda hugged Bobby and greeted Josh warmly. Bobby dropped a buck on the juke: Melissa Etheridge "Come to My Window." They sat at the bar and had a beer.

"Have you read *Sustainable Protocols*?" Josh said.

"I'm not much of a reader," Bobby said. "Orlok likes it. Why? Are you a greenie?"

"No. I keep seeing it around."

"Me, I'm deeply suspicious of anyone who wants to save the earth. Aim lower! Save your own damn self before you start telling the rest of us what to do."

"Amen, brother!" Josh said. "Amen."

They high-fived, the click of cue-balls intruding on the song. Bobby reached inside his vest and withdrew a fat doobie. "Want to join me?"

They went out on the front porch, sat on a bench and passed the joint. It was an overcast night with a hint of rain. Josh sat blitzed, listening to a million crickets inside his skull. Bobby grunted and pointed to a deer crossing the road.

A car cruised into the lot, the only sound coming from the crunch of its tires on gravel. Jane and Orlok got out of the Durango. On the porch Jane fixed Bobby with an accusing eye. "Did you just finish a joint?"

"Yeah," Bobby said. "Why? You want some?"

"Let me get a drink first," Jane said, pulling Orlok into the bar like a Cairn terrier leading a St. Bernard around by its collar.

Bobby and Josh sat in stoned silence until Bobby heaved himself up and leaned on one of the wood support pillars. "Walp ahmina cruise. I gots to snooze."

Josh remained where he was. "I'll catch up with you."

Bobby got on his V-Max and thumbed the starter shattering the peaceful night. Josh listened to his exhaust until it was subsumed by crickets. After a while he got up and went inside. The Rascals were on the juke, Jane was at the bar and Orlok played pool. Josh ordered another beer and sat next to Jane.

"Talked to Peggy today," Josh said.

"My neighbor Peggy?"

"Yeah. She's setting up a meet between me and Sheila Whoozis-whatshername."

"Sheila Livermore-Epstein? Why? She's evil."

"Yeah. I want to speak to her why she's supporting subsidies for GMOs."

Jane leaned back and regarded Josh as if he were a talking Weimeraner. "You? How do you rate?"

"I told her I could get a thousand bikers to vote for her."

"Seriously?"

Josh nodded. She drained her drink and signaled for another. "I would love to come to that meeting."

"I'll bet."

"Can I?"

"I don't think that would be a good idea."

"That's funny. You are a man of many parts, Josh Pratt. I'm going to go out and smoke a bowl. Want to come?"

Josh spotted purple paisleys in his peripheral vision. "Ah-mina just sit here and decompress for a minute."

Jane smiled, took her drink and sashayed out the front door. The Rascals gave way to Bob Seger. Billiard balls smacked into one another. At the edge of his hearing Josh heard a cut-off yap, the sound of a car door closing and the chirp of tires. It took a second for the circuit to close. Josh slid off his stool and went out front. No Jane.

CHAPTER 25

A CLEAN SWEEP

Josh opened his ears listening for some faint whine of engine, but the ambient sound drowned everything else. He went back inside where Orlok bent over one side of the pool table with his cue. Orlok looked at him and straightened up

"What?"

"Someone grabbed Jane."

"What? Who?"

"I don't know. She went out front to get high and someone grabbed her. I heard the car door slam."

Orlok threw his cue stick to the floor and headed for the front. "Josh, you and Marcus come with me. Panda, you and Feral head south."

"Wait a minute!" Josh said. "We can't go racing after her in the middle of the night! There are a thousand ways out of here. I'll find her. It's what I do."

Orlok looked at him with suspicion. "What do you

know, Pratt? Tell me the truth."

"Her old man asked me if I would snatch her. For deprogramming. I told him no. He must have hired someone else."

"You're shittin' me!" Orlok exploded. "That's kidnapping!"

"I know. Let me handle it."

"You? I know how to make him talk."

"Orlok—you're on parole. Let me handle it."

"You're a fuckin' ex-con like me."

"I got a pardon."

"I don't give a shit. No one kuips my old lady."

The others gathered around agitated.

"Orlok! Listen to me. I know how the system works. I'll find her! You've got to trust me on this."

Orlok looked around. "Where's Bobby?"

"He went home to sleep. There's nothing he can do right now. There's nothing any of us can do. They're not going to hurt her! Franklin may be a turd, but he loves his daughter."

"How?" Orlok said. "How you gonna get her back?"

"I'll talk to Franklin. He'll tell me where they've got her."

"What if that doesn't work?"

"There are other ways."

Orlok looked ready to crush. "Like what?"

"Go through the tax rolls and identify rural properties owned by Franklin, Franklin Farms, or any of Franklin's subsidiaries and dummy corporations. It ain't that hard. When we find it we'll go get her."

"What about tracking her via her cell phone?" Marcus said.

"Maybe," Josh said. "I know someone who can help with that."

"Maybe we should call the police," Panda said.

Orlok gave him a look of utter contempt and Panda shrank.

"Well fuck," Orlok said. "Forget about sleep. Let's get to the compound and figure out our course of action."

Josh said, "I'm heading to my place. I'll get on this first thing."

Feral jutted his chin. "How do we know you ain't in on it?"

"What?!" Josh said. "Are you nuts?"

"What do we really know about this guy?" Feral said.

Orlok looked from Feral to Josh. "What about that?"

"I work alone. You know that."

Orlok crinkled his forehead. "What's your plan?"

"I'll see Franklin first thing. There's nothing we can do now. We go roaring up into Pine Perch and they'll have every law enforcement officer in Dane County up our ass."

Orlok gripped Josh's bicep threatening to crush it. "You got twenty-four hours. Then I talk to the old man."

It was senseless to argue. Josh nodded and took off. When he got home, he phoned Franklin despite the late hour.

"What's up?" the breeder answered, with the sound of a cocktail party behind him.

"Did you have your daughter kidnapped?"

"Excuse me?"

"Someone snatched her from in front of Chief Konapacki's, out here in Grant County.

"What?!"

"Yes, sir." Josh told him what happened. "I wanted to check with you first to make sure it wasn't something you ordered."

"No! Absolutely not. Did you phone the police?"

"That's your call, sir."

Silence.

"Come over here."

"Sir, can't this wait until morning? I'm exhausted and there's really nothing we can do."

"How do we know Orlok isn't behind this?"

"Trust me, sir. I was with Orlok when it happened."

"That means nothing."

Josh could hear Franklin's teeth grind.

"Be here at eight o'clock."

A light rain began to fall around midnight, lulling Josh and Fig to sleep.

Josh rose at seven to a clear sky, kicked out at Pine Perch at eight. Franklin was waiting for him in a posture of impatience, legs spread, hands on hips. The breeder wore cargo shorts, leather sandals, and a pale yellow LaCoste shirt.

"They called an hour ago," he said. "They want a million dollars. They said if I contacted the police, they'd start mailing body parts."

Josh followed Franklin through the house to his office.

Marian was gone.

"Tell me what happened," Franklin said, sinking into a mesh office chair.

Josh told him. "Did you record the call?"

Franklin placed his phone flat on the desk and pushed a button. A wheezy, patently fake voice said, "We have her. If you want her back get a million dollars together in used, non-sequential hundred dollar bills. Do not contact the police. You do that, we're gonna start sending body parts. First, we'll send an ear. You have twenty-four hours. We are watching you."

The call ended.

"Do you have any enemies who might do such a thing?" Josh said. "Someone we haven't considered?"

"No! I'm not a gangster! The people I know are all legitimate."

"What about the people with whom you deal? Your clients?"

Franklin was silent for a minute. "Sometimes a little money changes hands, when dealing with international clients."

"What does that mean?"

"The Ukraine, for example, makes it virtually impossible to legally import bull sperm. The laws exist solely for the benefit of corrupt officials. It's cheaper and easier to pay them a little something under the table than try to jump through their hoops."

"I thought they paid you."

"We have to be licensed to deal in certain countries. Bribes are common. I keep a certain amount of cash on hand at the farm, but it is to be used strictly for that purpose. If I withdrew a million dollars, I'd have nothing. And we have deals coming up."

"Are you saying you can lay hands on a million in cash?"

Franklin spread his hands. "It's not my money! I have investors."

"Where is this cash?"

"It's at the farm. I'm the only one with access. Nobody has to know about this."

"Who else knows?"

Franklin grimaced. "Marian. My ex-wife. They just know it exists, and neither of them would ever say anything."

"I see," Josh said. "I'll get a guy out here, sweep your house."

"What do you mean?" Franklin said.

"Let's just make sure nobody got in here and planted any devices."

"I have home security."

Josh waved. "You can beat anything. Don't worry. My guy is state of the art."

"Call him," Franklin said.

Josh phoned Kleiser, who was at his desk at Dovetail in Middleton.

"Randall, can you come out here? I need you to sweep a house."

"Can't. I'm working on a deadline."

"Randall, this will only take an hour. We're nearby. Please."

"Okay. What should I bring?"

"Everything."

Josh hung up. "Sir, you may not want to hear this, but is there any chance Jane staged her own kidnapping?"

Franklin looked at Josh with a hint of sadness. "It's occurred to me."

"Do you pay her an allowance?"

"Yes. It's very generous."

"Sir, right now there's nothing we can do. When my friend arrives, we can ask him about tracing the phone call."

Kleiser arrived at nine-fifteen in his Mazda crammed with plastic cases containing electronic equipment. He wore khakis and a Call of Duty T-shirt. Franklin greeted him at the front door.

"Come on in the kitchen. You want coffee?"

"That'd be great."

While Kleiser fixed himself a cup, Josh told him what they needed done. Kleiser returned to his car and came back wearing headphones and holding a plastic cylinder with a thin plastic delta extending from one end, like a hand-held vacuum. He went methodically from room to room. It took a long time because there were twelve rooms, but in the end, he found nothing.

"No transmitters, no transceivers, no cameras. The device doesn't register transmissions, it registers combinations of metals that are common to all bugs."

They sat in Franklin's office with fresh cups.

"Dude's gonna call back tomorrow morning," Josh said. "Any way to trace the call?"

Kleiser looked at his watch. "Yes, but I'll have to rout that call from Mr. Franklin's phone to my computer and I don't have time to do that right now. I'll come back this evening, if that's all right with you?"

"Sure. I'd also like you to do a complete background check on Carl Kuhn. Calls himself Orlok and is prez of the Jugan motorcycle club."

Kleiser made notes in his laptop. "Ahmina have to charge you for that."

Josh looked at Franklin.

"Of course," the breeder said.

THE CANDIDATE

Josh called Fleiss.

"Fleiss," the lawyer answered.

"Steve it's Josh Pratt. Got a situation. When can we talk?"

"Come on over. My eleven o'clock canceled."

Josh rode downtown, up Monroe past chi-chi eaterias, new condos, Trader Joe's, and a decrepit comic book shop. Josh wheeled into Fleiss' tiny parking lot and wedged the Road King between a dumpster and the wall. Fleiss' office was on E. King St., the second floor of an ugly stucco two-story building that housed two other law firms and the Wisconsin Pub Association. Fleiss' office was on the second floor beneath a big skylight. His buxom secretary Sarah turned from her keyboard as Josh entered.

"Hello, Josh. He's in there."

Josh went into Fleiss' office where the lawyer was tilted

back in a black leather chair with levers, his tasseled loafers on the mahogany desk surrounded by computer terminals. He held up a finger as Josh came in.

"Not Shapiro! Anybody but Shapiro!"

Josh heard a faint voice through Fleiss' blue tooth headset

"All right," the lawyer said with resignation. "Shapiro." He turned to Josh. "I hate golfing with Shapiro. Hey! Where do hos go to buy clothes?"

"Beats me," Josh said.

"Joseph A. Skank!" Fleiss howled.

"Steve, you know Lewis Franklin?"

"I know of him. I don't know him."

Josh told him the story, leaving out nothing.

"Nobody saw her taken?" Fleiss said.

"No. We were all inside. I heard a car door slam."

"Tell the cops."

"Franklin won't do that. They may not get along, but he loves her."

"So, what do you want from me?"

"If I go after her I might get in trouble."

"Yeah but that's never stopped you before. You have my number."

"What if you're golfing?"

Fleiss grinned. He was a middle-aged former public defender with tight-cropped curly white hair and a nose like a conning tower. People had mistaken him for Gary Shandling twice. "For you, bubbie, I drop everything. Seriously. What are you planning? A little *pussy comitatus*? They don't like that around here, you know that."

"It's possible Jane kidnapped herself."

"If that's the case, why doesn't he tell the police?"

"I told you. He loves her. He's thought about hiring mercenaries to kidnap her so she can be deprogrammed. He thinks Orlok's a cult leader."

"So whaddaya want from me?"

"Isn't hiring mercenaries to kidnap your daughter illegal?"

"Ha!" Fleiss barked. "Not if you're part of the machine and Franklin is definitely part of the machine. Big Dem donor. He's pushing that Livermore-Epstein broad, you know."

"I didn't know but it makes sense. Franklin Farms could benefit from increased tax breaks for GMOs."

From Fleiss' office it was five minutes to Jane's apartment. Josh let himself in, trying to remember what he'd seen from his previous visit. Everything was the same. He couldn't tell if she'd packed for a trip or not. The only difference was, her passport was missing. When he got out, the sky was clouding up again.

Josh got home around four, grilled some chicken breasts for dinner, gave one to Fig. She downed it in three seconds.

"How did it taste?" Josh said.

Fig looked at him grinning and wagging her tail. Trading his bike in for the car, Josh drove to Franklin's as a light rain began to fall. Kleiser's Mazda was parked in the driveway with the tail gate open. Kleiser was inside seated at a card table in the office on which he'd set up some of his machines including a carbon fiber nacelle the size of a milk crate, several control yokes, and a six-rotor drone.

"I can put this baby in the air and track 'em with their heat signatures," Kleiser said.

"It's supposed to be overcast tomorrow," Franklin said. "Can that thing fly in the rain?"

Kleiser made a minute adjustment with a pair of needle-nosed pliers. "Does the Pope shit in the woods?"

"It can even fire weapons," Josh said.

"Not as presently configured," Kleiser said. "So, what's the plan?"

Josh stooped and opened a small cube refrigerator and removed a bottled water. "We'll have to wait for the call. Ideally, he'll offer to trade Jane for the money right there. On the other hand, he may try to give us the run-around. Send us somewhere else. If this is Jane and Orlok in cahoots, as I suspect, we'll find her in a room somewhere, and as soon as we free her, she'll throw herself into Daddy's arms and shout, 'Thank you, Daddy! Thank you!'"

Franklin grimaced, twisted open a bottle of Macallan's and poured two fingers into a cut glass decanter. He downed it and looked up, holding up the bottle.

Josh waved. "I'm good."

"I'll take a couple fingers," Kleiser said

Franklin poured.

"What time did he say he'd call?" Josh said.

"Tomorrow. Didn't say when."

"I'm going home," Josh said. "I'll be here by eight."

Kleiser saluted without looking up. Josh let himself out and rode home in the rain where Fig waited, greeting him with a fusillade of barks. Josh turned on the television. There was no mention of Jane on the six o'clock news. Josh wondered about Orlok. The Jugan President seemed honestly shocked at the news, and Josh was a good judge of character. Except for women.

"Pussy is like voodoo, son," his father Duane had told him. "It can make a man do anything."

Orlok had the Fort McCoy job lined up, but one million was a lot more than a hundred thou. No. Josh couldn't see it. Armed robbery was more Orlok's speed—not chicanery. Who had Jane enlisted in her little scheme? Some lovesick swain? Josh began to go through her Facebook friends, one by one. There were any number of sleazy local characters.

His phone buzzed. It was Peggy Albright.

"The candidate is willing to meet with you for a few minutes prior to her fundraiser at Monona Terrace at two."

"Thank you, Peggy. I'll be there."

Josh looked at Fig. "Did you hear! The candidate will meet with us! Gimme a high five!" Josh put his palm down low and Fig swiped it.

They watched television, Fig's head in his lap. Anthony Pettis fighting Ebson Barbossa. Pettis was among Josh's favorite fighters. They called him "Showtime" because of his insane flying kicking techniques, specifically, the "Matrix kick," when he bounced off the wall and knocked Benson Henderson down with a roundhouse. But tonight, Pettis seemed sluggish and a step behind. It made Josh sad. Everybody faded. Nobody stayed on top forever. At the commercial break, a young man with a beard appeared.

"I got struck by a car and the insurance company only wanted to give me ten thousand dollars. So, I got in touch with Steve Fleiss, and he got me two million dollars!"

Fleiss appeared, unctuous in a charcoal suit. "Of course, I can't guarantee that your case is worth two million, but if you have any questions, call me, Steve Fleiss, the Hammer!" Fleiss' phone number appeared in flashing chrome over hellfire to the sound of "Dead Man's Curve."

Josh knelt by his bed, hands pressed together, Fig looking at him worshipfully, her snout on the bed. "Dear Lord, please let Jane Franklin be safe. Amen."

They went to bed.

CHAPTER

27

Josh woke at six on Saturday and went for a run, Fig at his heel. It was a shiny new summer morning and the leaves on the trees glowed emerald. As he was headed back, Bass passed him going into town in a Toyota Armada and waved. Josh waved back. Suddenly Bass was beside him, cruising down the wrong side of the road with the window open.

"Did you think about our offer?"

"I'm thinking, Phil. I'm thinking."

"Good! Okay! Let us know."

Bass sawed the big car back and forth across the blacktop until he got turned around. Josh showered, checked his email, and jumped on the bike, arriving at Franklin's house at seven forty-five. Kleiser's Mazda was where he'd left it last night.

Josh entered without knocking and went to the kitchen where Franklin and Kleiser sat on stools at the island, where

Kleiser had set up his monitors.

"What up?" Josh said.

"Good morning," Franklin said. "Help yourself to coffee and doughnuts."

"Listen. When he calls, stall for time. Tell him it's Saturday and there's no way you can raise that kind of money on Sunday. At least hold him off until Monday."

"That's true."

Josh fixed himself a mug, grabbed a bear claw, settled into the breakfast nook and watched CNN on a flat screen hinged to a jointed metal arm extending from the wall. The sound was off, but the scroll carried the headlines.

43 DEAD IN KABUL BOMBING
STATE DEPT. TO ADMIT 10,000 MORE SYRIANS
57 ARRESTED IN PIPELINE PROTEST

Franklin stood behind Kleiser. "How much would it cost for you to set up drones to cover the farms, and to operate them?"

Kleiser, who wore headphones and a Shazam T-shirt, stared at his monitor. "I've already got a job, Lew, thanks."

"What do they pay? I can do better."

"No thanks, Lew. I signed a contract. I can recommend people."

The phone rang. Franklin, Kleiser and Josh stared at it. It was eight o'clock. Franklin picked it up.

He cleared his throat.

"Franklin?" a said a voice from a tin esophagus.

"Here."

"You got the mil?"

"No. It's Saturday! You have to know there's no way I can lay my hands on that kind of money on a Saturday!"

The speakerphone went silent. They looked at each other grimly. A minute later it rang.

"Hello!" Franklin said.

"We're giving you a forty-eight hour extension. We'll call you Monday. Will you have the money?"

"Yes! I'll have the money."

"You'd better."

"I want to speak to my daughter. How do I know she's even alive?"

Static.

Seconds later, "Daddy!" Jane wailed and was abruptly cut off.

"When will you have the money?" said the tin esophagus.

"I should have it by six."

Josh remained in the breakfast nook throughout this exchange, gazing out the window at a stand of elm, alder, northern birch. Birds flitted about Franklin's alabaster bird feeder. Something flitted behind a tree, too big for a hummingbird. Josh stood, touched Kleiser on the arm and pointed out the window.

Kleiser waved him off, intent on tracing the call so Josh ran outside just in time to see the attenuated black object fly up, over the trees and down the north-facing slope. Seconds later, Kleiser and Franklin caught up with him.

"What?" Franklin demanded.

"I think it was a drone. It flew north toward the highway."

"They're looking in my windows?"

"That's a distinct possibility," Kleiser said.

"It's drone versus drone out there," Josh said.

"What's to see?" Kleiser said. "They couldn't see in the kitchen and if they did, all they'd see was you and me.

"Exactly. They see that the police are not involved."

Josh looked at the hacker. "Did you get a fix?"

"Yeah," Kleiser said. "Middle of Hilldale."

Hilldale was a popular mall on the near east side, traditionally crowded on Saturdays.

Josh headed back to the house. "All right. I'll be back tomorrow at six."

"Where you going?" Kleiser called after him.

"Downtown. I got a meeting."

Josh went home and changed.

Monona Terrace was a faux Frank Lloyd Wright design hanging off the Isthmus over Lake Monona. Wright's views on waterfronts were well known. Wright despised cities that cut themselves off from their own waterfront via railroad track and highway. Monona Terrace skirted this prickly issue by building out over the water, but the tracks and highway still skirted the shore.

Josh cruised downtown at one-thirty, parked by the Monkey Bar and walked up to the monument commemorating Otis Redding's death. On Dec. 10, 1967, Redding was due to give a concert at Madison's Factory when his single-engine Beechcraft crashed into Lake Monona killing all aboard. Josh had seen the poster. The Grim Reapers had been the opening act.

He walked to the Terrace past ambulance chasers and upscale restaurants. At three-thirty he identified himself to a campaign worker inside and waited while the young man disappeared. A few minutes later Peggy Albright came out vibrating with self-importance.

"Sheila can give you five minutes." She turned to go.

"Wait a minute."

Peggy turned around.

"Have you heard from Jane recently?"

Peggy smiled quizzically. "No. Should I?"

"Just wondered."

Josh felt not the slightest twinge of guilt at his deception. Lying to a politician? Peggy led him through a series of rooms to a suite overlooking the bay, hot and pungent with bodies, where the candidate, a surprisingly diminutive figure in blue slacks and white blouse, looked over a speech on a clipboard while conferring with a slim, elegant man in a hairline mustache. She put the clipboard aside and took off her glasses as Josh approached, smiling broadly and extending her hand.

"Josh," she said with a firm clasp. "Thank you for coming. Peggy tells me you're interested in helping with the campaign."

"Thank you for seeing me, ma'am. I'll make this brief. Today's bikers are lawyers, doctors, and leaders of industry. The governor and two past governors are bikers. We believe wearing a helmet should remain a personal choice. What would it take for you to change your position on the helmet laws?"

"Got any money?" the candidate said. Josh liked her immediately.

He grinned and pulled out his pants pockets. "Have you ever ridden a motorcycle?"

"No."

"May I offer you a ride? Very slow, no traffic. I guarantee you'll enjoy it. It certainly won't hurt you with your constituency."

"What is it you do, Mr. Pratt?"

Josh gave her his card.

"You're a private investigator? How interesting. We may have need for you."

"References available."

Hairline mustache hovered. The candidate held up a finger.

"Whom did you say you represented?" she said.

"Just myself, ma'am. But I know a lot of people."

She considered it. Harley-Davidson was one of Wisconsin's bedrock corporations and a beloved American institution. "Let me give it some thought. I'll get back to you."

"Promise?"

"Promise."

She turned to the aide.

ON THE TERRACE

Josh took a seat at the back of the packed theater. It was a short talk followed by a meet and greet with three candidates vying for state rep: Livermore-Epstein, Bill Lawrence, a conservative businessman, and Angie Hightower of the Atheist/Anarchist Party.

Crews from three television stations stood at the back of the room. A dais had been set up in front of the curving, expansive view of Lake Monona with the Wisconsin state seal and a pitcher of water flanked by the American and Wisconsin flags.

Lawrence's platform was less government regulations and tax breaks for business. The response was lukewarm. Angie Hightower in her potato sack dress and shock hair proposed free marijuana, free bicycles to be provided by the city, free internet for everyone and free public transportation. She proposed raising taxes on private businesses and increasing the cost of parking to discourage the use of carbon-spewing death-mobiles.

Livermore-Epstein spoke of the economic climate and how she planned to make Dane County a high-tech mecca like Silicon Valley.

Josh broke early and went up to the terrace, leaned on the rail and looked out on the bright blue lake reflecting the bright blue sky, white triangles darting hither and yon. He looked down. Each brick on the patio had been engraved with the names of donors. Josh headed back to his bike, nodding to a cop he knew, crossing Willy Street at the tracks.

What was it like, he wondered, to love your child so much, you'd pay a million dollars to get her back? That she was openly defiant, scornful, and possibly treacherous, and you still loved her? Josh had never known love until Charlotte. His own father, Duane, had abandoned him at a Bosselman's Truck Stop in Ohio when he was fifteen years old. He'd bounced around from foster home to foster home until he'd joined the Bedouins at age seventeen. That was his real family.

All his life, Josh had believed there was a secret handbook on how to behave. Protocols, he called it. Everybody had a copy but him. When he was with Charlotte, whom he called Fig, for the first time he had imagined himself as a family man. A father. He wouldn't make the mistakes Duane had made.

Mistakes? Duane was a felon and sadist who regularly humiliated Josh. Why Duane kept Josh was a mystery. Certainly, there were other little bastard Pratts running around out there. That's just the way Duane was. It wasn't until Josh went to prison and Chaplain Dorgan talked to him of spirituality that Josh got a handle on who Duane was. He'd since looked into Duane's background, enough to find a rap sheet from San Diego to Portland, Maine. Car theft, drug dealing, assault, passing paper, rape, public indecency; it was as if Duane were trying to cross off a bucket list culled from the criminal code.

Josh hoped Jane was all right. He thought she probably was.

He called Kleiser.

"How's it going out there?"

"The Jugan just showed up."

"Fuck!" Josh spat, heading for his bike.

An hour later, he kicked out next to four other hawgs including Orlok's Victory and Bobby's V-Max. The oak front door was open and loud voices issued from within. Josh strode through the Spanish tile foyer into the rec room facing the patio where a red-faced Orlok squared off against the smaller but equally pugnacious Franklin in a shouting match. Bobby sat at Franklin's Steinway baby grand running his sausages across the keys, softly playing boogie-woogie that threatened to explode, while Marcus and Panda stared at the furnishings, picking things up, examining them, and setting them back.

"How do I know you aren't in on it?" Franklin spat.

"How do I know *you* aren't?" Orlok rumbled back. "Josh

told me how you were thinking of hiring some goons to kidnap her and deprogram her."

Franklin shot Josh a look. Josh shrugged and stepped between them, like a raccoon trying to fit between sheet rock and wall.

"What are you doing here, Orlok?" Josh said. "I told you I'd handle it."

Orlok lowered a squid-like eye. He was as dense as a meteorite and exuded his own gravity. "Don't talk to me like that, prospect."

"Sorry. I think we're doing everything we can to get Jane back safely. We haven't called the police. Franklin says he can get the money together Monday."

"Maybe," Franklin said.

"And what if he can't?" Orlok said. He turned to Kleiser. "What's this, some kind of tech expert?"

Kleiser gave a little wave without taking his eyes off the screen.

"This is my business," Josh said. "This is what I do for a living and I know how to handle it. The only thing you'll do by being here is spook them."

"How would they know, whoever the fuck they are?" Panda said. Suspenders spangled with badges held up his 44 inch waist Levis.

"They're using drones," Josh said. "We saw one this morning."

"I will shoot that motherfucker out of the sky," Orlok said.

"No, boys, that would only invite the police. Trust me. We know what we're doing. Go back to the ranch and chill."

"Did you just say the ranch?" Panda said.

"I meant the farm."

Bobby chuckled. Orlok chuckled. He turned on Josh.

"I want you to phone me the moment you know something, understand?"

"Aye-aye, boss," Josh said.

Orlok swirled his finger over is his head. "Let's go, boys."

A moment later, multiple loud explosions shattered the quiet neighborhood, drowning out the drone of the leaf blowers down the street. They listened until the sound of the unmuffled engines faded away.

Josh collapsed onto a sofa, heart beating. "Is that the first time you two have met?" he asked Franklin.

"Yeah. He practically ripped my front door off. The moment I opened the door, he bulled his way in here with his pals and started shouting. I'm a retired Marine. I don't let anybody push me around, least of all in my own home."

"Did you tell him you were a Marine?"

"No. Should I?"

"Yeah," Josh said. "He's a Marine too. I like how you stood up to him. Can I have some bourbon?"

"I think that's a good idea," Franklin said, heading to the wet bar against the wall. He brought back three shot glasses and a bottle of Buffalo Trace, poured a couple fingers in each. Josh threw a seat cushion at Kleiser.

"Hey! Take a goddamn drink!"

Kleiser came over, picked the shot glass up off the coffee table and held it up.

"L'chaim!"

"L'chaim!" Josh and Franklin repeated, and all downed their shots.

"Are you riding?" Kleiser said.

"One drink ain't gonna fuck me up. I have experience."

"What's the plan?" Franklin said.

Josh got up. "Randall will stay here until we hear from the kidnappers, that okay, Randall?"

Randall cocked his finger and pointed.

"As soon as you hear from them call me. I gotta go home and check on my dog. I'll call you tomorrow."

CHAPTER
29

THE COBRAS

Josh rode to church Sunday morning, kicking out next to Pastor John's Bonneville.

Wearing an L.L. Bean hoodie, Pastor John looked out at several dozen parishioners, a self-effacing middle-aged man with short brown hair and squint lines.

"Today's sermon comes from Timothy, 4: 1 -2. 'The Spirit clearly says that in later times some will abandon the faith and follow deceiving spirits and things taught by demons. Such teachings come through hypocritical liars, whose consciences have been seared as with a hot iron.'

"Sound familiar? Remember the Branch Davidians? Anybody watching that Leah Remini show on A&E? Of course, the Episcopalians swear that the Baptists are the anti-Christ, and nobody's sure about the Mormons."

Laughter.

"Some claim the United States is a Christian nation.

That may or may not be true. The Founding Fathers made no secret of their faith. But as the Bible predicted, we have come into an age of Babel, where a thousand philosophies demand your attention. It's Yaweh or the highway! Global warming. Militant veganism."

He bit his lip and looked up. "Mil. A. Tint veganism. What are they gonna do? Throw coconuts? Humans Off Planet. They're hoping for people to stop procreating so that Gaia will recover from humanity."

Pastor John threw up his arms and rolled his eyes. "Humans Off Planet!" The congregation loved it.

"This is why history is important. There is such a thing as the accumulated wisdom of the ages, and the Bible represents much of it. Is there a more perfect moral doctrine than the Ten Commandments? There is a tendency in our country, and throughout Western Civilization, to forget history, to pretend that the world began when we were born, and to make up our own rules. Universities no longer teach American history, and many of them are removing Shakespeare, Sir Walter Scott, and Herman Melville from their curriculum because those guys were all white males, and by definition, their work is tainted by racism."

Yes, Josh thought. Yes. He looked around. Others nodded, hanging on Pastor John's word.

"It may be," Pastor John continued, "that Western civilization has bred common sense out of our genetic make-up. We no longer do what is right for fear of being branded sexist, racist, homophobic, or some other demeaning term. That is not to say these things don't exist! I know many of you have experienced them because you have discussed them with me."

About a third of the congregation was black. They nodded vigorously along with the rest.

"George Orwell said 'The most effective way to destroy people is to deny and obliterate their own understanding of their history.'

"The Bible speaks of First Things and basic principles. When you hear something that sounds too good to be true, or feeds into common prejudices, take a step back. Ask yourself, what would Jesus do? Would he take the word of some wandering prophet, or would he find out for himself?"

Murmurs of ascent.

"Watch out for false prophets, folks. Don't bear false witness. Stay off Facebook! Now please join me in reciting the Lord's Prayer."

Monday morning.

The call came at eleven. Josh was in his garage rearranging the objects on the shelves over the workbench. Scale model Harleys, tin signs featuring Elvis, Coke, old Indians, a cathedral-shaped tube radio, stacks of CDs, match boxes, a bong, toys, paperweights, odd things.

"They just called," Franklin said. "I told them I wouldn't have the money until six. They'll call back then."

"I'll be there," Josh said.

Fleiss phoned. "Got a summons for you. Two hundred and fifty."

"I'm on my way."

Evan Northcote was a petty thief, ex-con, and curbside mechanic who worked out of his trailer in Arena, an hour west of town. He was also a member of the Cobras, a low-rent motorcycle gang that hung out at O'Dell's Irish Pub in Arena, population 2118. Evan owed thirty-five hundred dollars in back child support and his ex-wife Joy was suing him in Dane County Court. At two-thirty in the afternoon there were six chops lined up outside O'Dell's, about a quarter mile from the Wisconsin River. With its gritty tile walls and gun slot window, O'Dell's could have been ripped from Brooklyn and plunked down in rural Wisconsin by a tornado. Sun shone through the heavy canopy of oak, elm, cottonwood and willow that drooped and fuzzed all over the cracked blacktop parking lot. Josh backed his chop to the curb next to an S&R hard tail with a chain drive, painted flat black and ugly as a cockroach in milk.

Josh pushed his way into the cool gloom of the bar, inhaling cigarette smoke and stale beer. The click of pool balls drew his attention to the table at the far end, where two Cobras played ball while two watched from a booth, two more at the bar. Having looked at Northcote's mugshot, Josh spotted him immediately as one of the pool players. He was a big, rangy hillbilly type with jug ears, unkempt hair, and an Adam's apple the size of a baseball. His colors were neatly folded over the back of a chair.

Josh ordered a draft from the codger behind the bar. With his rosacea-ravaged face and rim of white hair, he reminded Josh of Archie Bunker. A ball game played silently on the ceiling monitor. Z.Z. Topp's "Legs" blared from the ancient Wurlitzer. The wall was decorated with black and white photos of the Cobras going back several generations, as well as tin signs advertising Indians and Harleys. A deceased Cobra's colors hung on the wall enclosed in glass. Josh sat with his elbows on the bar and watched Northcote line up a shot, one cheek bulging like a squirrel. He took the shot, sinking the three ball in the side pocket, hawked up a wad of liquefied tobacco and launched it an arc at a brass cuspidor on the floor. The wad sailed over the rim and splatted at the base of a booth.

"Nice shot, shit for brains!" brayed one of the guys in the booth, skinny dude with bad skin and a fifties DA, black leather vest over a filthy T-shirt, dungarees, boots. Northcote lined up his next ball. It bounced off the bumper and came to a stop in the middle of the table. "HAW HAW!" brayed the skinny dude, getting up with his own cue.

Josh stood next to Northcote, who finally turned toward him. His vest said Slimy, amid various patches.

"What?"

"Are you Evan Northcote?"

"Who the fuck wants to know?" Northcote said, spraying Josh with tobacco juice.

Josh handed him the envelope. "This is for you."

As Josh turned to go, Northcote ripped the envelope open.

"Hey, motherfucker! Hey! I'm talking to you! You think you can just walk in here and disrespect me with this shit?"

Josh ignored him.

"Fuck him up, Slimy!" Skinny said.

Josh spun and whacked Northcote's hand away an inch before it reached him. Northcote threw a hard right that Josh ducked, throwing a hard fist into Northcote's gut. The hillbilly folded.

Josh was halfway out the door when someone said, "Wait a minute! Are you Josh Pratt?"

Josh was halfway out the door. "Yes," he said, letting the door close behind him.

The guy was at the door. "Hey wait! Let me buy you a drink! They call me Bone!"

Josh didn't move. He went back inside.

Northcote, who still lay like a gaffed fish on the hardwood floor, looked up in surprise. "You're Josh Pratt?"

"How the fuck do you guys know who I am?" Josh said.

With Skinny's help, Northcote struggled to his feet. "Well shit! Why didn't you say so! I never would have hassled you, man!"

"Seriously. How do you know who I am?"

"Your picture was in the paper, dude," Skinny said, "when you had that beef with the Jizlams."

"Fuck," Josh said.

"You're a fucking legend, man," said a Cobra with a gut

that slow flowed over his belt like lava.

"Boys," Josh said, "I appreciate the respect. I would just as soon remain anonymous, know what I mean?"

They looked at each other and nodded.

"Right on, bro," Flow Gut said.

"Respect," Northcote and Slimy said. The others nodded.

"Now, Evan, the summons is from your ex-wife. You're behind in child support. That's no secret, am I right?"

Northcote looked down. "I know."

"How many kids you got?"

"Two," Northcote said with a touch of pride. "Johnny's eight. Junebug is six."

"Do you see 'em?" Josh said.

"My bitch of an ex-wife does everything she can to stop me from seein' 'em. Now she's shacked up with some fuckin' construction worker who says he'll punch out my lights if I show up."

Josh put his hand on Northcote's shoulder. "A man supports his family. That's what he does."

"That's right," a Cobra said.

"I know," Northcote said. "Sorry I swung on ya."

Josh slapped him on the arm. "No prob. Sounds you need to go to court and let the judge know what's happening. You got a lawyer?"

"Fuck no," Northcote said. "I ain't got jack since I got laid off."

"What were you doing?"

"Construction."

"I might have a few leads for you," Josh said, thinking of Newton Construction. "Let me have your phone number."

"I can't afford no phone." Northcote turned picked up a matchbook off the bar and handed it to Josh. "You can reach me here."

Josh tucked the matchbook in his vest and handed Northcote his card.

"Have a drink, bro!" a big Cobra with a full beard said, handing him a tap in glass.

Josh took the glass. "What is it?"

"Capital Kickapoo India Ale."

Josh drank. All the Cobras did the same.

Slimy took a postcard of beautiful Arena out of a rack on the bar. "Would you sign this for me? Make it out to Slimy."

Josh laughed and waved him off. "Fuck no!"

"What was it like, hangin' with Buffalo Hump?" said the guy with the gut.

"Buff's a down-home individual," Josh said. "A straight-shooter. Doesn't drink, doesn't do drugs, he fucks a lot."

Everybody laughed.

"He's got hepatitis from when he was a junkie. It's under control."

"What does he ride?" Northcote said.

"Buff doesn't ride, but most of the Seekers ride Harleys. Most of the Red Shirts ride Indians."

More questions. Josh waved a hand. "I gotta go, boys. I

got more paper to hang."

They back slapped him out into the parking lot, admiring his bike while he powered up and headed east. In the rear-view, they all waved.

CHAPTER

30

ANGELL PARK

Josh arrived at Pine Perch at five, as Kleiser was loading a drone into his hatchback.

Josh kicked out behind Franklin's Boxster. "Anything happen?"

"All he could scrape up was six hundred thou," Kleiser said.

Josh followed Kleiser into the house, into the kitchen where Kleiser opened the massive copper-colored refrigerator, removed two cans of Coke and tossed one to Josh. Through the serving window to the dining room, Josh saw Franklin brooding in the sunken living room, forearms on knees, staring at his phone which sat on the rosewood table before him. Marian sat next to him kneading his shoulder muscles.

A small TV on the kitchen counter was tuned to Fox Business, where a silent Neil Cavuto extolled the virtues of ginseng. Josh turned it up.

"Demand for ginseng continues to rise, as annual sales pass two and a half billion dollars. Here in the States, the number of ginseng farms has tripled in the last three years, particularly in the Pacific Northwest, with its ideal growing conditions."

Franklin's phone emitted a deep rumble. He touched his ear set as Josh and Kleiser hustled to his side.

"Franklin."

"Yeah," said the bizarre voice beamed in from Pluto. "You got the money?"

"I have six hundred thousand. It's all I could get! Most of my money is tied up in work. Please! Think about it! Six hundred thousand!"

Silence, as the heavy breathing resumed.

"All right. Now listen carefully. We'll make the exchange at nine-thirty tonight at Angell Park Speedway. You know where that is?"

"Yes."

"Come alone. We will be watching. Park in Section TT. Park with your taillights next to the fence. There will be plenty of room. Park the car off by itself. We will contact you once you arrive. Remember. We're watching you. If you contact the police, you'll never see your daughter again."

The call ended. Franklin looked spooked. He reached into his jacket, withdrew the spiral notepad and a pen, and wrote something down.

"Okay, listen," Josh said. "I'll get there ahead of time. Kleiser will put his drone up and we'll track you to the exchange. Once we get a fix on the guy, the drone will follow him."

"How?" Marian said.

Kleiser reached into his ditty bag and removed a can of aerosol marked "Infra-Red," and handed it to Josh.

"If you can spray paint an 'X' on the roof, that would be groovy. I'm also planting a transmitter in the satchel in case they ditch us."

"What if Jane's not with them?" Franklin said.

"That's why we follow them back, Mr. Franklin."

Franklin couldn't even summon any anger. He slumped on the sofa and looked defeated.

"Oh baby," Marian said, taking his hand.

"Where's the money?" Josh said.

Franklin pointed to a Gladstone bag on the table. Josh opened it. It was filled with stacks of hundred-dollar bills. He'd never seen so much cash before. He turned toward Kleiser, who hunched over his laptop on the table.

"Know where Angell Park is?"

"I'm looking at it right now. It's in Sun Prairie. Let me get the satellite view."

Seconds later Kleiser pointed to the screen, to a detailed picture of the park, a half mile oval, surrounded by bleachers, parking lots, and a city park also called Angell Park. "This has got to be what he means when he says back up against the fence."

The wedge-shaped parking lot extended south and east from the track itself, right up to a major road. "This is Bishop Street. They got the parking lot pretty well lit up."

"I've been there on a race night," Josh said. "It's a zoo. There are a half dozen ways out of that parking lot. I'm going to be on the ground out there when Franklin parks."

"I can't believe she'd do this," Franklin said to himself.

"Sir, we're going to run this as if her life were in danger. It may very well be. We don't know. Don't beat yourself up until you know the truth."

"Thanks," Franklin said. "Christ, I wish I could have a drink."

Josh wished he had more hands and thought of whom he could call. He couldn't very well call Orlok, since the Jugan leader might be in on it, the previous days theatrics notwithstanding. Josh had met men who would swear convincingly on their mother's grave that they were innocent, with a knife in one hand and a heart in the other. He decamped at seven, cutting around the city on Q, through Waunakee, east on 19, arriving at the race track a little before eight. It was midget night, and the ugly little beasts raised a din that made conversation difficult, even in the parking lot. Josh kicked out amid several other bikes near the main entrance. One thing about riding a motorcycle. Parking was seldom a problem. It was only a problem at Sturgis during Bike Week, when you could literally walk across town stepping only on motorcycles.

Josh pulled his binocs from the tank bag, stashed them in his backpack along with the aerosol, and paid the ten-dollar admission fee, got a wrist band, and entered the teeming oval, the sound a hundred foot cheese grater. He purchased a hot dog and a soda from a vendor and took a seat at the top of the bleachers while the ugly little cars, mostly engine and roll cage, raced around the dirt oval stirring up dust while an announcer bellowed incoherently over the PA system.

From the top of the bleachers Josh had an excellent view of the parking area and the strip at the back where the kidnappers had directed Franklin. Only a few vehicles had parked in the back. Josh turned around. Klieg lights lit the track like a Hollywood set. People drank, ate, yelled and cheered, all of it inaudible against the wall of sound. At nine o'clock, Josh watched the parking lot in earnest, sweeping from one side to another. He noticed a gray Toyota pull in, driving up one row and down another until it found an empty spot in the middle. Josh trained his binocs on the vehicle for five minutes. The driver remained inside.

Josh looked up and down the bleachers and spotted a dude a hundred feet away from him doing the same thing. It was just dumb luck that the guy hadn't noticed Josh first. Of course, they would have a spotter. Josh went down a few rows, found a spot on the end from which he was able to train his binocs up and get a good look at his fellow searcher, who wore a gray hoodie that concealed his face.

If hoodie saw Josh spray-painting on the roof he would alert the kidnappers. It was already nine. Josh went outside, backing off several hundred feet until he could hear himself think and dialed 911.

"What is your emergency?"

"I'm out here at Angell Park Speedway and there's a guy in the last row of the bleachers staring at young girls through binoculars. He's wearing a gray hoodie. I saw him drive up in a plain van and I just get a feeling he's up to no good."

"To whom am I speaking please?"

Josh hung up, went back inside to the top row. He didn't have long to wait. Within ten minutes, two Town of Sun Prairie police officers in short-sleeved dark blue shirts climbed the bleachers toward hoodie, who did a massive double-take and took off running, the two cops in pursuit.

Josh hustled back outside as the race ended and a blessed curtain of relative calm descended. He phoned Kleiser and told him what happened.

"Okay," Kleiser said. "I'm over on Bishop Street and I'm ready to go."

Josh checked the lot and spotted Franklin's Cadillac.

"Here comes Franklin. Put 'er up. I have to go make the 'X.' Keep an eye out, wouldja?"

"I'm on it."

Josh kept his head down, wending his way through the parking lot until he spotted the gray Toyota. The windows were too heavily tinted to see inside. Minutes later, a man in a hoodie emerged and headed toward the back of the parking lot. No Jane. Either they were dealing in bad faith or she was in on it. As soon as the driver departed, Josh ran up to the Toyota and sprayed an invisible 'X' on the roof. He went to his bike and waited.

Kleiser called. "Got 'em. No Jane. They're arguing."

"Do you see the 'X?'"

"Got it," Kleiser said. "The dude in the hoodie just wrested the bag outta Franklin's hands. He's walking back to his car. Okay, now Franklin is returning to his."

"Keep on it," Josh said. "Gotta go. Franklin's calling."

"No Jane," Franklin said.

"I saw. What did he say?"

"He said that Jane would be waiting for me at my place."

"Did you phone her?"

"I'm doing that right now."

Josh hung up and waited. Moments later, Franklin called back.

"There's no answer. Goes straight to voice mail. Marian says she's alone there."

Josh got on his bike. "Okay. We got the car marked. We're going to follow him."

Josh watched the Toyota peel out of the parking lot and head toward the Interstate. He started his engine and followed at a discreet distance, putting several cars between them. Josh was five minutes behind when the Toyota pulled into a strip mall with an Ace Hardware, an Albertson's, and a liquor store. He cruised up and down the mall until he felt his phone buzzing against his thigh.

It was Kleiser. "Dude just switched cars."

"Fuck! Do you have the second vehicle?"

"I'm sorry, man. They all look alike from on high."

"Okay. Meet me back at Franklin's. They said Jane would be waiting."

CHAPTER 31

PARAGUAY

They were all back at Pine Perch by ten-thirty, the house ablaze. No Jane. Kleiser ran the Toyota plates and learned that the vehicle had been stolen from Mitchell Airport in Milwaukee a week ago.

Marian poured Franklin a Scotch from a bottle of Glenmorangie and looked around.

"Who else? Josh? Randy?"

Josh waved it off as Kleiser held up three fingers.

"They ditched the bag. It's still in the parking lot."

Marian poured one for Kleiser and one for herself, which she gulped.

"Now what?" Franklin demanded.

"Sir," Josh said, "please don't worry that Jane is in any danger. From my experience, this would tend to validate my theory that she's in on it."

"That's supposed to make me feel better?" Franklin

snapped.

Marian kneaded his shoulders. "Lew, Josh may be right. There's nothing you can do."

"I can call the police."

"Sir," Josh said, "If that's what you want to do. I would wait twenty-four hours and see if she contacts you. In the meantime, I have some friends in national security agencies. I'll ask them to put out an alert. If she tries to go anywhere under her own name, we'll know about it."

"When?" Franklin said. "It's eleven o'clock."

"I'll contact them now if you like."

Franklin nodded. "Please."

Josh opened the sliding glass door to the patio and went outside where the pool glowed aquamarine from underwater lights. He looked up. Thousands of stars looked down. Josh dialed Roland Stoeckle, the NSA agent he'd met when he'd killed the Jesuit. Josh left a message for Stoeckle to call him and went home.

Stoeckle called at nine a.m., at Josh's turn-around point, two and a half miles from home. Josh stopped as Fig looked up quizzically, and explained the situation.

"I can do that," Stoeckle said, "but I need a reason that will satisfy protocol."

Josh could have told the NSA agent about Orlok's plan to rob Fort McCoy, but it felt like a betrayal to his biker brothers. Instead, he said, "Sir, have you ever heard of Heinrich Hochrein and Sustainable Protocols?"

"No."

"It's a global warming cult that's trying to make inroads in the U.S."

"Let me look into it and get back to you."

"Great. I'm sending you everything I have about Miss Franklin."

Fig wagged her tail.

Josh resumed running. "Let's book!"

Back at the house he showered, made coffee, and emailed Stoeckle Jane's vital statistics. The NSA had the power to canvass the internet, airlines, trains and buses in search of individuals. It was a long shot.

Franklin phoned. "Kuhn's here. Can you come over?"

When Josh arrived, Kuhn's Indian was in the driveway. Marian's car was gone. Kleiser had left. Josh found the two men red-faced and arguing on the patio. Kuhn looked ready to punch Franklin but the businessman stood his ground.

"Hey!" Josh snapped loud enough to get their attention. "Orlok, what's the problem?"

"You fucked up! That's the problem. You shoulda let me do the exchange."

"I'm her father!"

"Yeah, well, I'm willing to do things you aren't. I would have found out where they're holding her."

"And what if they had a fail-safe option?" Josh said. "They might have killed her."

"She may already be dead!" the Jugan leader yelled.

Josh held his hands up. "I've got my feelers out. Just hang on. These people don't want a capital sentence around their necks."

Orlok glared at him and for a moment Josh felt as he had when Dionysus was on his ass—about to be obliterated by a superior force. He involuntarily took a step back.

"What feelers?" Orlok said through clenched teeth.

"I got friends in law enforcement."

"What friends?"

Josh shook his head. "That's confidential."

Orlok pointed a brat-like finger. "If I find out you're a rat..."

"I ain't no rat!" Josh snapped.

Orlok shook off his anger like a wet dog. "I'm trusting you on this, Pratt. You find something out you call me."

"I will," Josh said to Orlok's back as he strode toward the front door. A minute later they heard him fire up the big V-twin as it roared away.

"What friends?" Franklin echoed.

"You don't need to know either. I don't suppose there's any point in calling the kidnappers back. You have that number?"

Franklin looked astonished as he dug for his phone. He poked at it, handed the phone to Josh as it was ringing. The ringing gave way to an electronic squeal.

"They used a burner," Josh said.

"Well what do you expect me to do?" Franklin said with a plaintive tone.

"Sir, I can't tell you that, but you've got a business to run. This is my top priority. I'm not doing anything right now but looking for Jane."

"But if Kuhn isn't in on it, how could Jane?"

"Sir, don't torture yourself. I just have a feeling she's alive."

"Christ, I hope you're right."

"It doesn't hurt to pray," Josh said, heading for the door.

"Thanks! Thanks a lot!"

Outside, Josh phoned Kleiser.

"I'm in the middle of something," the programmer said.

"Can you come over to my place when you get off?"

"I'll be there."

Josh went home and played with Fig. Phil Bass phoned at noon.

"Thought about that offer?"

"I'm thinking about it, Mr. Bass."

"Call me Phil, wouldya? Let's you and me get together for drinks. How does tonight sound?"

"I'm sorry, Phil. Tonight's booked. I'll call you tomorrow."

Josh mowed his lawn and stewed. As a federal agent, he was required to report threats to federal facilities such as Fort McCoy. Josh knew better than most that rules were made to be broken, but he had to weigh his options. The feds would only back him if he continued to be useful to them. How could he be useful?

Looking deeper into Sustainable Protocols, Josh learned that Germany had banned the group and issued an arrest warrant for Heinrich Hochrein, who had not been seen in seven years and was presumed dead.

Stoeckle called at two.

"Jane Franklin boarded United Flight #1224, non-stop from Chicago to Rio de Janiero, at four p.m. yesterday. She landed in Rio at ten-thirty, and purchased a ticket to Asuncion, that left at one-thirty in the morning."

"Asuncion?" Josh said.

"Paraguay."

CHAPTER

32

DEL FUEGOS

"What have you got for me?" the agent said.

Josh sighed. He'd made a deal with the devil, but a deal was a deal. "The Jugan are planning to steal guns from Fort McCoy, up near Stevens Point."

"For what purpose?"

"Money. They've got a deal with the Blackstone P Nation in Milwaukee."

"When?"

"I don't know. That was before Jane was kidnapped—or faked it. Orlok and Jane are an item. He's ready to go to war. At first I thought he was in on it."

"Who's Orlok?" the agent said.

"Orlok Kuhn, Jugan President. They're a cycle gang, mostly ex-military, headquartered in Western Wisconsin. I'll send you a profile. They have their own web site."

"What are you into, Pratt?"

Josh gave him the rundown, from his first meeting with Jane out at Zeke's.

"How long have you known about their plans?" Stoeckle said.

"Couple days."

"The Jugan, huh?"

"The Jugan."

Stoeckle made a squeaking noise with his lips. "They're not on any terrorist watch lists. In fact, there's hardly anything about them."

"They're not like other cycle gangs."

"Keep me posted."

As soon as Stoeckle hung up, Josh phoned Franklin and told him the news.

"I want you to go down there and bring her back."

"Paraguay, sir? I don't speak the language. I have no authority."

"Either you do it, or I'll contact some mercenaries. Your choice. I'll make it worth your while."

"Can I think about it overnight? I doubt she's going anywhere."

Josh felt Franklin's impatience and disapproval over the phone. "Call me in the morning."

Josh called Orlok.

"What are we going to do about it?"

"Franklin wants me to go down there and bring her back."

"I'll go with you," Orlok said. "Come on out here."

Fig laid her muzzle on Josh's knee and looked up. *Walk*

me! "I can't leave right now, boss. Waiting for someone, but you can come over here."

"What's your address?"

As soon as he hung up Josh regretted his decision. Just what he needed. The Jugan roaring up and down Ptarmigan Street. The only reason the cops hadn't warned him about the alarming phone calls from his neighbors was his close relationship with the department, mainly through gangs expert Detective Heinz Calloway.

Josh went out front and tossed a Frisbee, Fig leaping four feet in the air to snag the plastic disc. She didn't go into the street once. She loved tug-of-war and the only way Josh could get her to release the disc was to blow in her nose.

Kleiser's black Mazda pulled into his driveway a second before the roar of unmuffled pipes rolled down the street. Kleiser got out and looked back. Only Orlok and Bobby, but they sounded like a herd of mastodons.

As the Jugan kicked out, Phil Bass drove by, slowing down to stare in shock. Josh waved and led the bruthas through the house out onto the back deck. Josh went into the kitchen and got a four pack of Odell's Myrcenary, returned and handed them out.

Josh told them what he'd learned from Stoeckle.

Orlok squinted. "Who is this guy again?"

"Just a guy I know, works for the NSA."

"How soon you leaving?" Orlok said.

Fuck, Josh thought. Paraguay. Fuckin' Paraguay. He sighed.

"Tomorrow."

"You want me to take care of Fig?" Kleiser said.

"That'd be great, Randall. Thanks."

Orlok slammed his beer, set it on the table with a thump. "I'm coming."

Bobby put his hand on Orlok's arm. "Now ain't a good time, hoss. We got that thing comin' up."

"Fuck," Orlok said. "Fuck, fuck, fuck. You said you were gonna take care of this."

Fig laid her muzzle on his knee and Orlok automatically stroked her head.

Josh shrugged. "You know, man, she may have faked the kidnapping."

Orlok looked up at the glowing emerald shroud of forest in the afternoon light. "I know. I don't understand her. But I love her. She came to me. She sought me out when I was in the pen. That's how we met. Because she's a selfless, loving creature. But she's crazy. I know that. She's completely bug fuck. You think you can handle this?"

"I'll give it a shot," Josh said. "I don't speak Paragese, but I have some ideas."

Orlok looked at Bobby. "We know anybody in Paraguay?"

Bobby blew a Bronx cheer.

Orlok turned his wide-set eyes on Josh. "How you gonna bring her back?"

"Fuck if I know."

"Don't worry about it," Kleiser said. "That's what he's good at. Improvising and shit."

"You lost a couple clients," Orlok said.

"I loved Fig Newton the way you love Jane. Do you know how she died?"

Orlok backed off. "Sorry, brother, didn't mean to rake up any bad memories. I just don't want to lose her, know what I'm sayin'?"

Josh nodded. "I think Jane trusts me."

"She oughtta," Bobby said.

Orlok ruffled Fig's ears. "So this is the dog?"

"That's the dog. I call her Fig, after Fig."

"What about the dog?" Bobby said, so Josh told him about the dog, and Jerrel Moore.

Kleiser stood and picked up empty beer bottles. "Are we gonna eat or what?"

"Order some goddamn pizza," Orlok said. "I'll pay."

Josh shook his heads. "Sorry, boys. I gotta work. Kleiser, you gotta work. So you boys gots to go."

Orlok's eyes went wide. "You're kickin' us out?"

"Get outta here before the neighbors call the cops," Josh said.

Bobby stood, knuckled Orlok's shoulder. "Let's go, hoss. These guys ain't no fun."

Orlok heaved himself to his feet. "Fuck it."

Moments later, the cacophony sent blackbirds flying as the Jugan rode away. Kleiser had brought in a laptop and drives.

"Now what?"

Josh gave him everything on Jane including pictures.

"Do they even have internet in Paraguay?"

"It's everywhere," Kleiser said, entering data.

"You got some kinda tracking device? Something really tiny I can slip in a person's clothing and they won't notice?"

Kleiser stood. "Yeah. Hang on a minute."

He went out the front door and returned a minute later clutching what looked like a hearing-aid battery. "You activate it by twisting a quarter turn. Sends out a signal on an unused frequency that can be picked up by a NASA satellite."

Josh took the device. "Did you develop this?"

"Hell no. We're working on a replacement and NASA sent this as a model. Whatcha gonna do with it?"

Josh stood. "I'm going to plant it on Jane, if I find her."

"Whatcha gonna do?"

Josh headed into his office. "Find a friend in Paraguay."

Fig followed Josh in and settled at his feet. Josh googled "cycle gangs Paraguay," and the first hit was losdelfuegos.com. Their page was surprisingly sophisticated, with a half dozen Del Fuegos in colors standing behind their bikes in front of a stucco cantina with viga poles, Cerveza painted on the window in elegant script. An explosion of green framed the little building.

Josh clicked on the translation for their mission statement.

The Del Fuegos are a group of ex-Paraguayan military officers who enjoy riding motorcycles, helping charities, and having a good time.

Under contact he found President Yowel Yglesias. Josh wrote him an email.

> *Dear President Yglesias: I am a private investigator from Madison, Wisconsin, looking into the disappearance of a young woman who was last seen boarding an airplane for Asuncion last night. I don't speak Spanish or Guarani. My client offers more than adequate compensation. Do you know someone who could act as my guide?*
>
> *By the way, I own a heavily modified '96 Road King and have been riding since I was fifteen years old.*

Josh was looking at bikes when his in-box binged.

> *Dear Mr. Pratt: Yes! I am happy to act as your guide! I look into your background and find you are real bad ass! You killed fucking cougar with a pen knife! I speak Spanish and Guarani and am pleased to act as your guide. My telephone is 011 343 666 2798. Please let me know details of your flight and I will meet you at Silvio Pettirossi Airport. I remain, your obedient servant, Yowel Iglesias.*

CHAPTER

33

YOWEL

After a quick search, Josh found Yowel on Facebook, sent him a friend request, and was immediately accepted.

"Do you have Skype?" Yowel asked.

Josh's Skype handle was Biker1. Yowel looked like Tommy Chong, seated before his computer in a dark den with a poster for the Paraguayan National Soccer Team on the wall behind him.

"Comrade!" he boomed over the speakers. "I have followed your exploits since you kill the puma!"

"Where did you hear about that, Yowel?"

"It was on several biker boards, but that was years ago. Then I read about your battles with the Islamists..."

Josh felt sick to his stomach. He hated publicity and did his best to avoid it. But the upside was, bikers around the world knew and respected him.

"Okay, I don't know when I'm coming, but it's in the

next couple of days. The person I seek is Jane Franklin. I'll email you the particulars and some photos. She's mixed up with something called Sustainable Protocols. Ever hear of it?"

Yglesis lit a cigar and leaned back. "No. I will look into it."

"What about Heinrich Hocheim?"

"Hocheim? That does ring a bell. I will look into it. Tell me! What kind of bike do you ride?"

"It's a '96 Road King. Why?"

"I knew it!" Yowel howled. "Come see my beauty!"

Yowel's inked arms reached for the screen and the view shifted, a vertiginous mish-mash, a shaky image, and at last the laptop focused on a dark shape in a corner of the room. The lights went up and Josh looked at an old pan-head springer with an enormous round headlight over a big round horn, wheelbarrow bars, fishtail exhaust, painted red.

"Noice!" Josh said. "What year is it?"

"It's a '48! I restored it myself. But it is too precious for me to subject to these awful roads. This is my daily ride."

The camera swiveled to close in on an old four-banger Gold Wing with no front fender. "But do not worry! I also have a truck to pick you up. I will not ask you to ride pillion with me. Only the ladies!"

Yowel burst into laughter.

"I really appreciate this, Yowel, and like I said, my client will pay you a reasonable rate. What do you want?"

Yowel scratched his beard. "What about one hundred

dollars American a day?"

"Done," Josh said. "I'll be in touch."

He signed off and went into the living room where Kleiser was bent over his computer, earphones on, with Fig's head in his lap. She lay on her back with her legs in the air like a dead cockroach.

"Hey!" Josh said.

Kleiser looked up. Fig's tail thumped.

"Can you scrub any mention of me on the internet, while not messing with my Facebook page or email?"

Kleiser took off the headphones and set them down. "Say what?"

"There are news stories about me, and crap on biker chat boards. Can you create a program that finds them and deletes them? I'm sick of having my fucking life splashed all over the internet. I don't like it."

Kleiser picked up a can of Coke and glugged. "That's an interesting question. Let me look into it."

Josh found a frozen pizza in the freezer and put it in the stove. He dished out Canidae Grainless Salmon meal for Fig. After he and Kleiser ate, Josh sat on the sofa next to the programmer and turned on the television. A winsome young man with hair in his face looked at the camera.

"After my motorcycle accident, the insurance company only wanted to pay me ten thousand dollars. So, I went to Steve Fleiss, and he got me one point two million dollars. Glad I called."

Fleiss appeared in a sober suit. "Of course, I can't guarantee that your case will be worth a million dollars, but if you've been in an accident and the insurance company isn't giving you what you think you deserve, call me, Steve Fleiss—the Hammer."

Kleiser looked up. "Franklin landed in Asuncion at four-thirty this morning."

"Can you track her phone or something?"

"Negatory. Paraguay's not like the US, with phone towers up the yib-yob. You're gonna have to track her down the old-fashioned way. With good old police work! Pounding the pavement."

"All right," Josh said. "Get outta here. It's Fig's bedtime."

Kleiser packed his stuff. "When you going?"

"Tomorrow, I guess. And I'm not happy about it."

"Then why go?"

"A job's a job. Let me give you a key."

Josh found a duplicate in the kitchen, put it on a bottle opener keychain and handed it to Kleiser. Josh showed up at Franklin's house Tuesday morning at ten. Franklin handed Josh a thick wad of cash. "There's five thousand dollars for expenses and your tickets. Keep all your receipts. You have a passport?"

Josh nodded.

"You'll need to get a visa in Chicago to enter Paraguay."

"How long do you want me to stay down there?"

Franklin gave him a look of disgust. "As long as it takes!"

"Sir, I regret having to mention this, but what if she doesn't want to come back?"

"No. That's not acceptable. Look. You're a resourceful guy. I'm not saying to drug her or anything but do whatever it takes. What about her boyfriend? Is she just dropping him like a bad apple?"

"You're the client."

"All right. Let me know if you need anything. I had my secretary book you on United #5446, Chicago to Rio, this afternoon at four. You leave for Asucion at eight-thirty on Brasilia Air."

On the way back, Josh stopped in at Dovetail where Kleiser hunched in his office, shades drawn, working on a program. He held up a finger when Josh entered. Josh went down to the break room, snagged a bottled water and returned.

"Did you look into scrubbing me from the internet?"

Kleiser swiveled. "Depends on how many sources post stuff about you. I could create a crawler bot that searches for mentions, and then when it finds them, it initiates an attack to gain access to the hosting server and flags the person in control of the bot to take further action. If Josh Pratt is pretty famous and stories and posts about him get copied or re-posted quickly, it could never keep up and in the act of destroying information is almost certain to get noticed. If Josh Pratt is not very famous, and information on him is limited to just a few websites then it might be possible for me to react fast enough to clean information about you, but to not get noticed you wouldn't want to erase the data, you want to replace it with false information so that it is less likely the person who posted the data will notice. If you wanted to erase yourself from the internet, it might be better to go after the source of how people find you, Google or Bing, and see if you can trick them into making Josh Pratt a part of their censor list. Hacking or tricking Google directly would require quite a number of resources on the level of being a nation state, so this might not be the route to go. Cuz sure as shit, somebody at NSA is keeping tabs on what we do.

"A better way is to 'blind' the people who look you up. You create a honeypot server that has a really high match rate for Josh Pratt and put a ton of false information, but make it look plausible so that search engines will rate it very high in their rankings. The server hosting this site runs a bot that logs everyone that is looking at Josh Pratt 's false information, and when it notices a browser that is not Google or Bing, it flags the server owner that a person is looking up Josh Pratt and sends the computer links with browser exploits in them. If we can exploit the browser, we can replace search results of Josh Pratt with whatever we want. Thus it appears that Josh Pratt is just a fiction, or just whatever you want him to be. And since other searches give completely normal results, they would not think to look for a hack in their browser."

Josh's mouth opened but nothing came out.

Finally, he said, "Do whichever works best."

CHAPTER

34

ASUNCION

Josh thought about Kleiser every time he flew, and especially Kleiser's girlfriend Patty, who died aboard a SW flight from Denver to Austin. TSA gave her the full treatment, while waving through a woman in a burqa. The ship exploded in mid-air. Investigators concluded it was a bomb.

He got through Madison okay, but when he got to Chicago, he had an hour to kill, so he left the secured area to visit the aviation museum in the basement of the adjacent Hilton. When Josh passed through security, they pulled him aside, asked permission to stick their hands down his pants, sprayed his hands with some chemical, and then told him to follow them to a secure room where they repeated the procedure. They also went through his carry-on bag item by item, including the toothpaste and a floss box which they pried open. When they were done, they said, "Okay, Mr. Pratt. You can go now."

Josh drew a window seat in row 24 of the United 747. the man in the middle seat looked ordinary in every way. He wore glasses, a pilled knit shirt under a beige sport jacket, and carried an ersatz leather briefcase which he slid beneath the seat in front of him, first side to side, then end to end.

Josh waited until they were air born and then slumped in the corner. Something about the vibrations always made him sleepy. It was not long before his neighbor tapped his elbow. Josh looked up.

A blonde steward looked at him from the end of a drink cart.

"Would you like something to drink?" the steward said.

"I'll take can of tomato juice, if you have one," Josh said. "Just the can, no glass."

The stew handed him a can, poured a soft drink for his neighbor. Josh lowered the seat tray and pulled out the latest issue of *The Horse*. His neighbor looked over.

"So you going to Brazil too, huh?"

Josh didn't look up. "Yup."

"I'm going to visit El Racario, a notorious serial killer who slaughtered 24 people in a remote area of the Mato Gross."

The man looked over Josh's shoulder. "One of the serial killers I follow was a hard-core biker who abducted women on his motorcycle."

Josh looked up. "What the fuck?"

"Yeah. His name was John Ambrose. I'm Arnold Lubing, by the way."

Josh had no choice but to shake his hand. It was eight hours to Rio. "Josh Pratt."

"I'm a web designer, but serial killers are my hobby. I've talked to a lot of them. Charles Manson sent me several drawings. Would you like to see?"

"That's all right."

Lubing already had the briefcase open on his lap. "One of the reasons El Racario agreed to see me, he wants to see some of my trophies. Here. Look at this." He handed Josh two pages of rough foolscap taped together, covered with ritualistic spirals drawn in crayon, and drawn on top in black crayon, a crude skull. It was signed "Charles Manson" in the corner. Ambrose tried to hand it to him.

Josh shuddered. "No thanks."

Lubing gingerly took the drawing back, folded it in two, and carefully tucked it into a frayed manila envelope. He burrowed through his thicket and retrieved a Polaroid which he passed to Josh, showing a smiling Lubing with his hand on the shoulder of a porcine man in prison grays, inside an institution.

"That's me and John Gacy." Lubing handed Josh another photo. "This is the house they built on the site of Gacy's old house, which they tore down. I took this myself. Look. Up there in the window. What do you see?"

Josh stared at the photo of a gauche house with fake dormers. There was a blur in the upstairs window that could have been anything. Lubing's finger landed on it like a fat house fly. "See? That's the ghost of one of the boys he murdered. I also have a birthday card Squeaky Fromme sent me."

Josh looked around. He grabbed his over nighter. "Would you excuse me, please? I have to visit the head."

"Sure," Lubing said, standing. "Sure."

The man in the aisle seat stoically stood as Josh eased himself out, heading for the back. The 155 passenger ship was mercifully not completely booked. Josh found two empty seats in the very last row, next to a Brazilian woman with headphones on. Josh took the aisle seat. The seat back was fixed upright. Josh put down the tiny tray, set his over nighter on it, and leaned forward. Fifteen minutes later he was asleep.

This time, a stewardess woke him to ask if he would like a snack. She gave Josh two Hot Pockets, ham and cheddar in some kind of flaky dough. He woke again as they were landing at Santos Dumont. Josh stood and stretched, patiently waiting for the entire cabin to empty ahead of him. He walked out into tropical air, a hint of the ocean, aviation fuel, and garbage. He'd landed on the Second Concourse. His Azul flight to Asuncion was on the Sixth Concourse. With two hours to kill, Josh walked slowly, watching the bustle and flow of humanity at three o'clock in the morning.

Box-like shops were set into the inner concourse wall, like American airports in the seventies. A boy slept on a pile of burlap bags in the back of a food stand, sealed off from the concourse by a folding steel grate. Brazilian security forces in black berets walked German shepherds up and down,

joking with travelers. Josh passed Starbucks and McDonald's, stopped at a Giraffa's and bought a pork sandwich
on a Hoagie roll with an agreeably spicy, mayonnaise-type
spread.

The terminal was not air-conditioned but open widows
caught the sea breeze. His Azul flight was an ancient 737
with duct tape running up and down the interior fuselage.
A family with a pig on a leash and a chicken in a cage occupied two rows opposite. The airplane reeked like a barnyard
and served warm cans of Coke and potato sticks. The plane
landed at three a.m. Asuncion time, at a small, one-level
airport with six ports. It was hot. Amid the scrum of people
waiting at the gate to greet new arrivals, Yowel was immediately identifiable. With his wild black beard and colors, he
looked like an extra from *Hell's Angels On Wheels*. He fixed
his beady gaze on Josh, coming up the stairs, and waited at
the top with open arms.

"Hermano!" he exclaimed, enfolding Josh in an embrace
smelling of cohiba and Ax body spray. "Is this all your lug-
gage?"

Josh hefted the overnighter. "This is it."

Yowel took it from him. "Come, come. You'll be staying with me, of course." Josh followed the lumbering bear
through the nearly deserted terminal out into a rutted
parking lot lit sporadically by sodium lamps, to a 1974
Ford pick-up jacked two feet off the ground, sodium lamps
mounted on a roll bar that arched above the roof. Yowel
tossed Josh's bag in the bed next to an old raw-boned hound

curled up on a pile of blankets.

"Say 'allo to Fulgencio," the Paraguayan said, opening the driver's door. Josh used a handle to boost himself up into the shotgun seat. "I live in Tacumbu by the river. Fifteen minutes, this time of night."

Through the open windows the city smelled of diesel, burning trash, and fresh rain. Fifteen minutes later, Yowel turned onto a paved, narrow residential street lined with stucco houses, one running into the next, some with tiny yards fenced in by iron gates, most with red tile roofs. Mango trees lined the street, their fruit creating a slippery mess. Josh's shirt stuck to the small of his back. Yowel stopped outside a house with a scrap-iron goony bird, a mango tree and two chickens in the yard, released the padlock on the gate, drove the truck inside, shut off the engine, got out and shut the gate behind him.

"Don't slip on the mangos," Yowel said.

The old dog got up, put its paws on the tailgate and stretched like a ski jump before clambering out. Yowel grabbed Josh's bag and led the way, unlocking the door. Josh followed him into a surprisingly bright and airy interior, with a high ceiling, ceiling fan, skylight, Indian rugs on the hardwood floor, and a parrot on a stand.

"Fuck you!" the parrot sang.

"Hush, Renaldo!" Yowel hissed. "Forgive him, he is a stupid bird."

"And the horse you rode in on!" Renaldo sang.

Yowel's bike took up a quarter of the room, gleaming in

the light of several lamps. A six-foot leather sofa pressed the wall beneath a framed black velvet painting of a blonde in a bikini relaxing on a Harley, lit by a black light. Framed black and white photos showed Yowel solo and with his brothers, posing in front of some backwoods watering hole or on the road.

Yowel disappeared in the back and returned with a pile of blankets which he threw on the sofa.

"See you in the morning."

CHAPTER 35

DUE DILIGENCE

Orlok couldn't sleep. Bare-chested, sweating, he danced around his office to the O'Jays, slashing the air with a katana.

Overseas, he had routinely gone for thirty-six hours without sleep hopped up on a mix of meth, khat, and Captagon, which was mother's milk to the *muhajadin*. Nor was there much sleep in Waupun, where he'd served two years for manslaughter. He'd used that time to study the great philosophers, from Epictetus and Marcus Aurelius to Nietszche, Kierkegaard, and Von Mises. Orlok had been a warrior his entire life, from the seventh grade when Ron Barnett once tried to take his lunch money.

That was the last time anyone had tried to push him around. Orlok joined Eugene Field Junior High's Boys Wrestling Team and stuck with it through college, where he was NAAA Division 3 Heavyweight Champ.

As a child he'd gorged on books, dreaming of joining

his heroes, Jack London, Ernest Hemingway, Conan the Barbarian, Matt Helm and all the other doers and dreamers. Orlok began training in karate at age of fourteen with Kim Il Jung, a former Korean Army Captain who earned a decent living teaching the ancient martial art to sons and daughters of Milwaukee, while hitting on every attractive female who entered the dojong.

By the time he was twelve, Orlok was over six feet tall. From Master Sung he learned of the Okinawan karate master Mas Oyama, who felled bulls with a single blow. Orlok went to the shelf covering one wall and ran his finger down a series of ancient VHS tapes, choosing one with an illegible title scrawled on the end. It had been duplicated many times. Extracting the tape, he muted the radio and slid it into the creaky RCA unit attached to the flat screen on the shelf. The grainy, brown images flickered as words appeared.

14th January, 1954. Tateyama Coast, Chiba. Oyama was 173 centimeters tall, weighed 82 kilograms at that time. The bull was five years old. It weighed 450 kilograms and had a horn 9 centimeter in size, 40 centimeters long.

Orlok watched the burly Oyama wrestle with the bull for agonizing seconds before drawing back his hand in a shuto strike and shearing the bull's right horn. Seconds later, Oyama felled the bull with a palm strike between the eyes. As an animal lover, Orlok was appalled. As a karateka, he was in awe.

By the time Orlok was sixteen, he'd developed the massive bony ridges of scar tissue on both hands from repeatedly hitting his rope-covered makiwara. As defensive linebacker for the Wauwatosa Wildcats, Orlok led his team to an eleven and two season, and was scouted by the Packers and the Vikings.

He was far more interested in joining the Marines. The first time the drill instructor asked for a volunteer, Orlok knew he was destined to teach hand-to-hand combat. He was a corporal by the time they landed in Kandahar, always the first to volunteer on night missions so he could test his techniques. He'd killed eleven men with his bare hands and nine of them died without a sound. A strong punch to the center of the chest would stop their hearts. High on Captagon, some of those sand niggers weighed over two hundred and fifty and were six feet tall.

Orlok and Bobby formed the Jugan in the sand. Bobby was from the South Side of Chicago, steeped in the blues and wise in the ways of the street. When they got out, Bobby joined Orlok working construction for an ex-Marine in Whitefish Bay. "White Folks Bay," Bobby called it. One night they were drinking in a joint called The Outrigger, with a vaguely Polynesian theme, when some dude punched his girlfriend. Orlok stepped in, landed a haymaker, and the guy went down. Dead before he even hit the floor.

Orlok was in his thirteenth month at Waupun when Jane wrote him out of the blue.

Dear Mr. Kuhn: You don't know me, but I'm a patriot, and I read about your troubles in the Milwaukee Journal/ Sentinel. *I researched your past and learned that not only are you a war hero, but the circumstances of your conviction. I know I am not alone in viewing you as entirely justified in your action, and calling your incarceration a miscarriage of justice. I read your letter in the* Journal/ Sentinel *regarding genetically modified organisms and I couldn't agree more.*

Let me tell you a little about myself. I am a Peace Corps Worker currently in Paraguay, but I will return in three months to my home in Madison, where I plan to register for college. I will study animal husbandry with an eye toward natural selection, and the folly of genetic modification. I believe you are someone who understands me, and whom I can understand. I hope that you will write back to me and tell me of your plans when you get out.

Yours sincerely, Jane Franklin

She'd enclosed a photo. The letter's scent gave Orlok a raging hard-on, but he was no animal and would never spill his seed up another man's ass. He took care of business the old-fashioned way. He wrote her back and by the time he was released, eight months later, they were in love.

Jane was waiting for him when he walked out the gates. He couldn't believe his luck. It was like a fucking fairy-tale, how this beautiful young woman had zeroed in on him like a single grain of sand on the beach. What were the odds? They went to bed that night and had been inseparable ever since.

While Orlok was incarcerated, Bobby had incorporated the Jugan MC, and used the pooled assets of all one hundred Jugan, including Orlok, to purchase the 480 acre enclave that comprised the farm. The Ojibwa had farmed ginseng on that land for three generations, but the newest generation wasn't interested. Casinos were more lucrative. The Jugan bought the place at bargain basement prices, including the tractor.

Now, with both Jane and Josh in Paraguay, Orlok didn't know whether to shit or go blind. He was sick with worry that something might have happened to her. Yes, she was overly dramatic, but that was just another shade of her passion. Jane was a genuinely good person who cared about the downtrodden and the disenfranchised. She could have chosen any of a thousand different causes. She chose to fight genetically modified organisms because she had seen, firsthand, the results in Paraguay. An entire tribe of Guanari Indians wiped out by a rare form of thyroid cancer which researchers traced to genetically-modified cassava. Sustainable Protocols had done the research.

She might have been behind the kidnap hoax. He didn't care. It was no secret how she hated Lewis. That money would be hers someday, anyway.

"If only he were dead," she murmured in his ear at night, but Orlok wasn't buying.

Josh was another story. Orlok couldn't help but like the guy, but there was something about him. Like he was hiding something. Orlok asked Bobby to do deep background. It was ten o'clock at night and Orlok replaced the katana in its scabbard and withdrew a kukhri. Orlok popped the tape, returned it to its slot, and turned the Sirius XM up. Creedence's "Run Through the Jungle." They'd played that all the time in the sand.

"Yo," Bobby said from the door. Orlok whirled in a fighting stance, not that he intended to gut anyone. It's just the way it was. Grinning, he slid the kukhri back into its sheath.

"Whatcha got?"

Bobby walked in and sprawled on the leather sofa, which chirped back and hit the wall. "Our friend Pratt killed a mountain lion with a pocketknife."

Orlok froze. "What?"

"Yeah. I read it this little Wyoming newspaper. They charged him with killing an endangered species, but the charges were dismissed."

"What the fuck?!"

"I tried to get the whole story when the weirdest thing happened. I was reading this paean to him on the Crazy Bikers forum, when suddenly it blinked out. Page was no longer available. So I ran a search and where before, there were at least a dozen stories on the guy, they'd all disappeared. So I contacted my man at Army Intelligence. Couple hours later he gets back to me. He's got sources at Homeland Security, and they tell me Pratt's on the payroll."

"You're shitting me."

"No, hoss. Pratt's a fed."

CHAPTER

36

THE WILD WEST

Claws dug into Josh's chest. He looked up. The chicken looked down. Bright sunlight flowed in through the front windows and skylights. Yowel, wearing only Yogi Bear boxer shorts, marched into the living room, Fulgencio at his heels, waving a straw hat at the chicken which hopped to the ground and hopped up to the open window. The chicken jumped.

"Get out of here!" Yowel said. He looked like he was wearing a black cashmere sweater. Tribal tats covered both shoulders.

Josh rubbed his eyes and sat up. He looked at his watch. It was eleven o'clock.

"That's some ink," Yowel said.

"Thanks."

Yowel sat in a wooden chair beneath a portrait of the Virgin Mary. "Sustainable Protocols is located in the Alto, up near the Matto Grosso. That is a lawless area, my friend."

"How do you know?"

Yowel scratched his belly. "Brazilian millionaire accused them of brainwashing his daughter. He went up there with the state police last year and they had a stand-off for about a week. They finally sent her out and he went away."

"They never went into the compound?"

"No. They figure someone in the organization paid off an interior minister."

Josh stood and stretched. "So nobody knows what goes on in there."

Yowel shrugged. "Who knows? It is too late to start today. It will take us all day to get there so I thought I'd show you around town."

"That's fine. Where's the bathroom?"

Yowel pointed. "How do you like your eggs?"

"Scrambled."

Josh felt better after a shower. He and Yowel ate breakfast at a round metal table in the tiny backyard, surrounded by a six-foot stucco fence enclosing a patio and a yucca tree. It was ninety degrees with humidity that felt like a moist washcloth. Yowel served scrambled eggs with cheese, bacon, and onions.

Josh held his thumb up. "Good grub!"

"Let's get you some huaraches," Yowel said. With Fulgencio in the truck bed, they drove into town on Avenue Gral Maxico, a broad boulevard that led to Bahia de Asuncion, a bay off the Paraguay River. Yowel parked parallel to the curb among an odd selection of vehicles including many

American cars from the seventies.

Yowel handed Fulgencio a bone and pointed at him. "Stay."

They set off down the esplanade, separated from the sandy beach by a four-foot wall. Hundreds of Paraguayans and tourists had pitched blankets and umbrellas. Past the bay, steamers moved up and down the broad river. "Most people think of Paraguay as a backwater of Nazi scientists, but we are modernizing quickly."

"What about the del Fuegos?" Josh said. "We gonna visit?"

"Much as they would love to meet you, they are scattered to the winds. Figlio and Nestor are with the State Police."

"They don't mind that they're in a gang?"

Yowel shrugged. "This is South America, my friend. The lines get blurry."

The air was heavy with the smell of sewage and rotting fish. Mango trees lined the camino and Yowel pointed out squashed mangoes to avoid. They paused at a roadside stand with a thatched roof hut and bought glasses of fresh-squeezed cherimoya juice. They entered a broad zacalo across the street from the beach, with an ornate church and a marble fountain in the center that depicted Simon Bolivar on a rearing stallion. A dozen people sat on marble benches circling the fountain, while others, mostly Indian, trickled in and out of the church.

"Will you wait for me while I make confession?" Yowel said.

"Knock yourself out. I'll be on that bench."

Yowel headed for the Gothic arch as Josh grabbed a seat in the shade, vacated by an elderly gentleman with a Pomeranian on a leash. From here, he could see the avenue, a steady stream of rusted vehicles, smoke spewing mopeds, and bicyclists carrying improbable loads. Airplanes flew in and out of the airport, just past the horizon. A micro-bus decked out like a garden party, broadcasting an inane jingle, pulled up to the curb by the beach and was besieged by children. A stray dog came up and sniffed Josh's hand. When Yowel came out, they walked back to the truck and drove to the Palacio de Lopez, approaching on foot amid immaculately maintained topiary.

"Here, our beloved El Presidente charts a happy and prosperous future for all the peoples of Paraguay!"

"Yowel, we're wasting time. Why don't we take off for the Alto today?"

Yowel reeled back and gave Josh the hairy eyeball. He looked like Sergio Aragones. "There are no roads up there. I am not sure that we can even make it in one day."

"All the better to get started now, yes?"

Yowel warded off flies. "I forget how impatient you gringos are! There is the matter of my salary."

"I believe we settled on a hundred a day." Josh pulled out his wallet and counted off five hundred-dollar bills. "Here's an advance."

Yowel snatched the bills and stuffed them in his pants. "You have convinced me. We must stop at the house first to stock up on supplies, and then of course I will need to visit the service station to top off and fill the tires."

Two hours later, they headed north on State Highway 9, past broad savannas with grazing cattle, overtaking heavily-laden stake trucks filled with workers or produce. Yowel's neighbor had agreed to look after Fulgencio and the chickens.

Yowel slid a CD into the retro-fitted player. "You like the Rolling Stones?"

Let It Bleed bled from the speakers. The broad, four-lane soon gave way to a paved two-lane that ran between rolling grass and swamp lands, past cheerfully painted villages, plumes of smoke, and the occasional dead dog. Yowel leaned over and popped the glove compartment, the truck veering dangerously close to the side of the road.

"This is for you," he said, righting the vehicle.

Josh pulled out a Taurus five-shot .38 special and a box of cartridges.

"You packin'?"

Yowel reached inside his vest and withdrew a compact Beretta nine. "No one goes to the Alta without guns. It is still the wild west up there." He reached under the seat and handed Josh a sheathed Puma White Hunter with a six-inch blade. "Take this. I took it off a punk at a soccer game."

Josh stuck the gun and the knife in his backpack.

He reached back into his vest and pulled out a pack of Colorados, shook one out, and lit it with a Bic. Harsh tobacco smoke filled the cab. Even with the windows wide open, going sixty miles per hour, the heat was unbearable.

They passed a river.

"Let's stop and take a dip," Josh said.

Yowel grinned around the cheroot. "That is not advisable. There are caiman and anaconda in the river."

They rode in silence. Josh checked his cell phone. NO SERVICE AVAILABLE.

"Are you a religious man?" Yowel said.

"I recognize Jesus as my Lord and Savior."

Yowel thumped the wheel. "Aha! I knew it! We are mostly Catholic, as you can see. So tell me. What were you before?"

Josh gazed out the window at casava fields, a green furze of hills in the distance. "I was a hoodlum. My father abandoned me when I was fifteen. I joined the Bedouins, the only family I ever had. We did a lot of bad shit. They sent me to prison for assault. For the first time in my life, I started to think about things. Really think about them. They had a chaplain there, Frank Dorgan, who took an interest in me. I don't know why. He didn't push it, but he got me to thinking. Who made all this? Who made the stars and the people and the dogs? Did it just somehow come into being by itself? Didn't make sense. And what Jesus said made sense. Once I accepted Him into my heart and soul, I knew peace for the first time."

Yowel slowed for a herd of sheep crossing the road. "I, too, am an orphan."

They turned off the highway onto a rutted and swampy

road. An hour later, Yowel pulled the old truck into a clearing with a makeshift stone fire ring filled with discarded beer cans. The light was fading.

"We stop here for the night. Keep that pistol with you. This is the wild west."

CHAPTER 37

RAID

Twelve Jugan gathered around the big table in the dining room, looking down at a map of Fort McCoy. Orlok stood at the head of the table with Bobby at his side. The fort was triangular, with administration and a baseball field in the middle. Orlok used a rattan stick to point.

"This here's the main gate, on Sparta Road, but we're making our incursion here," he pointed to the northern end of the map, "through this gate off Bivouac Road. Bobby got us a sweet EMP drone that's gonna fry their circuits. We will use that window to infiltrate. Me, Bobby, Feral, Panda and Marcus."

Bobby stepped away and returned with the drone, a two-foot cross with a rotor sticking up out of the end of each girder. "This is the biggest and most powerful drone I could get. It runs two million volts through the pulse capacitor. Once that goes off, it'll fry every hard drive in the joint, it'll scramble every cell phone. They'll be confused, not knowing what's going on."

A thick Jugan with a red bandanna around his head stepped up. "How long that fry gonna last?"

Bobby twirled one of the rotors. "Hopefully, several hours until they can reboot and replace. They got emergency generators, so the place'll be lit up."

"We stop here," Orlok pointed. "Bobby gets out and does the drone thing. We pick him up on the way back."

Orlok pointed to a series of black rectangles. "The armory is here. We got a Stew & Steve 4X4 in the barn. Groover bought it off eBay in Missouri. All the electrics are shielded in lead tape. We got uniforms. We go in, we get out. We're grabbing M-4s, M-165s and LAWS rockets."

"Also," Bobby said, "land lines won't be affected. Hopefully, we'll get in and out before they realize something's up. We got a manifest. We got fake orders. We know how these things work."

The room smelled of pizza and dope, with four large Rocky's Pizza boxes stacked on a sideboard. Jugan chewed while they studied the plan.

"Gear up," Orlok said. "Leave your cell phones."

He, Bobby, Marcus, Panda and Feral left the room, returning shortly in green Army fatigues, three buck privates and Sergeant Kuhn. Fort McCoy was just outside Sparta, twelve miles north. Bobby's route was all back roads. It was twelve-thirty Tuesday morning when they left the compound in the khaki green truck. The prospect closed the gate behind them and saluted.

The noisy diesel combined with the thrash of gears to drown out ambient sound.

"Zis because of Josh?" Bobby said.

Orlok shifted up with another gnash of gears. "Whadd-aya mean?"

"Cuz you wanted to bring him along, remember? But now that he may be working for the feds, we do it without him."

"What do you think?" Orlok said.

They saw the glow of Sparta in the distance. By one they were in place. Orlok pulled off the road, Bobby unloaded with his gear, and Panda took his seat in the shotgun seat. Bobby came around to the driver's side and synchronized his watch with Orlok's.

"Five minutes," Bobby said.

Orlok flashed five fingers. The truck drove off, turning into Gate 3, at the camp's northwest corner. They pulled up to the guard station and a soldier came out to greet them with a flashlight.

Orlok stopped the truck, got out, and handed the soldier a clipboard.

"Here to pick up ordnance for Truax."

The soldier examined the papers with his flashlight. "I don't know anything about this. Wait here." The soldier went into his hut with the papers and reached for the land line.

The lights went out. The soldier looked up, then down,

stabbing ineffectively at the telephone. Orlok couldn't believe his luck. The EMP had slagged the land line.

The soldier exited the hut. "You're gonna have to wait here. I don't know what's going on."

"Corporal Adams," Orlok said, reading the soldier's tag. "This may be related to the terrorist attacks. Did you see the memo? It went out to all branches and law enforcement agencies."

"What memo?"

"Al Qaeda threatened a series of attacks for today in honor of some bumfuck terrorist shooting. That's why Truax needs the ordnance."

Adams went back into the hut and raised the gate.

"Mind if I hitch a ride?" he said.

"Soldier, I think you'd better stay here."

"Right! Right!"

They drove toward the darkened base, powerful flashlight beams flickering off the buildings. As they approached, they heard men shouting and the shrill pierce of whistles. No one looked at them as they rolled into the compound and turned right onto Constitution Boulevard. No one had tried to start any vehicles. They were too busy being confused.

Orlok pulled up to the armory where two nervous guards fingered their side-arms. Orlok got out and showed them the manifest.

"I don't know anything about this," said the corporal in green cam fatigues.

"Didn't you get the memo?"

"What memo?"

The others got out while Orlok explained. The corporal waved and yelled.

"Captain Barrett!"

A graying man with a mustache hustled over in captain's fatigues.

"I'm Captain Barrett. Who are you?"

Orlok explained.

"You think we're under terrorist attack?" Barrett said, nonplussed.

"That's my theory, sir."

Barrett examined the papers. "You know Colonel Gunderson?"

"Yes, sir."

"What does he look like?"

Orlok had served with Gunderson in Afghanistan. "He's a ramrod-straight six two by-the-book Charlie."

Barrett signed the papers on the hood of their truck.

"Corporal, help him out. We're still trying to figure out if we're under attack."

Barrett snapped off a salute. "Yes, sir!"

He held the door to the armory open. It was a red brick warehouse with a concrete door surround that said 1945. Inside, the long warehouse had a slick-as-glass concrete floor and was filled with nine-foot steel shelving. Barrett led them to a line of green racks chained with pad locks. The racks were four by four feet, containing M-4s and M-16s resting vertically in slots, ten to a rack. Barrett withdrew a key ring from his pocket.

"Or do you want to take the racks?"

"Truck won't hold 'em all."

Barrett began unlocking racks and they unloaded the rifles by hand, laying them on blankets in the truck bed, including two LAWS rockets.

"Thank you, soldier!" Orlok said as they were leaving.

Barrett and the other guard returned his salute.

Ten minutes later, they picked up Bobby and his drone.

CHAPTER 38

DO'S AND DON'TS

Yowel and Josh slept on air mattresses in the truck bed surrounded by mosquito netting. Even with netting the bugs found a way in and Josh woke several times during the night to fight them off, leaving blood skids on his skin. His sleep was shallow and punctuated by a frustrating dream, wherein he'd forgotten where he'd parked his bike and wandered all over Madison looking for it.

The night screamed with many voices, including what Josh was certain was a panther, plus some kind of howler monkey and birds that sounded like air-raid sirens.

They broke camp at dawn and headed northeast on roads that were barely discernible.

"You come this way before?" Josh said.

"Years ago, when I was with the state police. It was actual hell. But I'm curious, and I want to help you."

Plus a hundred a day.

Josh fetched his backpack and pulled out the manila envelope with instructions for prospects.

"What's that?"

Josh told him.

"I would like to see that when you're done."

"Sure. Lemme know when you want me to drive."

This is a critical point because the strongest and most representative form of rule is one in which the leadership comes from the bottom up. The figureheads of the Club are in place to merely carry out the wishes of the membership. Remember that the strength of a brotherhood rests with the membership at the bottom of the chain of command is passed up. This is why aggressive participation is such a prized quality that is expected from the Patch Holder and is looked for in the Prospect.

It is not possible to make a checklist of what is expected from a Prospect in all cases. There is no formula for success. However, it can be said that the key ingredient is ATTITUDE. Everything else can be learned in time, but a man's attitude has to come from the heart.

The testing of a prospect may come in many ways. It may be premeditated, or it may be spontaneous. In any event, when a Prospect is given a task the Patch Holder is going to be looking for the man's attitude and at the spirit in which he carries it out. The Prospect should be alert and attentive to the needs and comforts of the Patch Holders. He should be aggressive in always looking for more to do. If he is ever in doubt of his priorities or if he cannot find something to tend to, he should ask.

If a brother in another Chapter has negative feelings about you, the voting Patch Holders of your home Chapter will respect and trust their brother's judgment over any positive feelings that they may have for you. Their brother always comes first. So if you should find that a Patch Holder in another Chapter has a problem with you, it will be up to you to square things with him and keep the ball rolling.

SOME DO'S AND DON'TS

As a Prospect, strive to conduct yourself as a Patch Holder at all times.

Always display an aggressive positive attitude.

Participate more than what you think is the minimum.

If you should see a Patch Holder that you have not met, take the initiative to introduce yourself.

At a gathering make it a point to circulate and greet every Patch Holder there.

Don't wait to be told. Anticipate the Brother's needs and offer to supply them.

Don't get overly friendly with someone that is not a regular acquaintance of the Club. If someone has questions about the Club, refer them to a Patch Holder.

Never give out a Patch Holder's name, phone number, address, or any other personal information to anyone outside the Club.

Be security minded. Look around and see what is going on around you in public spaces and report anything that seems suspicious.

In public places, never, ever let a Patch Holder walk off unescorted. If he is going to the men's room, to make a phone call, across a crowded bar, out to his bike, go with him. Keep him in sight and always watch his back.

If you are at an open function and pick up some negative attitudes, especially from another Club, report it immediately to a Patch Holder.

If two or more Patch Holders are having a private discussion, do not approach them within earshot, especially if they are engaged in discussion with a Patch Holder of another club. If you need to interrupt, put yourself in a line of sight and wait to be acknowledged.

Never, ever use the term "outlaw club" when speaking to a member of another club.

Never, ever lie to a member of another club about anything. If you are asked something about the Club, it is totally acceptable to say that the subject touches on Club business and you really can't talk about it. If that doesn't put it to rest, make the offer to find a Patch Holder for him to speak with.

Never, ever establish what you think is a personal friendship with a member or associate of another club. Don't be naive and believe that you can separate your *personal life from your Club life, not that such a move on their part is not without purpose. Their club and their brothers come first, as should yours. Be on your guard as this sort of positioning occurs frequently.*

Always carry a note pad and pen.

Never ask when you may be getting a patch.

Never, ever call a Patch Holder "brother."

Show respect and courtesy to Patch Holders of other clubs, but don't come across like you want to be buddy-buddy. Be professional about such encounters. Keep it short and sweet, then move along.

Keep away from women that you have seen associating with other clubs.

In Closing...

Yowel nudged Josh with his elbow. "You want to drive?"

INTO THE ALTO

They pulled into Bahia Negra just after six, a river town with one foot in the jungle and one in the twenty-first century. The military base, a smart, modern, gleaming white structure, was the most impressive building. The streets were made of crushed gravel. Josh spotted a couple of stoned tourists stumbling down by the river wearing backpacks with the Canadian flag.

They gassed up on petrol for the equivalent of a dollar eighty a gallon, parked in front of a rickety roadhouse on stilts with a hand-painted sign over the door. Seguro's. Inside, a half dozen Indians sat beneath ceiling fans drinking beer. Josh and Yowel sat at the bar where a flat-faced, expressionless Indian served them cold beer from the tap.

Yowel's colors elicited praise and interest. Everybody loved tough guys. Yowel and the bartender chatted for ten minutes before Yowel belched with satisfaction and laid a ten-dollar American bill on the counter, which the bartend-er picked up and held to the light.

"Their camp is about forty klicks upstream from here, but the guy told me the road's washed-out in several places. But there is no worry, because Penelope is powerful, and God is with us!"

Two klicks on, the road entered a dense rainforest. Yowel occasionally hit the wipers because of the condensation. His shirt soaked through, Josh reached for two bottled waters, uncapping both and handing one to Yowel. The truck stopped. Yowel's hairy arm extended past Josh to the right.

"Look."

Josh looked. At first, he didn't see anything, but then he noticed the trunk of a tree was flexing and moving like an acid trip.

"Anaconda," Yowel said. "Big one."

John watched with dry-mouthed fascination as the snake spiraled down around the trunk and disappeared in the green riot.

"How did you spot that?"

Yowel tapped his large, porous nose. "I can smell things."

Monkeys and birds hurled abuse from above. It was louder than a Limp Bizkit concert. Josh caught glimpses of the river, once saw a caiman slither down a muddy incline and disappear beneath the green waters. They stopped oc-casionally to remove debris from the road, and once, while taking a piss, Josh thought he saw something slithering through the underbrush and practically leaped back into the vehicle. Yowel howled.

"Welcome to Paraguay!"

It was dark by seven-thirty, but the truck's lights turned the tunnel into green day and sent creatures scattering. Yowel stopped several times to check his map and try his GPS.

"Reception is terrible, but we are close. I can smell it."

A half hour later, two men carrying rifles stepped into the road and motioned for Yowel to turn off the engine. Yowel tucked his automatic into the back of his belt and got out. Josh did likewise.

"This is private road," a man said in English.

"We are looking for Sustainable Protocols," Yowel said.

"Who are you?" the man demanded. He was stocky, bearded, and wore a guayabera, cargo pants, and mud-caked Adidas, and carried an AK 47, as did the other one.

Josh stepped forward with his arms by his sides, palms forward.

"Sir, I'm a private detective from America looking for Jane Franklin. Her father hired me to find her. Her father is very concerned."

The gunmen exchanged a glance and came forward, lowering their weapons.

"Are you really a private detective?" said the thick one.

"I'm going to reach into my hip pocket for my wallet so that I can show you my license, okay?"

The thick one nodded. Josh dug his license out and handed it over. The two men studied it like it was the Rosetta Stone before handing it back.

"Yes, we know Jane," Stout One said. "She is a great friend to us. I am Raul and this is Damien."

Josh stuck out his hand. There was something about shaking a man's hand that made it difficult to dislike him.

"Is she all right?"

"She is fine, as far as I know," Raul said. "You may return to the camp with us and speak to Karl, but we must ask you to surrender any guns you may have. This is for your own protection as much as ours."

"You can't ask a man to give up his guns in this country," Yowel said.

Raul aimed his rifle at Yowel's knees. "Let me see."

Yowel reached behind and pulled out his auto, holding it upside down with just finger and thumb. "I will empty it."

He dropped the mag and ratcheted out the round in the chamber, which fell at Josh's feet. Yowel looked at Josh.

Josh removed the revolver from his belt, flipped open the cylinder and let the cartridges fall into his palm, then put them in his pocket.

Raul pointed at Josh. "You ride in the back with Damien. I will guide you to the camp." They got in the truck and headed into the jungle. Josh sat behind the cab's open rear window.

"Who's Karl?"

"Karl Hochrein, son of our founder, the scientist and philosopher Heinrich Hochrein."

"Is Heinrich around?"

Raul turned to look at him. He had a Mayan nose and a scar running from the bridge of his nose to the side of his mouth. "Master Hochrein accomplished all he could. He suffered from a rare form of lymphoma, and it is possible that had he gone to Brazil for treatment he would still be alive. But he chose to spend his remaining years out here in the forest with his work and his people. Now his son Karl runs the organization."

"How did he die?"

"He threw himself into the river and let the caiman take him."

"Jesus!" Josh said.

"Yes," Raul said. "He was a very great man. He left a letter behind outline his dreams and love for his people. He also arranged that no member of Sustainable Protocols need ever go hungry. We are largely self-sufficient as it is. We live off the land as Master Hochrein intended. We farm soy beans, coffee, and tobacco, we keep chickens, monkeys and some milk cows, and eat fish from the river."

"Monkeys?"

Raul laughed at the expression on Josh's face. "Only occasionally. The monkeys are mostly for research."

They rounded a bend and lights blazed on the walls of a series of tin-roofed huts on stilts, some connected by walkways two feet above the muddy ground. Beyond the camp lay a lake, possibly connected to the Paraguay River, reflecting stars. Josh checked his phone. NO SERVICE AVAILABLE. Under Raul's direction, Yowel pulled up in front of the largest of the huts, a shotgun shack, really, with a broad veranda. Lights gleamed through the mosquito netting in the open windows. It was nine-fifteen.

Raul opened his door. "Wait here. Damien, keep an eye on them. I'll be right out."

Damien was a raw-boned youth in his early twenties with a prominent Adam's apple and piercing dark eyes.

"Do you speak English?" Josh said.

Damian nodded.

"O-kay."

Raul returned a minute later with a man wearing a white Nehru jacket over camo trou. He stood at the top of the stairs with his hands behind him, looking down like a general inspecting his troops. Raul motioned for them to come up.

Karl Hochrein appeared to be in his forties, with piercing, deep-set eyes and a Frida Kahlo brow, prominent cheekbones highlighting the face, of mixed race.

"I am Karl Hochrein," he said in a surprisingly high voice. "Raul tells me you're looking for Jane Franklin."

"Yes, sir," Josh said. "Her father hired me to find her. I'm a licensed private detective from Madison, Wisconsin."

"USA," he added, pulling out his license and handing it to Karl, who studied it closely.

The camp leader turned with military precision. "Come inside. You must be thirsty after such a journey."

CHAPTER 40

GO TO SLEEP YOWEL

Karl led them into the big front room, its shutter propped open, ceiling fan whirling, and motioned to a pair of cane chairs facing the red velvet sofa on which he sat. A black cat immediately jumped up and sat in his lap.

Josh and Yowel sat.

"Raul, would you bring us some cold cans of Coca-Cola please?"

Raul nodded and left the room. Josh looked around. There were framed black and white photographs on the wall of various people lined up in front of the hut over the years, as well as a romantic painting of an Indian chief with a beautiful woman clutching his leg. Josh thought it looked familiar. He realized it was the painting on the cover of Malo II's album, the Latin jazz/rock band.

Expensive carpets lay on the floor.

"Is Jane here?" Josh said.

"She's using the camp as her base at the moment. Understand that Sustainable Protocols requires the individual to undergo constant soul searching, to maintain the path. Have you read *Sustainable Protocols*?"

"No, sir. I haven't"

Karl reached over his shoulder to the bookshelf behind him, pulled down a copy and passed it to Josh.

"Heinrich Hochrein was one of the great philosophers of the twentieth century. This century as well. He only died four years ago. His memory is still fresh."

"Was he your father?" Josh said.

Raul returned with four cans of Coke in a plastic yoke and passed them out, taking a seat on a wood bench against the front wall by the open window. There was silence while they popped their cans and drank. Only the chatter of monkeys.

Karl set his can down on a hand-carved bloodwood table.

"Yes. I am my father's only surviving son. I had a brother, but he died when I was very little. I attended university at Sao Paulo where I studied sustainable agriculture and husbandry. My father first began formulating his thoughts on Sustainable Protocols when he was a student at the University of Stuttgart, where he studied genetics and biology."

Karl pointed to a framed certificate on the wall. "There is his Master's Degree from the University of Heidleberg. He moved to Sao Paulo in 1975. I was born four years later. My father founded Sustainable Protocols as an agency of change and unity, to bring people together through their shared love of nature, and to understand our responsibilities as stewards of the land. We are a non-profit organization devoted to non-intrusive farming and animal husbandry."

"We are like Greenpeace," Raul piped up from behind.

"Exactly."

"We have a group meeting every morning at eight. As you are our guests, I would appreciate your attendance. It's in the amphitheater. Raul will show you to your cabin."

"Can we see Jane?" Josh said.

"As I told you, we do not control Jane. I wouldn't know where to look for her. But you're welcome to look for her, for twenty-four hours. After that, we must ask you to leave."

Josh stood. "Thank you, sir." He shook Karl's hand, as did Yowel.

Raul led them outside. "Leave the truck here."

Yowel and Raul grabbed their bags and followed Raul down the raised boardwalk past six cabins in a row to an arc of three cabins a little ways off from the rest. He showed them into the middle cabin, turned on a bare bulb that hung from the ceiling. One door in the back led to a bathroom, the other to a smaller bedroom.

"Where do you get electricity?" Josh said.

"Paraguay Electric. Most of our electricity is hydro-generated, but we have generators which we use when there's an outage. For the refrigerators in the lab, mostly."

Josh tossed his bag and backpack on a bench. "What lab?"

"The monkey lab. I'll show it to you in the morning.

Buenas noches."

Yowel sat on the other bed, reached into his leather satchel and removed his works, a film canister filled with pot and some Bugle rolling papers. He used an ancient issue of *Popular Mechanics* off one of the press board dressers and quickly, expertly rolled a joint, which he lit with a pocket lighter, inhaling deeply. He handed the joint to Josh.

Josh let the *mota* fill his lungs and exhaled through his nose, feeling the familiar skull expansion and hyper-sensitivity to sound. "Yeah, man." He passed the joint back to Yowel.

Yowel took another hit. "What do you think they're hiding?"

Josh exploded in laughter. "He is kinda creepy."

"I didn't see any vehicles, did you?"

Josh shook his head, inside which ferocious blue beetles rubbed their legs together.

"I'm worried about my truck. They may try to disable it."

"Why?" Josh said. "Like they plan to kill us, or what?"

"I don't know."

Josh took the joint. One more hit. That was it. "Why would they let us keep our guns?"

Yowel reached into his waist band, withdrew the automatic, and inserted the magazine. "That's right. Maybe they're coming to finish us off once we fall asleep."

"Man, you know this shit makes me paranoid to begin with. Don't start with that shit." Josh took out his revolver and put the cartridges back in the cylinder. What if it was a cult? What if Karl commanded dozens of brainless zombies to attack them in the middle of the night? They were just minions. They were expendable.

Josh laughed.

"What? Yowel demanded.

"I'm freaking myself out!"

Yowel raised his pistol to eye level and swept it in an arc making guttural plosions in the back of his throat and making Josh nervous.

"Put that down, Yowel! You're stoned."

Giggling, Yowel slid the gun into his over nighter. They sat on bare, thin mattresses resting on springs.

Josh got up and looked in the closet, finding a stack of khaki green blankets. He tossed several to Yowel and put the rest on his bed.

"Let's try to get some sleep."

They spread the blankets and Josh turned off the light, lying there, gazing out the window screen at dim points of light.

"You still up?" Yowel said.

"Yeah."

"You know what bugs me?"

"What?"

"The horns they put on bikes. They're so fucking polite! You know why? Because Japanese society is so fucking polite. And as a result, some fucker swerves into your lane, you lean on the horn, he doesn't budge, you go down, you break your leg, the bike is totaled, all because the Japanese are so fucking polite!"

"Go to sleep, Yowel."

CHAPTER 41

THE TOUR

Clanging and crowing woke them with light shining in through the window illuminating a universe of dust. The clanging came from an old-fashioned cook hall triangle. The crowing came from chickens. They heard thumps movement, furniture sliding and the shriek of monkeys.

Josh looked at his watch. It was eight. He got up, visited the John, pulled on his jeans and a Norton T-shirt while Yowel did the same. They went out on the front porch to see dozens of people, mostly young, some with babies, some obviously pregnant, heading for the long, low, wide and deep mess hall where the cook swirled a steel spoon.

Josh and Yowel tromped along the boardwalk but had to step down into the mud to cross over to the meeting hall. Most of the young people looked exceptionally buff, and were extremely friendly, welcoming Josh and Yowel to the camp. Some of them looked oddly familiar, but Josh couldn't put his finger on it. They reminded him of that Malo cover.

Inside, about two hundred campers filled row after row of folding chair, with a line in the rear kept empty for visitors. Josh and Yowel sat down. They did not have long to wait.

Karl Hochrein stepped up behind a makeshift podium wearing a white, Nehru-like robe that fell to mid-calf held shut by frogs, wearing sunglasses. He looked like the young Elton John with dyed hair. As he began to speak, Yowel leaned in and translated.

"Students and warriors of Sustainable Protocol, give thanks to Gaia for this beautiful morning, can I get an amen?"

"AMEN," roared back.

A chill ran down Josh's spine.

"Recently, the European Union outlawed all genetically-modified foods. They are the first to do so. Unfortunately, our leaders in Asuncion have not achieved that level of wisdom and continue to allow the use of chemical fertilizers, growth hormones, and other untested products to flood our country. Our ancestors did not bleed and die so that Paraguay could join other Western nations on suicide watch!

"Once we perfect our food, we can perfect ourselves, and eliminate every physical hurdle, every sickness, every disease. We will eliminate aging itself and create a truly modern human being whose life we will measure in centuries!"

Josh held a hand up to Yowel. "You can stop now. I get

the gist."

Josh looked around for Jane but there wasn't a blonde in the place. Most of the kids had dark or black hair, a definite Indian/Spanish tint. After twenty minutes, Josh's shirt stuck to the small of his back and he was thirsty. He wanted out. Several men stood with their arms crossed at the rear of the room and although no weapons were visible, Josh recognized sergeants at arms when he saw them.

The crowd frequently interrupted Karl with shouts of praise and pumped fists. It made Josh's skin crawl. He'd read about the Reverend Jim Jones and the Jonestown Massacre. The group's ardor for Gaia easily matched that of evangelistic Christians Josh knew. Karl spoke so forcefully, and with that classic all and response rhythm, Josh was tempted to join in the hosannas himself.

Everyone else was rapt. When Josh looked back, Raul nodded at him. Josh pulled out his phone and scrolled through the pictures he'd downloaded from Jane's FB page, trying to see if he could recognize anyone. He spotted several with Karl and one with Raul.

The words "Josh Pratt" and "detective" snapped Josh around.

Raul leaned in. "We have two visitors today. Josh Pratt, a detective from the United States, and Yowel Yglesias, El Presidente of Del Fuegos Motorcycle Club. Say hello to our guests!"

Everyone twisted in their seats to smile and wave. They were a good-looking bunch. Many of them could be brothers and sisters. They smiled, waved, and cooed hello and *buenas dias*.

Josh tuned out the rest of the boilerplate and was relieved when Karl finally wound it down. Forty-five minutes. Felt like a week. As Josh and Yowel exited the meeting room, Raul was waiting.

"Gentlemen, there is no smoking marijuana at Sustainable Protocols. I must ask you not to imbibe while you are with us."

Josh slapped Yowel in the belly with the back of his hand.

"No problem," Yowel said.

"Karl tells me to give you the tour. So, if you follow me please."

Yowel sprinted for his truck. "Wait a minute!" He returned a minute later with two ball caps and handed one to Josh. Colorado Rockies.

Raul walked over a bridge connecting the meeting room to the next big wood shack. "This is our warehouse, where we store and prep sugarcane, soy, coffee and tobacco."

He opened a door and ushered them into a deep, dark room redolent with the fragrance of coffee and tobacco. You could bottle the air and sell it.

"Raul," Josh said. "Are you familiar with the Nazis?"

"What kind of question is that?"

"It's just that Karl's appeal to create a perfect human being, an *ubermensch*, if you will, reminds me of the Third Reich."

Raul clucked with disdain. "Look around you. Do our

people look anything like the master race? Half of us are descended from Indians, including me."

"There's no selective breeding?"

"That's ridiculous."

"I meant no offense, but speaking of this crowd, they're all so good-looking and healthy."

"We live a vigorous, sometimes strenuous life. Physical activity is encouraged. We have a soccer field."

"Yes, but aren't there any ill people? No cripples or those with deformities?"

Raul's face clouded. "Why would you ask such a question? You are our guests."

"You're right and I apologize."

"You know, if you want the Nazi tour, there's an outfit in Asuncion. They'll take you to Mengele's farm."

"I'm sorry, Raul. I won't mention it again."

Raul showed them the various drying and processing areas, then led them back out into the sunlight. They all wore sunglasses. It was over ninety. They traversed a twenty-foot rope bridge to the next building, a pole barn that shrieked and chattered like a zoo.

NIGHT MONKEYS

The smell hit them as soon as they entered the air-conditioned building, a combination of feces, Lysol, and some unidentifiable wildness that made Josh want to flee. An Apple computer rested on a desk beneath a double-pane glass window.

"This is our monkey lab, where Karl does his genetic research. We use *dourogoulis*, aka 'night monkeys,' whose DNA may contain the secret to human longevity."

"Tell me you don't use selective breeding here," Josh said.

Raul smiled. "Here we do. As you can see, we have several dozen monkeys. The cages are color-coded so we know which group is which. We are feeding them a variety of natural organics, such as the bark of the *quebracho* tree, which produces tannin, and may have medicinal properties, as well as the *srirota* vine, which we believe maximizes muscular development. We believe their brains produce an enzyme which may offer a cure for Alzheimer's. We are also experimenting with a rare type of orchid found only in this area. We study native plant remedies and have adopted some of them into our own health and safety curricula, such as the *yungas polypore*, which the Guarneri have taken for centuries for overall well-being. They boil the dried fungus and drink it with their coffee."

"Do you drink it?" Raul said.

"Of course. If you drink our coffee, you will drink it too. I have been drinking it for years without effect."

"Who does the research?"

"Karl."

"What do you mean, maximizes muscular development?" Josh asked.

"We believe it suppresses regressive genes which inhibit muscular development, while favoring genes which encourage it."

Josh pointed at the computer. "Who's your provider?"

"We have satellite feed through BGAN."

"Do you have free wi-fi?"

"You would have to ask Karl about that. He's very protective of our system."

"Who runs your website?"

"Ask Karl."

The din was overwhelming. Raul ushered them back out into the steamy heat, down some steps onto spongy ground, through a glade to a raised area filled with grass, with goal posts at either end. A dozen campers, men and women, wearing either red or blue shorts, scrimmaged.

"We used crushed rock to raise the field so that it remains dry. We have two teams, the red and the blue."

Sharp shouts drew their attention to where two men in blue shorts brawled with two men in red shorts. They fought like pros with straight punches, kicks, and attempted take-downs. Raul strode up the foot-tall incline onto the field, pulling a whistle from beneath his shirt.

He blasted shrilly. The brawlers stopped and looked, immediately backing off. Josh and Yowel followed as Raul berated them in Spanish. Yowel translated.

"You stupid bastards! You know fighting is against the rules."

The men hung their heads sheepishly. They all had black hair and tinted skin but did not look like brothers.

"All four of you are on monkey duty next week. Come see me at five for your instructions."

The long walk around the camp took them past casava and tobacco, bamboo stands, and a rivulet which brought them full circle back to the camp. It was eleven.

"That's everything," Raul said. "You're free to walk around." He headed for the meeting room.

Yowel looked at Josh. "Now what?"

"He said to ask Karl. Let's ask him."

They walked over to the administration building and mounted the steps, Yowel wiping off his face with a red ban-danna. Josh felt the sweat on his face and back. It was almost worth it to hang out in the monkey lab for the air-conditioning. Maybe Karl would let him use the computer.

They entered through the screen door. Karl looked up from his desk where he was working on a flat computer screen, the ceiling fan on high. The black tabby was on the desk, swishing its tail.

"Sorry to bother you, sir," Josh said, taking off his hat. "Could I talk to you?"

Karl motioned to the two chairs. "Any luck finding Jane?"

"No, we haven't seen her."

"You have today. After that you must go."

Josh and Yowel sat.

"We understand," Josh said. "I wonder if we could use your wi-fi."

Karl stared at him unblinking. "You want the password?"

"Yes, if it's not too much trouble."

"I'm sorry, but that is for Sustainable Protocols only. Understand, there are powerful forces arrayed against us. Drug companies. Governments."

"You know about Jane's father, right?"

"I'm aware of his breeding service. It's one of the reasons Jane joined us. She despises hypocrisy as do I. She has a good heart. Have you read any of the book?"

Josh's mind went blank for a second. He remembered. "Workin' on it."

"I think if you read that book it will answer all your questions."

Thumps on the deck and Damien appeared breathlessly in the door, speaking in urgent Guaneri. Karl stood.

"Gentlemen, please excuse me. I'll be back shortly. You may help yourselves to cold drinks from the kitchen if you wish."

Josh looked at Yowel.

"Those bastards are fighting again," Yowel translated.

Josh went over to a large aluminum framed bulletin board covered with notes, most in Spanish, business cards, and articles. There was a computer printed flyer for the Illumina HySeq, a gene sequencing machine that cost one million dollars. Josh examined the framed photos carefully. They were black and white, some of them taken some years ago. Karl as a youngster was immediately identifiable by his face and piercing black eyes standing next to a misshapen youth with black hair wearing coveralls. Their proud patriarch, Heinrich Hochrein, Josh supposed, stood behind them with a hand on each of their shoulders. Hochrein's face, if it was he, was hidden in shadow beneath a broad-brimmed straw hat.

There were dozens of them. In a later photo, this one in color, Jane was as apparent as a glass of milk on a bar. It had to have been taken within the past two years. Karl stood next to her beaming proudly.

"Keep an eye out, wouldya? Go out on the deck and if you see Karl, bang on the wall."

Yowel rose warily. "What are you doing to do?"

"I'm just poking around."

Yowel headed out, tapping a cigarette into his hand.

Josh examined the desk from Karl's perspective. He was reluctant to touch anything unless he had to, but it was unlikely SP was going to dust for fingerprints. Josh looked up and all around the room for cameras. He peered closely at an intricate zebra wood carving showing a small fishing village. He returned to the desk. The monitor paused at the SP home page. Josh held the mouse and clicked on the previous page. Images of lithe young men engaging in imaginative and gag-inducing sex.

So Karl liked the boys. Josh stuck his head into the hall. There were two rooms to the rear. Cautiously, he opened a boa wood door on a bedroom, queen-sized on an intricately carved frame, big flat screen TV mounted on the opposite wall, an armoire overflowing with men's clothes, a dresser piled high with men's cologne. Josh went to the end table next to the bed, where a framed photograph lay on its face. He turned it over. A stern-faced father with a hand on both his son's shoulders. Karl was one, the misshapen giant next to him was Axel, and the proud father, Heinrich Hochrein, was Hans Gruber. Josh was about to slide open the table drawer when Yowel pounded on the wall. Josh was out the door and back in his seat in an instant. A minute later, Karl entered with Yowel.

"Some of our people are a little hot-headed. Part of it is their Mestizo blood, to be sure. We encourage them to be sexually active at an early age because we are trying to grow the colony."

"What's your population?" Josh said.

"There are two hundred and nineteen registered Sustainables which is how we refer to ourselves. Gentlemen, we take dinner early because it isn't healthy to go to bed late on a heavy meal. I will see you in the mess hall at sixteen hundred hours."

Josh stood. "Thanks for your time, sir."

MY HERO

Yowel wanted to go into the trees and get stoned but Josh refused.

"Let's not piss 'em off, dude. We're not teenagers."

They grabbed bottled water from the mess hall, put them in their backpacks and hiked east toward the river. It took them forty-five minutes through jungle paths, vines snatching at their clothes and shoes, before they heard the river, a low rumble through the trees. Josh placed each foot with the utmost care. As far as he was concerned, everything in the jungle was lethal. The sight of the anaconda oozing down the tree had spooked him.

Several times they spotted monkeys and colorful birds in the trees, but nothing on the ground. They could smell the river before they saw it. As they topped a small rise and glimpsed their first view of the swiftly moving brown water, something crunched through the underbrush on their left.

Josh drew his pistol and whirled.

"What the fuck was that?!"

Yowel laughed. "Put the gat away, tough guy! It was probably an anteater."

They slid down a sharp trail to the riverbank, dotted with discarded bottles and plastic. Josh toed an empty bottle of Peppermint Schnapps.

"It blows my mind that people make such an effort to come here so they can leave their trash."

Yowel pointed to a ring of stones around a heap of ash and more litter. "They may have come by boat. This is a popular stop."

Josh looked around. Apart from the trash it was wilderness. "Why? Why would anybody come here?"

"We came here."

Josh laughed. Yowel pulled out a doobie and lit up, inhaling deeply and passing the joint to Josh, who inhaled. Old habits. Within seconds someone turned up the volume and he could hear birds chirping, honking, the chatter of monkeys, the burrowing of things. He looked across the river which was twenty-yards wide, as a log detached itself from the opposite bank and left a rippled wake as it headed toward them.

Josh whipped out the gun. "Fuck! A goddamn alligator!"

Yowel laughed, but he drew his pistol. "Careful. Those caiman are mighty hungry."

"What's a caiman?"

"It's a little alligator."

"It didn't look little."

"Well your black caiman can grow to about a ton, but they're not from around here."

"Neither are we! If that fucker comes up on shore, I'm outta here."

"It is hard to believe you killed a mountain lion with a pocketknife."

The ripples turned abruptly and headed upstream.

Josh took off his backpack and stooped. "Maybe we should pick up some of this junk." He gathered a half dozen flattened tin cans and some plastic bottles and put them in the pack.

Yowel stooped and did the same. They heard a rumble to the west. Yowel looked up.

"We'd better get back. It rains here all the time."

Josh looked at his watch. It was five p.m. They'd missed dinner. There was always the food they'd brought, in a cooler in the back of the truck. As the sun disappeared, they marched west. The first fat drops hit them halfway back, as water flowed from every leaf and branch. Instead of millions of drops striking the face, it was thousands of rivulets. They put on their plastic rain tarps, which didn't prevent their pants and shoes from becoming completely soaked.

Yowel turned and looked at Josh. "Another thing I would like to address is contemporary motorcycle styling."

"What about it?"

"Have you seen the new Yamahas and Kawasakis? They look like Jack Kirby drew them. They've got all these attachments and fake scoops and falanges and shit. Looks like some shit from a manga or something."

"I don't really pay attention."

"The only motorcycles that look like motorcycles are Harleys and Triumphs."

"I like the new Indians."

"Yes, yes, they're beautiful. There is one dealer, in Sao Paulo. But who has the money? What do you ride?"

Josh drew a deep breath. "Engine: 88 with oil cooler. Changed the cams to S&S gear drives with .510 lift. Took out the fuel injection and replaced it with an S&S Super E, Yost Power Tube, S&S manifold and Pingle High Flow petcock. S&S Tear Drop air cleaner cover with a K&N filter. Screaming Eagle Hi Performance ignition unit with a 6200 rpm rev limiter. Accell Super Coil, Fire Wire plug wires and spiral wound metal core wires. Accell Platinum tip plugs…"

A branch of a tree went limp and fell into a fat loop. A thick branch. Josh pulled out the pistol and gripped it in both hands. "Watch out!"

Yowel turned and observed the anaconda droop to the ground and slither off the trail. "Put the gun away. They are more afraid of you than you are of them."

Josh reluctantly replaced the pistol in his waist.

"And?"

"And what?" Josh said.

"You were telling me about your ride."

"Right! Right. Five speed tranny with Barnett kevlar clutch, self-adjusting hydraulic chain tensioner. Screaming

Eagle dualies. Progressive springs in front with higher viscosity, Progressives in back. Changed the rear swing arm
bushings to "STA BOW" nylon high density. SBS semi-metallic disc brake pads and the brake lines are stainless steel
braids. Went to tubeless wheels."

"You took out the fuel injection?"

"Yeah. I like carburetors."

They trudged on.

"I'm so hungry, I could eat that anaconda," Yowel said.

"We'll hit the commissary."

The rain poured mercilessly as they traversed the savanna
back to the camp, which glowed like a jewel box in the distance. There was no hot water in their bathroom, but it was
still in the eighties as Josh washed and toweled off. He put
on his other pair of fresh jeans and found a Red Sox T-shirt
in the old pressboard dresser. He put his gun on top. He was
still blitzed and went out on the porch to stare at the rain.
The ground was soaked, as a handful of campers made their
way grimly through the mud.

As quickly as it came, the rain stopped. There was momentarily an eerie silence. Light flared to Josh's left and he
looked over at the adjacent cabin, and there she was, lighting a cigarette.

"Jane!" he said.

She looked at him and threw her arms in the air. "My
hero!"

CHAPTER 44

VOODOO

She motioned with her hand. "Come over here!"

Yowel came out in fresh pants with suspenders, bare chest like a bear rug. "What's going on?"

"That's Jane," Josh said. "Go on without me. I need to talk to her."

Yowel stared appreciatively and slapped Josh on the back.

Josh crossed the rickety rope bridge ten feet to the adjacent cabin, which had a wood bench on the porch. He let Jane hug him. "I'm so happy to see you."

"How did you get away from the kidnappers?" Josh said.

"Oh that. That was Orlok's idea. I was just so upset about the whole thing I had to get away. I mean far away. You don't know what it's like living with him. He's a control freak. He's insanely jealous."

Her perfume drove him insane. She wore a yellow sundress that clung to her like a Porsche on a mountain road.

He took a step back and thought of crawling through broken glass. One of Duane's tricks. "Son, you got a hard-on you don't want, picture yourself crawling through broken glass."

"Are you telling me Orlok engineered that kidnapping scheme?"

Jane inhaled and blew it out through her nostrils. She looked like Veronica Lake. "Yes. He wants to buy the adjacent property."

"How could you put your father through that?"

Jane shrugged. "My father is an evil man. You see what he's doing, pumping chemicals and what-not into his stock, splicing in genes from buffalo, water buffalo, rats, for all I know."

"He loves you very much!"

Jane held the pack out to Josh. He shook his head.

"He may think so, but Lewis doesn't know what love is. Our mother left us because he was such a cold-hearted son of a bitch. When I was a child, we had a yellow lab. Kaiser. I loved that dog. One day Lewis decided that Kaiser was just too old, so he put him in the car and dropped him off at the Humane Society."

"I find that difficult to believe."

"Believe it. They told me you were here. Poor Daddy is so concerned! He's only concerned about his reputation. He's only concerned that I'm going to embarrass him somehow. How much is he paying you to come and get me?"

"Not enough," Josh said. "He's worried sick about you. You have to at least let him know that you're all right."

"You'll tell him, won't you? Come inside. I have a little Scotch." She turned and sashayed through the screen door.

Josh looked after her hungrily.

He followed her into the cabin, much better furnished than his own, with bamboo mats on the floor, rattan furniture, a ceiling fan, and a king-sized bed with a brass headboard jutting into the middle of the room.

Jane gestured at the sofa. "Have a seat." She went into the tiny kitchen occupying one corner of the large room, got out two clean tumblers, pulled down a bottle of Johnnie Walker and poured a couple fingers into each. She stooped to open one of those cube refrigerators found in college dorms and pulled out an old-fashioned aluminum ice tray, the kind with partitions, and whacked it on the kitchen counter, returning with two tumblers.

She handed one to Josh and flopped on the sofa next to him. She held up her glass. "Sustainable protocols!"

Josh clinked and drank. He was afraid to pray, afraid to move, like a mouse caught in a snake's gaze. What the fuck was he doing? He hadn't been laid in six months. He wondered if she was a sociopath.

Of course she was! He was angry and aroused. Her hand fell to his knee.

"You know, Josh, I was attracted to you the first moment I saw you."

They clanged together like magnetic dollars, him drawing her down across his lap. He clambered clumsily to get on top and they groped each other and locked lips.

"Let's get over on the bed," she whispered huskily.

Pussy is like voodoo, son.

He followed her as she peeled off her sundress in one movement and turned toward him, naked. "I never did thank you properly for saving me that night."

He peeled off his shirt and she traced the tat around his torso with her finger, right down to the tail. She de-pantsed him and when at last he hovered over her, naked in bed, she said, "Wait a minute," reached over to the bedside table, pulled open the drawer and took out a condom.

"I'll put it on," she said, tearing the envelope open with her teeth, looking at him mischievously, and then she rolled it down his cock, her hands caressing his balls. His lizard brain took over.

"Oh, oh, oh!" she cried out as he came, and they clung together silently for several minutes before Josh rolled over and pulled out, as her hand came up and held the condom in place.

She stood with the used condom. "I'll be right back. Don't go away."

He watched her go into the bathroom, rolled over, retrieved the tracking device from his pocket, activated it and buried it in her backpack. He heard the water running, and then she returned, sliding into his arms like a seal.

"Josh, Josh, Josh," she said, that finger tracing the dragon. "I have a thing for bad guys."

"I used to be a bad guy. I hope I'm not anymore."

"You are. You are! Don't you have someone back home?"

"My dog Fig. I love her. She's my best friend."

"Really? What kind of dog?"

"She's kind of a border collie/German shepherd mix."
He did not say Fig was named after his late girlfriend.

"Who's taking care of her?"

"I got a friend staying at the house."

She put her palm on his chest. "I'll get us a drink."

He watched her walk to the kitchen, then fell back staring up at her lazily-turning ceiling fan.

God forgive me, he thought.

She returned with two cold cans of Coke, handed one to Josh. He sat up and tilted back, guzzling half the contents.

"You're not going to mention this to Orlok, are you?"

"Don't be silly. It will be our little secret. Maybe we'll do it again sometime! Tell me about your house."

Josh told her how he'd bought the house, off the proceeds of an insurance settlement when a little old lady had T-boned him on his bike, how an uber-rich neighborhood had sprung up around him.

"Now I'm an eyesore and they're trying to buy me out."

"How much have they offered?" Jane said, her voice sounding like it was coming through a tube from the next room.

"Not enough," Josh said. Weariness washed over him. His last conscious thought before he slipped into dreamland was, *you idiot*.

CHAPTER 45

THE DEAL GOES DOWN

The exchange was set for two a.m. on 12th St. in the industrial valley that ran east/west south of Interstate 94, by the Menomonee River. Bobby air-googled the place ahead of time and determined that they were meeting in the parking lot of Visko Turbine Systems, a company that supplied turbo-chargers to trucks.

Jerrel agreed to pay fifty thousand dollars for the guns. Orlok didn't mention the LAWS rockets. Orlok, Bobby, Feral, Panda, and Marcus arrived at midnight in a Ford van Feral had boosted in LaCrosse the previous day. The eerie, sodium-lit industrial valley contained the main rail corridor, sewage treatment plant, and featureless warehouse after featureless warehouse containing everything from farming equipment to toys.

Orlok stopped the van outside the gate. "Panda, you and Marcus find some altitude, call me when you're in place."

Panda and Marcus bailed out the sliding door, each carrying an M-4 with a sniper's scope. Both were dressed in black, graduates of the Marine Sniper School, and carried grappling hooks. Marcus headed north, Panda south. The parking lot and the streets glittered with shattered glass. The sodium lights created little islands of illumination with most of the valley hidden in darkness. It was an overcast night. Orlok turned the van around and they drove north, into the Marquette neighborhood, where Orlok parked on the street a couple doors down from Vern's Tavern.

Vern's was a well-known biker hang-out, with a half dozen chops parked at the curb. The boys swaggered in and every head in the place rotated to check them out. Initially it was too dim to read the patches but the Jugan were not concerned. They were honored and respected throughout the Northern Midwest.

Bobby grabbed a booth as three students picked up their laptops, iPhones and back packs and headed out. Two Outlaws rotated on their bar stools to look them over. Bobby nodded and one of them nodded back. The Outlaws had a rep as the baddest gang in the state. Headquartered in Illinois, the Outlaws first incorporated in 1936 making them the oldest outlaw motorcycle gang in the nation. Vern's was Outlaw territory, but the Jugan weren't fronting or acting big.

One of the Outlaws detached himself and came over. He had a gunslinger's face with a handlebar mustache and luxurious sideburns, something out of a sepia-tinted photograph. His colors said Quinn, Enforcer. He stopped at the end of the table, thumbs hooked into his belt above a buckle the size of a dessert plate which spelled out OUTLAWS and ENFORCER in diamonds set in gold.

"You boys a little outside your territory," he observed.

"Hell yes, Quinn. You want a drink? We're just killing time."

"Killing time 'til what?"

"'Til it's time to go."

Quinn nodded. "Carry on." He returned to his perch at the bar. A UFC fight showed on several monitors hanging from the ceiling. The waitress, a bookish-looking young woman with a bluebird tat on her arm, took their orders, returning minutes later with four beers.

Panda called first. "I'm on the roof of Berman Electrical Contractors. It's a fifty-yard shot."

"I slap the top of my head, put one at their feet," Orlok said. "I rub my stomach, you know what you got to do. And if that don't scare 'em, put the little red dot on their chests."

Marcus was on the roof of Garrison Automotive, opposite Panda. Orlok told him the same thing.

Panda called back at one-thirty. "I got company. Brother named Troke, he's got a Remington, one tour of duty."

"One of Jerrel's?"

"Yes, sir! He got the same idea, set snipers in case things go bad, but I'm pretty sure they're on the up and up, 'cause Troke and me are sharin' a joint."

"Put him on," Orlok said.

"Troke here."

"You boys ain't plannin' to rip us off, are you?"

Troke chuckled deep in his throat. "I doubt it. Just a little insurance, y'know what I'm sayin'?"

"Well that's good to know. Tell Jerrel we'll be there shortly."

Marcus called while Orlok was on the phone. Orlok called him back.

"Panda's got company."

"I know. I talked to him, and I talked to one of Jerrel's boys named Troke. My gut says we're cool. They're doing the same thang as ussins. Anyone else?"

"No. I'm all by my lonesome and I got a clear shot. And here comes a black SUV. Looks like a Tahoe. And a Chevy pick-up truck."

"Okay. We're on our way."

Orlok paid the tab and left a ten-dollar tip. He, Bobby, and Feral got in the van. Ten minutes later, they pulled up at the entrance to the lot where one of Jerrel's boys wheeled back the railed gate. They drove through and he shut it behind them. Jerrel leaned against the front of the SUV next to two bangers. Orlok parked and got out.

He'd met Jerrel a couple months back at a nightclub. They slapped palms and bopped fists.

"Jerrel!" Orlok boomed.

"My brutha!"

"You know your man Troke is sharin' a joint with my man Panda."

Jerrel touched a finger to his chin. He was a trim, dark-skinned black man with hair shaved close, a Cab Calloway mustache. "It do seem odd, but judgin' from their action, I would have to conclude that you are on the up-and-up."

Both men laughed.

"Show me the money," Orlok said.

As Jerrel pointed, a tall dude wearing a knit Jamaican cap fetched a briefcase, set it on the hood, and popped the lid. Inside were banded stacks of hundred-dollar bills. Orlok worked one out and smeared it with a felt tip marker.

"Looks good. Marcus, Bobby, show 'em the guns."

Marcus and Bobby opened the double rear doors and began passing the rifles, wrapped in blankets, to the guy in the knit cap and a howitzer shell-shaped man in coveralls. Jerrel backed the pick-up to the rear of the van. As the van got higher, the pick-up got lower until all the guns were transferred.

Orlok and Jerrel swapped skin.

"Pleasure doin' business with you," Jerrel said and turned to go.

"Hey Jerrel. Is it true Josh Pratt got his dog from you?"

Jerrel turned with a surprised expression. "Yeah, I gave him a bitch. How's that motherfucker doin'?"

"He's a pledge. That's all I can say."

"Say hey to him."

"Hey Jerrel. You got any more pups you want to sell?"

"Not at the moment, my man, but I'll keep you in mind next time I breed Miss Lollipop."

They were on the Interstate headed west when Doughboy called.

"Man, don't come back here. The Feds are raiding the farm."

CHAPTER 46

OVER THE RIVER AND INTO THE TREES

Josh fought his way up from sleep against a terrible languor that clung to his ankles like a succubus of the deep, trying to drag him back under. It was urgent that he woke, and it was through sheer force of will that he opened his eyes. He was alone in the bed with a drug hangover that weighed on him like a chain mail suit.

"Stupid motherfucker," he said under his breath, looking around. It was still dark.

He struggled to sit upright. It was wrong, very wrong. He'd dived dick, line and sinker into Jane's trap, but he couldn't figure it out. If all she'd wanted was to neutralize him, why'd she fuck him? Was it some psycho-sexual problem, a daddy fixation, getting back at Orlok? Josh was no daddy figure. He was just a stupid, horny son-of-a-bitch who couldn't be trusted and lacked sound judgment.

Josh forced himself into the bathroom where he pissed

and drank a quart of tepid water, pulled on his clothes, and staggered back to the cabin he shared with Yowel. That ugly protein smell struck him as he entered. Yowell lay on the blood-soaked bed, ripped collarbone to crotch. Flies and other insects filled the air in noisome constellations. Why did violated bodies smell like shit? Where was the dignity?

Josh had to get out. He went to the dresser. The guns were gone.

"Fuck!"

Adrenaline burned through him, mitigating the drug.

How could he have been so *stupid*?

Faint chanting emanated from outside. He went to the door. A dozen campers with torches were headed his way chanting something unintelligible.

Josh quickly threw on his shoes, grabbed his backpack and bailed, running toward the trail that led to the river. He ran. Within five minutes he'd left the camp, the chanting and the torches behind and he stopped, breathing deeply. Years of running had conditioned him for the long haul. Were they going to track him down like *Hard Target*?

The backpack contained two twelve-ounce bottled waters and a water purification tube he'd ordered from Bud K for twenty bucks. The LifeStraw. Bud K was chock full of cheap jackknives, brass knuckles, war axes and fantasy swords for thugs on a budget. Josh never expected to use it. Now he was sorry he hadn't sprung for a more upscale model from the North Face. He buckled the Puma to his belt.

Chanting. They were coming after him. Shrugging on

the backpack, Josh set off at 4/5ths, running easily in long strides until he entered the rainforest. The sky turned gray in the east, but it was dark under the canopy and Josh slowed down. He didn't want to startle a feeding jaguar or trip over an anaconda. An involuntary shudder rippled his spine. He'd always hated snakes.

"Run Through the Jungle" played in his head. The brothers loved that song in Waupun, especially the old ones who'd been in Vietnam. Something crashed through the brush on his right. Josh drew the knife and crouched in a fighter's stance waiting for a jaguar to leap at him, but the crashing stopped. Josh ran on, pausing every now and then to listen. At least the chanting had stopped. It was all plain to him. They'd planned to kill him as soon as he'd arrived. Now they were willing to let the jungle do it. They were pretty damned sure he wasn't getting out alive.

He wouldn't want to bet against them.

The canopy lightened to a hazy green as thousands of birds cawed, trilled, and chirped the dawn. Josh kept an eye out for hanging vines the size of his thigh and when he saw one, he stopped and waited for it to move. It just hung there. He threw a rock at it. Another. Finally, it looped lazily to the ground and wound away. An hour later Josh heard the river and paused to finish off the second of the two water bottles, replacing the empty container in his backpack.

The sun broke through the trees at the riverbank, lighting the water like liquid gold. Josh unslung his pack, pulled out the LifeStraw, crouched by the river and pulled back on the handle, carefully filling his two water bottles. The LifeStraw promised to remove 99.9 per cent of waterborne bacteria and parasites. Josh tasted the water. A little gamy, but potable. He shrugged on the pack and looked around for the safest way to cross sixty feet of river. Josh couldn't see beneath the surface of the swift-flowing brown water. He had no way of telling its depth, but he was determined to put the river between him and the camp.

"Fuck it," he said, preparing to walk across. Something wrapped itself around his right leg. He looked down in disbelief at the thick coils climbing his thigh.

"FUCK!" Josh danced back trying to shake the reptile off but it tightened its grip like a vise, cutting off the circulation, the arrow-shaped head eyeing him with tiny, black eyes. Even the diamond pattern repulsed him.

Josh laughed. "Lord! Why does this keep happening to me?"

Its jaws were too small to swallow him, but the thing was long—over ten feet—and would crush him to death if he didn't do something. Josh grabbed the head in both hands and held it back from his body as it thrashed in his grip, dragging him down into the mud, enabling it to throw a loop around his torso. The sewer pipe tightened, crushing a water bottle in the pack, soaking his shirt.

Josh held the head off with his left hand, seventy-five pounds of pressure, muscles cramping in the heat, as the creature's jaws opened wide showing Karambit teeth. Josh lay on his back, right hand going to the knife as the snake tightened its coils, forcing him to exhale. It tightened its grip on his torso so that he could hardly breath, swaying and thrashing, making it impossible for him to cut. He forced his fingers through the coils, trying to grip the knife. As his fingers struggled for purchase, he realized the snake's skin was smooth and dry. Not slimy at all. It fought him the whole way but at last the knife came free.

With a supreme effort Josh flopped over on his knees, got one knee on the snake's neck just below the head, and drove the blade longitudinally into its neck. It was all neck. Its thrashing intensified, rocking Josh side to side like a pom-pom, the coil around his thigh cutting off all feeling to his foot, the one around his torso squeezing out his breath. With blood flowing from the deep gash he had made, Josh turned the blade and began sawing through the neck, using the serrated edge next to the guard. It was like trying to perform brain surgery on the deck of a storm-tossed ship. The snake grew slippery in its blood and nearly thrashed free. Josh grimly sawed, bearing down with all his weight. With a final effort the head came free, jaws snapping, while the body gyrated for long seconds and went still, coils loosening their grip.

Josh lay back, breath churning in and out like a bellows, staring at the green canopy above, the blue sky through chinks that opened and closed with the breeze. He lay there for long minutes, waiting for feeling to return to his legs, for the coils to slacken, blood pounding in his skull. He got to his knees, then to his feet, and hurled the snake head into the middle of the river. A caiman rose on the opposite bank and slid into the water.

Josh fell to his knees again.

A stunned silence segued into monkeys and birds all a-twitter as someone turned up the volume. Josh took out the remaining bottled water and drained it. His cell phone was crushed. Josh took his time refilling the remaining bottle, dragged the snake carcass to the river, and shoved it into the current with a long stick. It weighed well over a hundred pounds. Two caimans broke from the opposite bank. Josh waited, scanning the opposite bank for reptiles. Using a stick to probe, he entered the river.

A LITTLE WALK

Five feet out the bottom fell off. The current swept him along like a leaf as he swam toward the opposite side at an angle, pulling harder than he ever had, glad he'd worn only the light tennies. With every stroke he expected gator jaws to rip him apart. A hundred feet down, he grabbed some overhanging branches. Crawling out, he squish-walked away from the bank, collapsed on his ass, breathing hard, and pulled out his cellphone and his passport, both sealed in multiple zip-loc bags, both still dry. The LifeStraw and the cell phone were crushed. Josh's ribs throbbed with metronomic regularity. The real pain was coming. The same fucking ribs he'd broken several years ago taking down Moon. Well if wounds healed stronger, he was well on his way to becoming the Wolverine.

Josh's skills as a woodsman were nugatory. The closest he'd come to camping was pitching a tent at the Buffalo

Chip in Sturgis. He bushwhacked east until he came to a game trail, which twisted north parallel to the river, water squishing from his shoes. It was already warm enough that he wasn't cold, but he was hungry.

He pulled the last granola bar from the pack. Crushed. Josh tore the end open and poured it into his mouth. Fruit wasn't exactly falling to the ground. The only edible animals he saw were monkeys high in the trees, and he had no weapon with which to reach them. However, he knew how to build a bow, which he'd learned from an Indian named Sammy Paul in prison.

He hoped it wouldn't come to that. With any luck he'd run into someone before the day was out and hitch a ride back to civilization. A plague of insects descended, causing him to apply a handful of Cutter's from a tube in the pack. The Cutter's lasted until he sweated it away and the bugs returned. Occasionally he caught glimpses of the river through the trees, and was tempted to throw himself in. Once was enough. He'd been lucky. He walked all day without seeing another living soul and as the sun began to lower in the west, "Born on the Bayou" running through his head. Josh was born too late for Nam, and as an ex-con, was ineligible for service. Viet cats in the joint regarded Creedence as the war's official soundtrack.

The ground was free of undergrowth, the thick canopy blotting out the sun. Josh spotted scat that might have come from a big cat. He paused to watch an armadillo waddle across the trail. Were they edible? What part?

Josh walked all day. He walked until he came to a squarish rock, covered with green furze, jutting three feet above the ground, gently concave surface holding rain from the previous day. Josh used the knife to cut fronds, used those to sweep the water out of the shallow depression, crawled up and lay on his back, knife in hand. Monkeys screamed at him. It was going to be a long night.

He had the usual anxiety dream in which he forgot where he'd parked his bike and searched the city in a grid pattern hoping to find it.

He woke with his right foot throbbing. When he pulled off his shoe, he found an insect had burrowed in, raising a half inch lump. Wiping the tip of his blade back and forth on his shirt, Josh dug into the foot until he unearthed a half inch black beetle and flicked it into the trees. Now he had a gash in his foot. Fortunately, his steel-cased first aid kit survived, along with anti-bacterial cream. He worked the cream into the gash, covered it with a large bandage, replaced his sodden sock and shoe, and limped north.

At least he hoped it was north. He could hear the river to his left and had looked at a map before the journey. The Paraguay River ran north for miles. He was bound to encounter someone. Missing pieces were starting to fall into place. Jane had convinced her mentor to work at Franklin Farms to advance their agenda at Daddy's expense. Now Hochrein had access to gene-testing hardware and a lab to test his theories. But why cattle? Weren't monkeys adequate? Josh knew nothing about biology or anthropology but thought that monkeys were better subjects, if humans were the intended recipients.

Hochrein and Jane planned the kidnapping. The dude who showed at the racetrack could be any True Believer, possibly that dick Josh had seen at the Sustainable Protocols table in front of the Union. Perhaps Hochrein needed the money for the gene-splicing machine Josh had seen advertised in Karl's office. By now Jane was back in Wisconsin spreading lies. Had she bothered to contact her father? Josh understood how she could hate her old man. He hated his own. Josh hoped Duane was dead, in a pauper's grave. Frozen to death in some back alley clutching an empty bottle of peppermint schnapps.

Forgive me, Lord, for my hateful thoughts.

He trudged wearily onward. When thirst overcame him, he searched for depressions in rock. The river terrified him, but thirst finally drove him to the banks where he scooped out a hole a foot from the water, waited patiently until the hole filled, then scooped it up and drank it from his hands. Images from two nights ago. Even in his present condition, he couldn't forget the feel of her writhing in his arms.

Why did she do it? It wasn't his animal magnetism, although many women found him attractive. Was she just a whore? Was that even the proper word? Biker culture regarded women in old-fashioned ways, to put it charitably. But Jane was far too smart to throw herself at him. Not if she valued her relationship with Orlok. Unless she knew he was going to die.

*P*ussy *is like voodoo.*

He felt feverish, foot throbbing, sweating constantly, wasting time searching for water. He thought about drinking from the river, but common sense asserted itself. The trail branched away from the river over undulating land, a series of gentle swells and depressions. He went into a zen trance, one foot after the other, marching in rhythm to the throbbing in his foot and ribs. When something thrashed through the forest, he froze.

Through the trees he glimpsed an impossible ziggurat, lush green and purple spilling from terraced gardens, feathered priests on top, arms raised to the heavens. He heard them chanting. Civilization! Josh bushwhacked his way off-trail toward the vision, came to a slight rise and saw nothing before him but more jungle and shadows. He was hallucinating.

His guts rumbled and he barely had time to lower his pants and squat, hanging onto a tree limb, as his bowels voided in a stinking rush.

It was the water. Some organism attacking his system, breaking him down. Even if it was nothing more than a bad fever, it could be lethal. He had no source of fresh water to flush it from his system. Thinking of the terrible hours he'd spent in Moon's dry well, Josh envisioned cool, limpid water cascading down a mountain stream. He had to get back on the trail. If he collapsed in the brush, it was only a matter of time before some predator had him for lunch. He lurched back the way he'd come, tripping on a vine and falling to the ground, painfully scraping his elbow.

Josh got to a sitting position and laughed. He heard a low chortling sound to his right and turned to stare into the eyes of some kind of wild pig. The word peccary popped into his head. Christ he was dizzy. He lay back and sleep leaped on him.

CHAPTER

48

SAFE HOUSE

Bobby drove, Orlok at shotgun, Marcus, Feral and Panda behind them. Panda took the entire back bench for himself.

"You thinkin' what I'm thinkin'?" Orlok said.

"Shee-it," Bobby said. "I keep turning it over and over and I can't get around it. Musta been Pratt."

"I will kill that motherfucker," Feral snarled.

Orlok threw his sewer pipe arm over the back of the chair and turned. "No. I will."

Feral showed his teeth. "Where we goin'?"

"We're headed toward command post Zulu," Bobby said.

"What's command post Zulu?" Marcus said.

Bobby pulled to the right to let a pick-up pass. "Bitty farm we bought back in '14 with the money from that deal. Just in case. Now in case is here."

"Can they track us?" Panda said from the rear.

"No," Bobby said. "It's registered to a dummy corporation we set up in the Caymans. Checks go through a Swiss bank. They'd have to be awfully good to find it."

"Well fuck," Marcus said. "What are we going to do?"

They passed a sign that said Delafield, Next 3 Exits. Orlok tapped Bobby on the shoulder. "Pull off there. Let's lose these phones."

Bobby took an exit that led past a restaurant built from an old barn, with an honest-to-God phone booth outside. Orlok tapped him. "Pull in there. I gotta phone Del."

Bobby pulled up next to the phone booth while Orlok got out and pulled loose change from his voluminous cargo pants. The parking lot was empty at that time of night.

Orlok spoke into the phone for a few minutes and got back in the van.

"Wha'd he say?" Bobby said.

"He was pissed, but he'll see us. Up ahead—you see those white fence posts? Pull in there. Everybody give me your phones."

The boys handed up their phones. Orlok got out of the van, squeezed past the white fence posts, which were connected by a chain, and walked fifty feet up a shaded trail to the lip of the Delafield reservoir. He had six phones. Bobby carried two. Gripping each phone like a flat stone, Orlok spun them flat out over the water and watched them skip, two, three, four, five times, before sinking.

An hour later they pulled into the cracked driveway of a duplex in Lake Mills, a couple blocks from the lake. A hard tail with an S&S engine leaked oil in the adjacent spot.

"Wait here," Orlok said, getting out.

Marcus opened the sliding door. "I gotta take a piss."

"Me too," Feral said.

Panda followed them out. The three of them chose their respective corners and let fly as Bobby knocked on the door.

Del the Dealer opened the door with the chain on, his large, pale forehead reflecting the streetlight. The eastern sky began to lighten. Del unlatched the door and let Orlok in. Bobby followed. The house smelled of reefer and cats. A large orange tabby lounged on the threadbare cloth sofa Del had rescued from the junk yard. Del was fifty-ish, with thinning blond hair spread over his dome, and wore glasses. He flopped down next to the cat and reached for a hand-blown bong on the scarred coffee table in front of him, which contained an electronic scale, a number of amber plastic vials, a bag of weed, rolling papers, and several issues of *Southwest Art*.

"Whaddaya need?" he croaked.

"Five burners. Ten if you got 'em."

Del exhaled smoke through his nose. "I'll haveta check. I also got some primo blow, reefer, oxy and crank."

"Just the burners, Del."

With a sign, Del heaved himself up off the sofa and the orange tabby took his place. Del went into a back room and returned with a Woodman's grocery bag which he set on the table, reached in, and tossed Orlok a generic black flip phone.

"They need batteries. I threw in five packs, should be good to go."

"How much?" Orlok said.

Del made a show of counting on his fingers. "Five hundred."

Orlok extracted his Harley wallet, connected to a belt loop by a chain, peeled off five Benjamins and laid them on the table.

"You know the drill."

Del scooped up the bills and stuffed them in his shirt. "You were never here. I don't know you."

Orlok made a circle in the air with his index finger and the Jugan rose and trooped out the door. In the car, Bobby held a pen light in his teeth as he examined a map of Wisconsin.

"Turn north on Exit 34, twelve miles to Simkins Road."

From the back, Panda quietly crooned, "Who's the cat that won't cop out / When there's danger all about (Shaft!) Right on! You see this cat Shaft is a bad mother..."

"Shut your mouth!" Bobby said.

"Can ya dig it?" Marcus said.

Orlok laughed. They'd always done this, even in the field. "Shut the fuck up, you guys."

They rode in silence, save for Panda beating out a rhythm on his sequoia-thighs. Ninety minutes later they pulled off Valley Road in Vernon County where a chain stretched between two steel poles set in concrete across a dirt driveway which twisted out of sight behind a stand of cottonwood in the dawn light.

Bobby got out of the van, opened the combination pad-lock, relocking it after the van passed. The farmhouse was a hundred yards down the road, another fading, listing two story wood frame with a sagging deck. Behind it, the gray barn had long since collapsed. The fields, leased to a neighbor, contained orderly rows of waist-high corn. Enough of the barn remained for Orlok to conceal the van, the sliding door shutting with a horrendous shriek.

Orlok turned to Feral. "Throw some WD on that thing."

Feral saluted and rummaged around in a cardboard box in the back, coming up with a can of WD-40. Bobby grabbed a key ring from the glove compartment and used it to unlock the deadbolt in the front door. The others followed him in, using personal flashlights to set the gas lanterns. There was no electricity or water in the house, but the hand-pump out back worked.

Marcus went into the basement and returned a minute later with a case of bottled water and REMs in olive drab foil.

"You gotta be shittin' me," Panda said.

"Eat it," Orlok said. "It's what's for breakfast. We're laying low. There's going to be an APB out on us across the Upper Midwest. Stay inside unless it's absolutely necessary. If you gotta go, use the trees."

Through the open screen window, they heard the faint rumble of a tractor.

Marcus jerked a thumb. "What about that guy?"

Orlok jerked a thumb. "Don't worry about him. He doesn't come over here. Grab some kip. Bobby and me are in the master bedroom. Feral, you take first watch."

Feral took out his auto and ratcheted. Bobby and Orlok climbed the steep stairs to the second floor, straight back to the master bedroom which had been retrofitted with two army cots, which groaned when they sat on them. Bobby pulled the blinds and opened the windows and they lay back on the cots.

After a while, Bobby said, "I hate to bring this up."

"I know."

"She may have been playing you."

After a while, Orlok said, "I know."

CHAPTER

49

WATER TAXI

Josh was in the oubliette, staring up as the edge of the massive plastic dog cage extended over the rim. He knew what was coming. Dog boy would open the gate and drop a mountain lion on him.

And here it came. A hairy arm reached out to the front of the cage, undid the latch, and swung it open. One hundred and twenty pounds of angry puma hurtled at Josh. He brought his arms up and found himself grappling with many hands.

He woke up. Two brown faces topped by thatches of black hair looked down at him with concern. The man on the left wore an old Rolling Stones T-shirt three sizes too big. The man on the right wore a Miami Heat tank top that fell to mid-calf. The man on the left, who smelled of graphite and fish, held a cup with a straw to Josh's mouth. Josh sucked greedily, all the way to the bottom. He tried to ask for more but could only issue a harsh croak.

The other man gestured and Rolling Stones guy turned away to refill the cup. After the second cup, Josh croaked, "Where am I?"

"Sapuriucu Village," Miami Heat said. He could have been anywhere from thirty to fifty, walnut-colored, with a sloping forehead, pronounced occipital ridge, and W.C. Fields nose.

"How..."

"We find you in forest, three days ago, bring you back here."

Josh's head swam. He felt as if he were far underwater, pressure pushing in from all sides. He must have collapsed on the trail and gone delirious. If these guys hadn't come along he'd be dead. No inert protein lasted for long in the jungle.

Thank you, Lord.

Josh tentatively lifted one hand and pointed at himself with his thumb. "I'm Josh."

"We know who you are, Josh Pratt," Miami Heat said. "We looked at your passport. My name is Leotho. We are Guarneri. We have no phone, no internet. The only reason we know about such things is because I volunteer for Peace Corps in Pedro Juan. You also have bad infection in your foot, but we treat that."

Josh had forgotten all about his foot, which throbbed with a warm pulse of healing. He tried to sit up and became nauseous, falling down and controlling his breathing so he wouldn't vomit. Not that there was anything to vomit.

"Thank you," Josh said. "You saved my life."

Leotho bowed and pressed his hands together. "We are Guarneri."

"I'm a Christian," Josh said.

"I know. You recited the 23rd Psalm in your sleep."

"What day is it?"

"June twenty-three."

"Shit," Josh murmured. Well there was nothing he could do about it. Whatever happened had happened. He was just glad to be alive. Jane would have returned to Wisconsin now and told some story how she'd been abducted, or had a nervous breakdown, and no, she hadn't heard from Josh, why do you ask?

Josh had one advantage. They thought he was dead. But who were they, aside from Jane? He couldn't picture Orlok orchestrating so convoluted a scheme, and in fact thought Orlok had nothing to do with the kidnapping.

That left Jane's mentor knock-off Nazi Heinrich Hochrein. Pieces clicked together. Heinrich needed a fast mil or so to buy a new gene-splicing machine. Heinrich was after the elusive *Ubermensch*.

"I have to get to Asuncion. Can you take me? I can pay."

Leotho displayed teeth like a vandalized cemetery. "Maybe you better wait a couple days. You weak."

Josh sat up and swung his feet over the side, regretting it immediately. A wave of nausea threatened to consume him. He lowered himself carefully on his back and practiced controlled breathing for several minutes while Leotho watched like a research scientist. Josh regained his equilibrium and sat up again, slower.

"You know about the breathing," Leotho said.

"I can breathe, if that's what you mean."

Josh stood shakily, almost fell, regained his balance as Leotho stepped up and took his hand.

"Not today. You no can walk."

"Okay. Maybe not today. But tomorrow for sure."

"Not so sure," Leotho said. "Water taxi is only way. Half day to river. Then we wait for water taxi."

"Do you have any phones?"

Leotho showed his gravestones.

"What about radio or television?"

Grinning, Leotho shook his head.

"Electricity?"

Leotho shook his head.

"Shit," Josh said.

Leotho smiled gleefully. "We primitive."

That night they ate monkey stew, surprisingly tasty with hot peppers and a mango chutney. In the morning there were tortillas, mangoes and bananas. The Guarneri had preserved Josh's meager belongings including the crushed cell phone and binoculars. They'd burned his clothes and supplied him with some sequined blue jeans and a Jo Jo Gunne T-shirt.

They set out slowly, walking east through the forest, sun rays slanting in at an angle. After twenty minutes Josh's conditioning reasserted itself and he strode without breathing hard, accompanied by Leotho.

"I really appreciate what you've done for me, brother," Josh said. "How can I repay you?"

Leotho waved at the woods. "No problema. Help somebody else."

They reached the river shortly after noon and came upon a lively scene on the broad banks, with native Guarneri waiting in colorful garb, a pair of wicker booths selling tortillas and monkey on a stick, some river men hauling fish from a boat, and naked children running, squealing up and down the bank. When a little butterball ventured into the water, his mother swooped down on him like a hawk and carried him off, chattering in Guarneri. Two rickety piers extended into the fast-moving, muddy-brown water. Directly across, perhaps one eighth of a mile, the broad muddy slope exited the river between two more piers. A dirt road wended east. Two small fishing boats were pulled up on the near bank, one a dug-out, the other a shallow aluminum skiff with a small outboard in the up position.

Josh looked upriver, half-expecting a side-wheeled steamer. "How long before the taxi comes?"

Leotho shrugged.

Josh pulled out his wallet, surprised that everything was intact, and extracted three hundred-dollar bills, but when he tried to hand them to the Indian, Leotho held his hands up and backed away frowning. So Josh grabbed him by the shoulders and pulled him into a man hug, smelling graphite and a faint undertone of Mennen Skin Bracer.

Leotho smiled and hugged Josh back, let go.

"Come visit if you're in the neighborhood," he said.

Josh laughed. He bought an *empenada* from a vendor crouching on a jute mat, serving out of an old Klondike ice chest. Fifteen minutes later, the water taxi arrived. It might have been a reconverted landing craft, fifty feet long with a makeshift canopy made from rain ponchos, tarps, and old tents, at least three dozen on board including goats and dogs, mostly sitting on black benches with an aisle running down the center. The wheelhouse was at the rear, slightly elevated. A yellow on black sign above the wheelhouse said, Taxi.

Josh joined a cue of a half dozen waiting at the end of the rickety pier as the taxi rumbled close with its inboard engine and bumped into an old tire as the first mate/conductor/ticket collector threw a rope to the man at the head of the line. The conductor helped people aboard, collecting the fare.

Josh got to the head of the line. "How much to Asuncion?"

The man held out his hand. "Twenty dollar."

Josh handed him a twenty and was getting on the boat when his heart froze. There in the second row, showing his unhappy neighbor a drawing by Charles Manson, was Arnold Lubing.

CHAPTER

50

RIVER CRUISE

Josh didn't know what Lubing was doing there, and he didn't want to know. With his face turned aside and his ball cap pulled low, Josh made his way down the aisle to the back row where there was a space in front of the wheelhouse. Josh sat down, sliding his backpack beneath the bench beneath him. His ribs felt better but he'd lost weight. His belt was on the inner hole and his pants were slipping.

The boat pulled away from the pier and chugged to midstream, heading south. Josh caught occasional glimpses through the trees of simple shacks. They passed fishermen laying out the day's catch on the broad and muddy banks, some hauling in nets alive with silver fish. Josh worried about piranha and *candiru*, the so-called "toothpick fish," that swam up a stream of urine to invade the urethra. It had been a hot topic of conversation in prison. You'd think *candiru* were a much bigger problem than they were. A rifle shot startled Josh and he looked up to see a *paisano* aiming at a group of caimans on the shore, now piling into the water. Josh guessed it was sport. Ten miles downriver the boat pulled into another rickety pier, a line of Indians waiting to board while others got off. Josh had to relieve himself. He turned toward the captain, pointed to his seat and to his backpack.

He reached into his wallet and peeled off a damp ten. "Watch my stuff?"

The captain spoke no English but smiled, showing yellow teeth, made the OK sign with thumb and forefinger and pocketed the ten. Josh made his way warily to the gangplank, turning away so that Lubing wouldn't see him. The last thing he needed was to hear this fool blather on about his serial killer friends.

Josh joined the line at a primitive outhouse that radiated stink like a force field. He purchased some monkey on a stick from a vendor and hot-footed it back to the taxi. The captain had been good as his word. His seat and backpack were still there. The taxi pulled to the middle of the river and resumed course, as a handful of children wearing bright, hand-knit clothing, ran up and down the center aisle squealing. One of them wore a faded Plimsouls T-shirt. The air was rich with the smell of loam, rot, and fish. People waved from the shore and the captain tooted his horn. The first time he did it, Josh nearly leaped from his seat. It was right behind him. He turned and pointed to his ears. The captain shrugged and grinned.

Around three in the afternoon, Josh guessed from the shadows, the engine made a low croak and died. Everybody turned around. The taxi continued to drift south in the middle of the river but at a much slower rate and was of course, not steerable.

"Of for fuck's sake," Josh muttered, twisting in his seat to watch the cabin lift the wooden hatch concealing the engine, and staring down as if into the abyss. He reached down into an ancient red metal toolbox and pulled out a hammer. Josh got up.

Josh faced the captain and pulled up his shirt, showing the tats. "Let me do that, hoss."

The captain stood, giving Josh his spot. The engine was an ancient four-cylinder Puegeot, weeping oil from its blown seals. Josh pawed through the toolbox which contained a dozen mismatched wrenches including an adjustable, and vise-grips. He checked the oil. There was no way to check the compression without equipment so he concentrated on things he could check. He pulled a spark plug. It looked like a used Cohiba. The rest of the spark plugs looked the same. One by one, he used a steel brush to file away the carbon build-up, applying a little motor oil to the tips and the screws. He refitted them and checked the fuel. The tank was a third full. He checked the oil. It was sludge, but there was plenty of it.

He unhooked the much-abused car battery and gave the posts and the hook-ups the wire-brush treatment. He primed the engine with a retro-fitted bulb on the fuel line.

"Are you running with me, Jesus?" he muttered, hitting the start button. After a few grinding turn-overs, the engine rumbled and resumed its nautical chug. Applause and *vuvuzuelas* filled the air. Josh looked up. Everybody on the boat was looking back at him, some standing, cheering and clapping. Rising, Josh smiled and bowed, resuming his seat. The boat continued its progress downstream as Josh leaned back, trying to find a comfortable position. He was tired. He wondered if he could sleep on this heap. He shifted this way and that, tugging the bill of his cap down over his nose, and was about to drift off when he felt a presence next to him. Josh raised the bill.

Arnold Lubing sat next to him grinning, clutching his portfolio of horrors.

"I thought it was you!" Arnold sang.

"Hello, Arnold."

"Did you find that girl?"

"No."

"Seriously? That's too bad! It's been what, six days?"

Josh shrugged willing the pest away.

"Remember I told you I was visiting a serial killer in Brazil?"

Josh turned away.

"Well he told me about a giant caiman that has taken over twenty-five lives up here! I was just in the village of Perandu gathering eyewitness testimony! The natives are so pissed the government won't do anything. They say the government doesn't believe them. I made some sketches.

Want to see?"

"Go away, Arnold."

"Well that isn't very nice."

"I'm not very nice. I feel like shit. All I want to do is rest. Take your creepy serial killer shit and go bother someone else."

A look of red rage rippled Arnold's face, which was gone in an instant, replaced by a bland visage. "Okay."

Josh watched him walk to the front of the boat thinking, there goes a potential serial killer. He just doesn't have the guts.

Josh finally drifted off, waking when the boat bumped into a concrete pier ringed with used tires in Asuncion. Josh sat up and watched the passengers gather their kids, bags, goats and dogs and make their way down the gangplank. The pier was jammed with friends, relatives, travelers, and a couple *federales* in high-peaked caps sporting MP5s, just in case there was a terrorist attack. He watched Lubing walk down the gangplank and work his way up the pier.

The captain tapped Josh on the shoulder. Josh turned. The captain held the tired ten-dollar bill out in his hand. Josh smiled and waved it off. "You keep it."

The captain placed the bill between his palms and bowed.

Josh slipped his knapsack on and got off the boat, working his way to the end of the pier with the wedge, arms extended in front of him, palms together.

Now what? At least he had a few bills to hail a faded yellow Chevy Citation with mismatched door panels and a hand-lettered cardboard sign in the rear window. Taxi.

"American embassy," he told the old man behind the wheel. The ancient Citation chugged into traffic leaving a thick chemtrail in its wake, the driver navigating the roundabout, in the center of which was a statue of Alfredo Stroessner on a rearing stallion, speeding down a broad avenue of tony, neo-colonial and Spanish architecture, to stop at the iron gate outside a two-story white stucco mansion with a soaring tower set off by a pinnacle at each corner. American Embassy read the brass plaque on the wall, as an American Marine in dress blues and white cap stepped up to the car.

"Sir?"

Josh paid the driver, got out, handed the Marine his passport. "I need to contact my employer so I can get back to Wisconsin."

The Marine studied the passport, looking up to make sure Josh matched the picture, motioned him inside the gate. "Wait here."

The Marine went into a little hut and picked up a phone. A moment later he emerged. "Come with me, Mr. Pratt."

Josh followed him into the vast yard, around a central, exquisite circle of grass and topiary with a flagpole in the center, past Greco-Roman columns into the cool interior.

"Wait here, sir."

Josh sat on a marble bench admiring the heroic paintings hung in gilt frames in the main hall: Simon Bolivar on rearing horse, Alfredo Stroessner on a rearing horse, George Washington on a rearing horse. Minutes later, a trim, fifty-ish woman with a white Prince Valiant wearing a blue suit came out.

"Mr. Pratt? I'm Olivia Evans, Assistant to the Ambassador. Won't you come with me please?"

CHAPTER 51

SEARCH CONTINUES

Jane took a United flight out of Rio using a forged passport under the name Stella Adler, prepared for her by Sustainable Protocol's document division. She paid cash. She had just settled herself into her window seat in the business section when a gigolo with a hairline mustache, Armani suit, reeking of Paco Raban, sat next to her. Her hope that he wouldn't turn out to be a creep was dashed ten minutes into the flight when he turned to her with a million-dollar smile.

"Ma I buy the lovely lady a glass of champagne?"

"Fuck off, creep."

He looked startled, as if she were speaking Urdu. "Excuse me?"

"Fuck off, creep, or I'll tell the flight crew you were jacking off in your trousers. Find another seat."

His eyes closed to slits as he leaned in. "You fucking whore. Who do you think you're talking to?"

She punched him in the nuts and turned on the help light. A steward was there in an instant. "Yes?"

"Sir, this gentleman was masturbating. Would you please make him move?"

The snarling gigolo turned from her to the steward, but there was nothing he could do. The steward's lip curled in disgust. "Sir, I must ask you to move."

"She's lying!"

"Sir, you do not want to cause a disturbance on this flight. Please find a seat in the back. There are several vacancies."

The steward stood with his arms crossed while the gigolo slid out, showing Jane his middle finger. The steward followed him all the way to the back of the 757. He returned a moment later.

"Are you all right, ma'am? Should we notify the authorities upon arrival?"

"No. Thank you so much. It's not like I've never been hit on by creeps. Just so long as he doesn't bother me."

"I assure you he will not move forward of his seat during the flight."

A half hour in, she washed down a Valium, tilted back, and drifted into sleep, waking only when the steward tapped her shoulder. "We're beginning our descent into Miami, ma'am. You'll have to put your seat back up."

Feeling groggy, Jane made her way to the forward lavatory, returned to her seat and buckled up. It was nine p.m. as she looked out the window at Miami glittering below like a diamond necklace running from the Everglades to Palm Beach.

She breezed through Customs spent an hour at the Miami Airport waking up via coffee, recharging her devices and checking her mail. Her work was done. Now now she had to smooth things over with Daddy and Orlok.

Orlok was like a great, gentle bull. For all his violence he was a romantic at heart and desperately needed to believe in true love and soul mates. Daddy, well she was Daddy's little girl. He wasn't about to bail on her now.

She arrived at O'Hare at five in the morning and took a bus to Madison, departing at the East Side Terminal. Her Uber driver was waiting as promised, behind the wheel of a Nissan Leaf with a Bernie Sanders sticker. The middle-aged, bearded, tie-dyed T-shirt wearing overweight driver put her bag in the trunk and held the door for her, dry-mouthed at her beauty.

He got in and cleared his throat. "Uh, where to, Miss? I mean ma'am. I mean Mizz."

Jane laughed. "Just call me Stella. Twelve thirty-four Piebald Lane. That's down near New Glarus."

The driver punched the stats into his GPS. "Go south on East Washington four miles."

Jane leaned back, longed for a joint, looked out the window at the passing strip malls, kung fu studios, insurance companies and bowling alleys. The closer they came to the Square, the tonier the buildings. They circled the square via Webster and Doty and headed out West Washington toward the Beltline. The driver's name was Simon Burke, according to a placard on the dash, and he had a Masters

Degree in Comparative Sociology. Terrorized into silence, he kept his eyes on the road except for the occasional look in the rear view, where she could see his lizard tongue darting in and out.

The disembodied voice guided them to a ranch house in the hills east of Mount Glarus, one of those odd little neighborhoods consisting of a half dozen mismatched homes on a winding road in the middle of nowhere. A beat-up Rav4 with a Sustainable Protocols bumper sticker sat in the driveway. Jane paid the fifty-five dollar tab and threw in a twenty-dollar tip. The poor slob could barely croak thank you and stayed to watch her carry her bag to the front door and ring the bell.

A kid in a hoodie with a billy goat beard opened the door.

"Hello, Arlo," Jane said, breezing by him and tossing her bag on the sofa in the living room. "Where's Heinrich?"

Arlo stood gap-mouthed. He was President of the local Sustainable Protocols chapter and regularly set up shop at the entrance to the Union. "He's at work. Does he know you're here?"

"No. Would you be a dear and call him for me? And then hand me the phone?"

Arlo pulled his phone from inside the hoodie, dialed, waited.

"May I speak to Dr. Gruber?"

He waited. Jane crossed her arms.

"It's Arlo, doctor. Jane would like to speak with you."

He handed the phone over.

"I'm back. And I have a bonus. I'll tell you when I see you."

Jane turned away, listening.

"Great," she said, hanging up and returning the phone.

"He'll be here in an hour. Would you be a dear and give us some privacy?"

"Uh, sure, Jane. Sure! I was just doing a little yard work."

Minutes later, The old Rav4 fired up and dwindled away. Jane went down the hall, threw her clothes onto the king size bed, and took a shower as hot as she could stand. Toweling off, she pulled a black and pink velour jumpsuit from the dresser and put it on. She wasted no time on makeup. She didn't need it and wore very little. Every time an ad came on telling how to tighten skin, get rid of wrinkles and age spots, she chuckled at the suckers who bought that shit. The research Heinrich was doing would obviate any need for that.

When his research became public, the whole world would want in. Everyone. Because no one wished to be weak, ugly, stupid, or insane. There was no need to round those people up. Sustainable Protocols was not a malicious organization. Those people would take care of themselves. All you had to do was show the way.

She went into the retro kitchen, pulled a glass from the cupboard and opened the refrigerator. A six pack of Diet Coke sat in front of a rack of stoppered test-tubes, each containing an amount of fluid and a bar code. She peeled off a can, went into the living room, plopped down in the Lay-Z boy, feet up in the reclined position, and reached for the stack of *Wisconsin State Journals* which Heinrich kept neatly folded in chronological order in a magazine holder next to the chair.

SEARCH CONTINUES FOR BIKER GANG

CHAPTER 52

THE PRODIGAL DAUGHTER

The sound of the garage door opening woke her. For a minute, she lay in the nearly horizontal Lay-Z Boy, an Afghan pulled up to her chin, and wondered where she was. Then she remembered. She heard the garage door opening and a minute later Heinrich strode in from the kitchen, tossing his Tyrolean across the room onto a chair. Jane rose as he enfolded her in his arms.

"My queen!" he cooed, cupping her buttocks as she leaped up and threw her legs around him. They went into the bedroom. There was no talk of condoms. As they lay in the afterglow, her hair splayed across Hochrein's hairy chest, he lit a cigarette.

"How'd it go down there?"

"Pratt came out to the camp, donated, and now he's dead."

"How did he die?"

Jane chuckled. "The entire camp drove him into the jungle with torches, like Frankenstein's monster!"

"Did you confirm that he's dead?"

Jane brushed her hair back with her hands and sat up. "No. I was gone when that happened, but no one can survive on their own out there. Why? Has he showed up?"

"No, but Pratt is unique. That's why I wanted to add him to the bloodline."

"I knew he'd come. I knew he'd fuck me." She ran her index finger around Hochrein's nipple. "You know about genetics. I know about men. I like him. It's too bad, really. He would have made a great addition to our team."

"Not in a million years."

"Where's Axel?"

"He's at the farm. I need him on site at all times. My time at Franklin Farms is coming to an end. Soon I will leave with my findings and return to Sustainable Protocols. I had hoped we'd be able to pick up that gene-splicing machine by now. I really can't proceed without it."

"There's always the slush box."

Hochrein exhaled. He thought American cigarettes were crap. "That will be our last act, but surely you have milked Lewis for all you can."

Jane laughed. "Oh Heinrich! Daddy loves his little girl! In fact, I'd better go see him before he has a thrombo."

"Why not phone him?" Hochrein said.

Jane swung her long legs out of bed, threw on a yellow silk kimono, and swept into the bathroom. "Oh Heinrich!

That would set all sorts of things in motion! Much better if I surprise him. Do you know where he is?"

"He is most likely still at the Farm. Would you like me to phone and make sure?"

"No. I want to surprise him. May I take your car?"

"I'll drive you into Madison and you take an Uber."

By the time they had both showered and dressed it was five-thirty, and Franklin would have left the farm for his home. Jane had the entry code, so it didn't matter. She could let herself in. She had Hochrein drop her at the Student Union, a riot of activity on a Wednesday afternoon. Jane used one of the free terminals in the second-floor library to summon an Uber driver, to take her to Pine Perch. Out front, she stood with one leg on a marble bench showing a glimpse of thigh through the slit in her ekru dress. She toted a beat-up backpack. Exactly on time, a Nissan Leaf with a Bernie Sanders sticker pulled up at the curb. Simon Burke burst from the driver's side, practically running around the front of the vehicle to hold the door.

"Miss Franklin! Hello! I gave you a very good review!"

"Thank you, Simon! I gave you a good review too."

She slid into the cool interior and gave him the address.

Burke pulled away from the curb, turned left at Science Hall and right on University. "Do you mind if I put a record on?" he said, beady little eyes in the mirror.

"Knock yourself out."

Rage Against the Machine filtered through the speakers. They headed west through Middleton on Twelve and Eighteen, turned south on County Trunk TB, drove through the brick pillars advertising Pine Perch in gold letters, up the winding road to the butte, to the ancestral home.

As Jane stepped out of the car, the front door opened and Franklin came out, froze, and then came to her with long bold strides, clasping her to him.

"Thank God, thank God."

"Hello, Daddy. I'm sorry I caused you so much worry."

Arm around her shoulder he steered her toward the house. "Are you all right? What the hell happened? We were worried sick!"

"I know. I'm so sorry, Daddy. I was confused, and frightened."

They entered the house. Marian came out of the kitchen and hugged Jane.

"We are so relieved!" she said. "How did you get away from the kidnappers?"

"May I have a drink, please?" Jane went into the expansive living room and flopped on a sofa.

Marian went to the sideboard and poured two fingers of Scotch in a tumbler. "Ice?"

"Yes please," Jane said.

Marian gestured at Franklin, who nodded. She poured two more glasses. Jane waited until they all sat, Franklin next to her.

"It was Orlok's idea."

"I knew it! That son of a bitch didn't fool me, not for one second. By the way. Your boyfriend is on the run. The Feds raided their compound a couple days ago. They've probably all fled the state."

Jane went wide-eyed. "What?"

"Yeah. They want 'em for gun-running and robbing Fort McCoy. Tell me about the kidnapping. You must know, we were worried sick. Why did he not release you when he got the money."

"Oh, Daddy. I was so confused. He talked me into going along with him. I'm so sorry. I had a lot of time to think when I was down in Paraguay, and I know now how much grief and anguish I've caused you with my crazy behavior. I'm so sorry, Daddy. Never again. This whole thing has caused me to reevaluate my life. I'm through with Orlok. Once I was away from him, it was like I was coming out of a fog. Like he had me under some kind of spell."

"But why did you go to Paraguay? Why didn't you tell us?"

Jane looked at her lap. "I don't know. I guess I've been behaving like a child. I guess I've still got some growing-up to do. But my friends in Paraguay, they helped me see the light."

Franklin put his arm around her shoulder. "We're just happy to have you back."

"Never again, Daddy. I swear. I'm going back to school. I'm going to get my degree and I'm going to make you proud of me."

"I've always been proud of you."

Jane stopped herself from rolling her eyes. "Daddy, I hope you don't mind if I stay the night."

"Are you kidding? Move back in if you want! You don't need to maintain a separate residence."

"Well let me think about that. I have to phone my neighbor and see if Goldberg is okay." Goldberg was her cat. She stood.

"Excuse me one minute."

Jane went into Franklin's office and removed the cordless phone, opened the sliding glass door and went out to the patio where she phoned Peggy Albright.

"This is Peggy." She sounded businesslike. Jane heard chatter and clinking glassware.

"Peggy, it's Jane."

"Jane! Where have you been? Everybody's looking for you!"

"I know. It's a long story. I'll tell you when I see you. How's Goldberg?"

"Goldberg's fine. I want to thank you for sending Josh Pratt our way. Josh is going to help get the bikers behind Sheila."

"That's great. I can tell you're busy. I'll talk to you later."

Clutching the phone to her breast, Jane looked to the woods and smiled.

Across the street from the Franklin residence, it was quitting time. A crew of eight had been working the 4900 square foot mini-manse designed by Taliesen Associates. A man in his mid-thirties with a buzz cut took off his gloves, packed his tools in a leather satchel which he bungeed to the back of his FXLR, and took off down the road.

CHAPTER

53

SPLITSVILLE

Orlok was in the kitchen sharpening a knife when his beeper buzzed. It was an eighties-era beeper among a dozen that Bobby had found and repurposed for a handful of patched members only.

Orlok flicked the button and tapped out "go" in Morse code.

"Jimmy here. Jane home half hour ago."

"Thanks, bro," Orlok signaled. "Working tomorrow?"

"I'm on it. I'll let you know."

Setting down the beeper, Orlok sat with a thousand-yard stare for long minutes. Bobby found him like that when he went into the kitchen looking for his Bears hat.

"What?"

"Bad Jimmy just phoned. Jane just walked into Franklin's house."

Bobby put his hat on. "What do we do?"

"Bobby, I don't know. I have made many bad choices in my life, but Jane takes the cake. God help me, I loved her so much."

"And now?" Bobby said.

"I need someone to cruise by Pratt's place and see if he's back."

"If he is, he's layin' low. No net activity. You think Pratt's behind this clusterfuck?"

"I don't know. I've always been a good judge of character."

Bobby barked.

"Pratt gave us up."

"There's another possibility."

Orlok dipped his whetstone in a bowl of water and drew it carefully along the edge of the blade. "I need to talk to her."

"How you gonna do that, brother? What if she's the one gave us up? What if she's worked you for all she can get and she's moving on?"

Orlok was so still Bobby feared he would explode. Finally, he inhaled deeply, swelling like a hot air balloon, and let it out through his nostrils. "If so, it would be the biggest mistake of my life."

"Don't beat yourself up," Bobby said. "She woulda gave the Pope a woodie. There's no defense against someone like her, unless you're gay. And even then..."

"I want to hear what she has to say."

"How you gonna do that, brother? They're looking for us. You know how that works. Sooner or later they're gonna find us. In fact, I'd say we've about burnt this place to the ground. We gotta think about splitting up and going underground. You know I got that shit in the basement."

Orlok looked at him. "What shit?"

"Wigs. Clothes. Make-up. I learned that shit at ninja training camp. They're looking for a bunch of skinhead military types. You put on a pair of glasses, a wig and a mirror, put on one of them long coats, all of a sudden you're a gaming nerd."

"Aw not this shit again."

"Don't laugh. It works."

Orlok got up, poured himself a cup of coffee from the pot on the hot plate, which linked to an electrical cord which linked to an external power line, and sat down again. "Show me."

Bobby went into the basement and returned with a suitcase and a make-up kit. He opened the suitcase on the table and selected a Beatle wig, the type of thing Johnny Carson might have put on for a skit. He put it on, adjusted it, looked at a mirror affixed to the inside of the suitcase lid, turned and struck a pose.

"It's you," Orlok said.

Bobby took the wig off and handed it to Orlok. "No. It's you."

Orlok put the wig on and rotated the suitcase to take a look. He had to admit it completely changed his look. Bobby handed him a pair of horn-rimmed glasses with flat lenses. Orlok put those on.

Feral entered the kitchen and did a double-take. "What the fuck!"

"Get used to it, bro," Bobby said. "We're splitting up. We're pushing our luck staying here."

Feral ran a hand through his hair. "I'm too pretty to mess up."

Bobby tossed him a bottle of hair dye. "Use this shit. And shave the sidewalls."

Panda entered. "Whassup?"

Bobby explained. "I don't have enough to give you all a makeover, but a coupla things. Wear long sleeves to hide the tats. Skip the muscle shirts. Wear coveralls and hats. Stop swaggering. Remember when they were teaching infiltration? Carry yourselves like you don't want to be noticed. Soft-peddle it, you understand?"

"Yeah, mon," Panda said. "Where we goin'?"

"Boys," Orlok said, "You get the hell out of Wisconsin. I don't care where you go, but git! Don't leave the country—pretty sure they're watching all ports. Try to blend in. Lay low. Maybe you got relatives who'll put you up."

"My fucking sister would turn me in for the reward," Feral said.

"What reward?" Panda barked.

Bobby looked at his hand-held. "Don't know. There might be a reward. We'll contact you when things quiet down."

"Things may never quiet down," Orlok said. "Bobby and me gotta figure this out. We'll let you know when it's safe. We may end up rendezvousing in California or something."

"What're you gonna do?" Feral said.

"I got a little unfinished business."

Feral palmed a small automatic and ratcheted a cartridge. "Let me take care of that motherfucker. I'd love to do it."

Orlok put up a hand. "Put that thing away."

"It's my job," Bobby said. "I brought him in."

"No," Orlok said. "It's my job. I'll do it. Bobby, I don't want you hanging around either. You need to disappear. You all got your burners. I'll be in touch."

Bobby pointed to the basement door. "Go down there and check it out. There's enough clothes to fill a Goodwill. Remember—the goal is to fade in, not stand out. Y'all got to act like citizens now."

"Sheee-it," Feral said, heading for the stairs. Panda followed, his feet on the old wooden steps reverberating through the house.

Bobby and Orlok exchanged looks at the sound of rummaging, cursing, and hilarity. A few minutes later Panda came up wearing XXXL Oshkosh coveralls, a Renk Seed cap pulled low over his howitzer head, and a pair of aviation sunglasses. He pirouetted like a runway model.

"Whaddaya think?"

"It's a look," Bobby said.

Minutes later Feral emerged wearing a red nylon jacket with Griffin Lanes stitched on the breast, and a picture of a bowling ball striking pins on the back. He'd traded his blue jeans for carpenter pants and wore a straw farmer's hat.

Orlok reached into his hip pocket, withdrew his Harley wallet and counted out hundreds. He gave each man a thousand dollars.

"Maybe you oughtta split it all up," Feral said.

Orlok looked at him. "Maybe you're right." He got up, went upstairs, and returned with a gym bag holding the cash. When he was done counting, each man got twenty thousand dollars.

"I'm holding onto the surplus," Orlok said, stuffing it inside his pants.

"How we moving?" Panda said. "All's we got is the van."

"We'll drop you. Bobby, you drive."

Twenty minutes later, the van exited the barn.

CHAPTER

54

Josh thought long and hard about emailing Franklin via the embassy computer but decided against it. She was either back in Daddy's loving arms or she wasn't. He would have to wait until he got back himself for Kleiser to find her.

He emailed Kleiser. On a secure server.

> *Randall: I hope to be home within forty-eight hours. I ran into some trouble, but I'm find. How is Fig?*
> *Fig's fine. What the fuck happened?*
> *I'll tell you when I see you.*

Josh contacted the Paraguayan State Police and told them about Yowel. They sent a car to bring him to State HQ, but Josh refused to leave the embassy. They sent two detectives. Josh was grateful that Olivia insisted on being present during the questioning, translating for both parties.

When the detectives were finished, they thanked him.

"What're you gonna do?" Josh asked.

"Rest assured, we take these allegations very seriously. We will look into them."

Josh was able to get his bank, the First National Bank of Wisconsin, to wire him funds to get home. Olivia Evans drove him to the airport. He arrived in Rio at four in the afternoon and bought a ticket on United to O'Hare, for eight hundred and fifty dollars. When he boarded the plane, he half-expected Arnold Lubing to take the adjacent seat.

Josh slept most of the nine-hour flight, arriving in Chicago at one in the morning. He took a bus to Madison, arriving at the East Side Station at four. He took a Union Taxi to his home on the far southwest side, getting out just as the sun was rising. Fig began barking before his hand touched the doorknob. Somehow, she knew he was there.

Josh let himself in and slid to the floor for a fusillade of barks and kisses, happy scampering and rollovers. Kleiser came out of the guest bedroom wearing Rocky & Bullwinkle boxer shorts.

"Hey, man." He squinted. "What the fuck happened to you?"

Josh hadn't looked at himself in a mirror in a week. "What?"

"You look like you been put through a woodchipper."

Josh reached for a hand. Kleiser helped him to his feet.

"I had to bushwhack through the jungle. I had to kill a fucking anaconda."

"Come on," Kleiser said, going into the kitchen and filling the coffee maker.

"Seriously, man. I had to kill a fucking anaconda. It was gonna kill me. Lemme get some coffee going and I'll tell you what happened."

While the coffee brewed, Kleiser found some Jimmy Dean Breakfast Biscuits With Cheese and Bacon and nuked them in the microwave. Fig buried her head in Josh's lap, her tail a metronome.

Josh gulped down a big mug and ate the biscuit. He told Kleiser everything that happened.

When he came to Arnold Lubing, Kleiser said, "Are you fucking shitting me?"

"No sir. Showed me a drawing by Charles Manson. Looked like something a vicious child would scrawl. But that ain't nothin'."

Josh got to Jane's sudden appearance and their night of love making.

"Are you fucking shitting me?!" Kleiser said.

Josh put up a hand. "Wait. It gets better."

He got to the anaconda.

"What the fuck!"

Josh put up a hand. When he came to Lubing's reappearance, Kleiser spewed coffee.

"You're having me on."

Josh put a palm to his chest. "Cross my heart and hope to die. I told him to take his creepy ass elsewhere. Now I need you to turn on your gizmos and tell me where Jane is at."

"I have to tap into the Defense Dept to do that, so it'll have to wait until I get to work."

The sun shone in through the living room window. "So, go to work."

Kleiser got up. A moment later Josh heard the shower running. He turned to Fig. "Want to go for a run?"

Fig jumped up and down on her front paws, barking, tail wagging. Josh changed into sweats and hit the road, Fig at his heel. He went the other way so he wouldn't run into Phil Bass. By the time they returned, Kleiser had gone to work. Josh showered, long and hot, toweled himself and looked in the mirror. The tats tended to hide most of the bruising, but there was a green/purple tint to his ribs and a gash over his eye. He looked unusually lean. He stood on the little bathroom scale. One seventy. He was down fifteen pounds.

His mail was mostly bills, the latest *The Horse*, *Easy Rider*, *Maxim*, and a new *Atlanta Cutlery* catalog. He'd bought all but Maxim from a Boy Scout going door to door.

Josh waited until nine to phone Special Agent Roland Stoeckle, using Skype. He'd left his old phone in the jungle.

"How'd it go?" the agent asked.

"Well I found her, but she got away from me. Pretty sure she's up here."

"What's the deal with Sustainable?" Stoeckle said.

"They're a weird fucking bunch. Their head man faked his own death and now he's up here running research for Franklin under a fake identity. Franklin has no idea."

"Seriously?"

"Yes. His real name is Heinrich Hochrein. His son Kurt is in charge of the camp down there. Looks like Jim Jones or the Branch Davidians, only they haven't started the killing yet."

"You know we raided your buddies," Stoeckle said.

"What?"

"A joint task force—FBI and ATF hit the Jugan compound the same night the boys were in Milwaukee selling stolen army guns to your old pal Jerrel Moore."

"Did you get 'em?"

"We got shit. A couple of pledges and a couple hundred pounds of decent reefer. Some guns. But the big boys are in the wind. I doubt very much they'd be stupid enough to hang around here."

Josh got an itch between his shoulder blades. "Does Detective Calloway know about this?"

"Everybody in the world knows about it except you, and now you know. Listen. I'm out at the compound now. I'd like you to come out here."

Josh felt an instant of vertigo. "What are you doing there?"

"Looking into possible ties to terrorist organizations, like your buddy Jarrel."

"Jarrel's not a terrorist!"

"He just bought an arsenal big enough to invade Guatemala and we can't find him. So get your ass out here."

"I'm on my way," Josh said.

CHAPTER
55

OLD FARN

Josh kicked out in Dovetail's visitor's lot twenty minutes later, went in through the front, took a Visitor lanyard from the receptionist, and waited for Kleiser to come out and get him. They went to Kleiser's office overlooking the employee parking lot and a picnic table, where Kleiser handed Josh a tablet.

"Okay. We are currently tracking her. Let me show you how it works."

Using Defense Department comsats, they located Jane at Franklin's house in Pine Perch.

"Well thank God for that," Josh said. "I'd have loved to be a fly on the wall when she came home."

"You can leave it on, and it will provide continuous coverage, or turn it off to save battery life. Here. Take this charger."

He handed over a cord and a plug which Josh stuffed

into his vest.

"Again, thanks for staying at my place."

Kleiser waved a hand. "De nada. I caught up on Vikings."

Josh headed west on fourteen. The entrance to the Jugan compound was blocked by sawhorses and two federal cars. An ATF agent checked his ID and let him through. Josh motored up the drive and kicked out on the concrete apron next to a crime van. Stoeckle stood on the front porch talking to an agent. Stoeckle was lean, six feet tall and balding. He wore a Packers cap, sunglasses, a sports jacket and slacks. Josh went up the steps and they shook hands.

"Okay, I'm here."

"Do a walk-through with me and tell me what's what."

They went into the house. "I guess you found all the guns and drugs."

"We didn't find any guns."

Josh pointed at Orlok's office. "You didn't find a .357 in that desk?"

Stoeckle shook his head. "Nope. Found a lot of marijuana, half ounce of coke, some meth, and oxy."

They went into the office. Orlok's computer was gone and the desk drawers were empty. Stoeckle waved around.

"Tell me what you saw."

Josh described everything, down to the copy of *Sustainable Protocols*. Stoeckle made notes in a pad.

"You know your way around?"

"Yeah. Bobby gave me a tour."

"Show me."

Josh led the way out the kitchen door, past the barn, toward the trees and the ginseng patch. The marijuana farm was picked clean. Someone had set up yellow crime tape around the effigy mound.

"We're checking with the State Dept. of Natural Resources and the NPS."

"For what?" Josh said.

"For permission to probe."

"Mannnn, it's an effigy mound. There's nothing buried under there."

Stoeckle shrugged. Josh took him to the astonishing sandstone formations.

Stoeckle adjusted his hat, leaned back and looked. "This place is beautiful. They should make it a state park."

"What's going to happen to it?"

"We'll confiscate the property on behalf of Interior, and probably sell it for back taxes."

"You mean Interior has more suck with this mound than the FBI?"

Stoeckle shrugged.

"What the fuck? They could have a case of dynamite buried in there."

"Somebody sent an unauthorized photo of the mound to Langley, and somebody there forwarded it to Interior. We're trying to find out who. In the meantime, we've been ordered not to touch the mound."

Josh turned back toward the farmhouse. "Well fuck it. I don't think there's anything in there anyway. The Jugan loves Indian shit. They bought this place from an Indian."

An hour later they circled back by the barn. Josh pointed. "What's in the barn?"

"Don't know. Let's take a look."

Dust danced in shafts of light through gaps in the wood. An old John Deere with mud caked on the wheels stood to one side next to a spiral plow pushed up against the wall. The three horse stalls were filled with old tack and tools including saws, pitchforks, and shovels. Midway back, two old Harleys leaked into the floor.

Josh pointed. "Panhead. Shovel head."

"They worth anything?"

Josh shrugged. "There's no shortage."

Someone had affixed paper targets to a hay bale in the corner, punctured many times. Next to it was the old pick-up covered with a tarp. Josh dragged the tarp off from the back. The bed contained two old tires, a tire iron, and an ancient, grease-stained galvanized toolbox with a Case padlock. They used the tire iron to bust the padlock and opened the box. Inside were crisp, stiff combat fatigues still smelling of wax, and several pairs of brand new combat boots.

"Probably kuiped these from some base," Josh said.

Stoeckle opened the driver's door with a skin-crawling creak. The old cloth seat was grease-stained and torn in several places, revealing crumbling foam-rubber padding. There were mouse turds on the seat and on the floor. A Ford fob dangled from the key, still in the ignition. Stoeckle climbed inside, pulled on some gloves, made sure the four on the floor was in neutral. He didn't touch the steering wheel. He turned the key.

After a few cranks the engine roared to life, spewing a dense gray cloud into the barn, which a light breeze quickly whipped away.

"Got a half tank of gas," the agent observed.

Josh opened the glove compartment revealing the butt of an old pistol.

"Take a look at this."

Stoeckle leaned over, snagged the pistol with a pen through the trigger, guard, and pulled it out.

"It's a thirty-two. Still loaded. Hang on."

Stoeckle went outside the barn, talked to an agent who removed a zip-loc bag from his pocket. The agent deposited the pistol in the bag and returned to the barn. Josh found a box of shells shoved to the back of the glove compartment along with old AAA maps of Wisconsin and Illinois, and the registration, in a crumpled, soiled white envelope.

He pulled it out. It was registered in 2012 to Arlen Lovejoy, the Ojibwa from whom the Jugan bought the farm. He showed it to Stoeckle.

"Why would he leave it here? It's got to be worth something," Stoeckle said.

"Yeah. And they must have been using it for something too. Look how easy it started."

"We'll have to get a crew in here to dust it and check the residue in the bed."

Stoeckle looked at his watch. "I've got a conference call.

Thanks for your time. If you can think of anything else we should check out, or anything useful, give me a call."

"Will do, boss," Josh said, watching Stoeckle head for the front. He was about to follow when he thought to check one more thing. He went around to the front of the truck and looked at the grill and bumper.

He ran after the agent.

CHAPTER

56

COMPANY GUY

The grill and front of the hood were crumpled, fibers clinging.

"I'm guessing this is the vehicle used to kill Pat Murphy," Josh said.

"Who's Pat Murphy?" Stoeckle said.

Josh explained. "Match these fibers to the clothes he was wearing. I think probably Jane Franklin was at the wheel."

Stoeckle looked up. "Jane Franklin killed Pat Murphy? Why?"

"Because she was the one talking him into stealing bull sperm and selling it on the side. He was hopelessly in love with her and he would have squawked if they grabbed him. So, he had to go."

"That's beyond our purview."

"What's gonna happen to this land?"

"Probably sold at auction," Stoeckle said.

"Any way to find out when that is?"

The agent peered at him. "That's beyond my purview too."

Josh waved a hand. "I'm on it." He went from the barn into the farmhouse, into Orlok's office and picked up the cordless house phone. Calloway wasn't available so Josh spoke to a homicide detective he knew who promised to send someone out.

Alone, in the privacy of his office, he checked Jane's whereabouts. Still at Daddy's house. Since the tracking device belonged to the Defense Department, he couldn't talk about it. The cops didn't need his help finding her. All they had to do was talk to Franklin.

Josh used the house phone to call Peggy Albright.

"What?" she said, sounding breathless.

"Have you seen Jane?"

"No, I haven't seen her in days. Why? What's up?"

"She's back."

Peggy turned away to talk to someone, possibly the candidate. "I'm sorry, back from what?"

"Oh, you didn't know. She went to Paraguay. I just wondered if she'd picked up her cat yet."

"Oh my god! I forgot to feed the cat!"

"She'll survive," Josh said. "When's Sheila gonna take a ride with me?"

"Soon. Listen, I'll have to get back to you."

"That's fine," Josh said.

He sat back in Orlok's chair, put his feet up on the desk and wondered what the fuck was wrong with him that he didn't have a woman.

Oh, he knew all the reasons. He was a loner, didn't know how to talk to women, and had never used a pick-up line in his life. Prior to Fig Newton, every woman he'd had was either crazy or a drug addict, sometimes both. He cringed when he thought back to times he'd been with girls as young as sixteen.

He'd only known Cass Rubio for a month before Moon killed her. It was the longest relationship he'd ever had. He hadn't known Fig that long, but he was smart enough to recognize a good woman in a dynamite package. He wondered what would have happened if she'd lived.

Josh would have married her, spawned, try to raise his kids into worthwhile human beings. He would never be like his father.

Never.

Nor would he be like Franklin, who'd raised a spoiled, amoral brat. He wanted to look in her eyes.

How could you?

He must have dozed off because the next thing he knew, a Madison detective named Norm Schuit was shaking his shoulder.

Josh opened his eyes. "Huh?"

"Josh. Norm Schuit. Where's the truck?"

"Oh yeah." Josh got up and led the detective to the barn. By now it was late afternoon and the front of the barn cast a long shadow. Just inside the entrance, Orlok's Indian and Bobby's V-Max sat next to a build-up in progress. Josh pointed them out.

"Oh yeah," Schuit said. "The crime lab's been all over those. Nice panhead."

"You ride?"

"I got a Road Glide. Every summer, me and the wife take a little road trip. This year we went to the Smoky Mountains."

"Nice. Take a look up here."

Schuit used an LED flashlight he held in his teeth to examine the smashed grill, a pair of tweezers to deposit fibers in a small zip lock. He stood, brushed off dust, and put the objects in his jacket pocket.

"Anybody touch the steering wheel?"

Josh thought back. "I don't think so."

Schuit pulled out his phone and requested a lab team, just as an unmarked van pulled up out front. They went outside into the slanting afternoon light as two guys in coveralls got out of the van, which had federal plates. They opened the sliding side door, removing four carbon-fiber cases, and carried them into the barn.

"That's the fed crime crew," Josh said. "Maybe they can dust the truck too."

"HA!" the detective woofed.

"I been out here all afternoon. I'm outta here."

"Okay," Schuit said. "Thanks for helping us out."

Josh got on his motorcycle and headed home through the rolling hills, descending into pine-cooled grottoes, slowing down for the blind curves. He paused to let a string of wild turkeys cross the road in front of him. It was seven by the time he pulled into his driveway, cars trickling home around him. Josh keyed the garage from his bike, rolled inside and went in through the kitchen.

Fig was waiting. They played ball for five minutes, then he picked up the dog shit, double-bagged it and put it in the trash. He took a shower, put on clean clothes, and went into his office and checked Jane's whereabouts. She was at her apartment. Good. He was worried about the cat.

He debated phoning Franklin. He was supposed to be working for the man, but he didn't want Jane to know he'd survived. He didn't need Franklin's money. He was on the NSA's dime. He'd done his job. He'd ratted out the Jugan.

They would come after him.

He dialed up Kleiser on Skype. The programmer sat in his gloomy den.

"What?"

"I need a new phone."

"Try AT&T."

"I thought you could maybe provide something that was shielded and couldn't be tracked."

"Not now. Maybe not ever. I just got off the phone with a senior Defense Department official. He wanted to know if I was using their technology for personal gain. I don't know how much longer I can hang on here."

"Randall, I understand. And I wouldn't ask you to risk your own liberty on my behalf."

"Good. 'Cause I'm making plans."

"I just wonder if you could tell me where Kuhn is. He's gonna try and kill me. He has to. I fucked him good."

"I'll do what I can, but my days at Dovetail are coming to an end."

"Well damn. I'll be sorry to see you go."

"Me too, pal. But I always knew it would end like this. I'm just not a company guy."

CLEANING OUT THE HOUSE

Jane packed a few things, jammed them in the trunk of her Prius, and returned to the ancestral home, the cat beside her. She set the kitty litter up in the laundry room and made certain Flip had access to food and water before going into her father's office with a glass of chardonnay and methodically leafing through the spiral notepads. Each was dated, going back ten years. Franklin was dyslexic, and had trouble remembering things. He often extolled the virtues of taking notes.

"It fixes things in your brain. It uses muscle memory to remember."

Jane had first learned of the existence of the slush fund five years ago, when she overheard Franklin talking to an overseas buyer. He'd often gone overseas to finalize deals, just as he'd often hosted foreign investors. They loved the farm. They loved the cattle, the smells, and the cowboys.

They loved it when Willoughby did horse stunts, or lariat tricks, even though he didn't sound like a cowboy. She'd seen the way he looked at her and knew she could have had him in a minute. But Willoughby was too loyal to be of any use to the cause.

Jane sipped from a glass of Chardonnay at her elbow as she went through the notepads page by page. There were women's names and phone numbers, up until he met Marian.

It took her two hours, but she'd narrowed it down to three combinations. One of them belonged to the safe at Franklin Farms, containing over a million dollars in cash. She could tell from the combos all the safes were electronic. There were several safes at Franklin Farms, for salaries, formulas, refrigerated safes for sperm, lab safes.

She knew where some of these safes were, but not the slush fund safe. Franklin's office was the most likely location, but her father was capable of subtlety. It could be anywhere. She jotted the numbers down on a piece of paper and put it in her backpack. Out of habit, she went through all the unlocked desk drawers looking for spare change. She'd sometimes found as much as a hundred bucks.

At four, Franklin phoned to let her know she was on her own for dinner.

"Thanks, Daddy."

She used her father's computer to send Hochrein an email.

I *have the combo. C U at midnight. Then we're outta here.*

My balls ache for you, he replied.

Jane felt a frisson between her legs. Until she met Heinrich, she'd had no idea what a man could be. He was every inch a man from his head to his well-formed toes, but what really separated him from the mass was his brain. Genius. There was no other word. From the first evening she spent with him, in a hut in the rain forest, a hut with a tin roof on which rain poured like Judgment Day.

The instant he opened his mouth she was mesmerized, and as he explained Sustainable Protocols, she squeezed her hands and thought, yes! Yes! Here was everything she'd thought coalesced into a life-affirming philosophy. The Earth was perfect without Man.

Man was a virus which had to be contained, managed. Man's natural instinct was to chew up the earth. Poison it. Burn it. Rip the roof off the sucker to make a buck. People came in all shapes and sizes, from the lowest, grunting animal, to geniuses like Stephen Hawking and Heinrich Hochrein.

Heinrich had showed her that with nature, all things were possible. He gave her orchid petals that eased her menstrual cramps, and a strange new mint that blew away headaches when rubbed on the temples.

His latest generation of night monkeys were devoid of imperfections and as intelligent as a ten-year-old child. Within five years he expected to teach them to mine the fields. The young people he'd gathered, dreamers and idealists like Jane, were utterly dedicated to their brave new world.

When Hochrein asked her to write to a convict named Carl Kuhn, she was reluctant. Then she saw his profile, in an armed forces publication dated ten years ago, about how his elite team had taken out an Al Qaeda leader in Mazar e Sharif.

"Kuhn styles himself after Ghengis Khan. He quotes Nietzsche and Edmund Burke. His men say he is a gourmet chef who can work wonders with canned food."

What woman could resist such a force of nature? Had she not sworn her soul to Sustainable Protocols, she might have married him, had two kids, moved to Whitefish Bay or Shorewood Hills. She thought about it for fifteen minutes, but all it took was one call from Heinrich to make her forget.

Orlok was a great big friendly bulldog, a man of character and grace. Were it not for her cause, she might have felt a twinge of guilt. How she loved riding on the back of his hog, her arms around his barrel-like belly. She would never see him again. Too bad. Orlok was in the wind, probably out of the country.

And Josh? Snake food or killed by one of the savage tribes that lurked in the jungle. She'd miss him too. She'd had the good fortune to know some truly extraordinary men in her life, and none of it would have happened if not for Hochrein. Only a man of supreme confidence and intelligence would dare lead her to those others. Heinrich never doubted her love and had no need to test it. Orlok and Josh were mere soldiers in the service of Sustainable Protocols, the philosophy and lifestyle which would ensure the safety and health of the very Earth itself.

Jane methodically gathered every dime in the house, including the cash Daddy kept in his wall safe and the spare change jar in the kitchen. She went into his bedroom and removed the .32 revolver which he kept in a nightstand. She'd known nothing about guns until she met Orlok. Now she could hit the bullseye at thirty feet. She slipped the pistol in her backpack, left the house, locking the door behind her, got in her Prius and booked.

Across the street, work lamps still burned around the construction of a new house, where one worker remained, sitting cross-legged with his back against the concrete foundation drinking beer. Seeing Jane leave across the street, he rose, walked over to his Harley, reached in the saddle bag and removed a simple binary transmitter. He flicked it on. Using morse code, he wrote, "Jane leaving. Will follow."

CHAPTER 58

YOU MOTHERFUCKER

Josh couldn't sleep. Sensing his mood, Fig whined and nuzzled into his armpit. He got up, went online, and looked for news of the Jugan's apprehension. There was nothing since the APB three days ago. He put on his jeans and an old sweatshirt and went into the garage where the Basket Case Harley was almost good to go. He'd been working on it for five years. It was a one-month job. He'd just been so busy.

He swung a leg over and sat on the custom leather seat with the Badger claw and gripped the apes. He'd attached the new tank a week ago, as soon as it had arrived from Monte Michael Moore in Colorado. Against a crimson background, Moore had expertly painted the Badger claw on both sides. The springer front end felt supple. All that remained was for Josh to install the chain drive. Josh wondered if a little reefer might help him go to sleep.

Who was he kidding? He was wired. He could feel the

Sword of Damocles hanging over the whole damn country. He flipped on the cheap-jack fat tube TV on the work counter and watched demonstrators burning Berkeley, apparently in reaction to a conservative speaker. At the break, a woman with fine cheekbones who looked like an aging model appeared. "I got hit by a truck and the insurance company only wanted to give me ten thousand dollars. So, I went to Steve Fleiss, and he got me five hundred thousand dollars!"

Cut to Fleiss. "Of course, I can't guarantee you five hundred thousand dollars, but if you wonder what your case is worth, call me, the Hammer."

"Yeah," Josh said. "But what about getting hit by the truck? Were you crippled? Was it worth it?"

He turned to Fig. "I think that woman's bogus."

Fig barked in agreement.

He futzed around with the motorcycle for a half hour and went back inside. Still not tired. Josh was not a big book reader, although he wanted to read more. He'd never really read books until Pastor Dorgan got him reading in prison, and even then, he'd concentrated mostly on history and philosophy.

He had a copy of Anna Karenina somewhere, left by a house guest. He went into his office looking for it and spied the tracking device Kleiser had loaned him. It was blinking. He picked it up and brought up the image. Jane was on the move. Josh quickly pulled on boots and jacket, slid the tracking device into the window pocket of his tank bag. He shooed Fig into the house and shouldered into his backpack.

"Guard the fort!"

Josh followed her north on the Beltline, Highway Twelve to Sauk City, then west on Thirty-Three. She was headed to the farm. He caught up to her about fifteen miles west of Baraboo, turned off his headlamps as he passed through a wooded cove. There was no hurry. He knew where she was going. He slowed way down and rode by the light of the half moon and a million stars, stopping for a minute in a valley and turning off the engine so he could listen to the crickets. The air was rich with the scent of alfalfa and honeysuckle.

After a while, he started the engine and rode on. He'd been hired to do a job and by God he was going to do it. He had a thing about people who tried to kill him. Usually he killed them back. But he'd never killed a woman, in fact, he'd never struck a woman. His father had done it and Josh vowed to never be like his father.

He just wanted to look in her eyes and say, "Did you intend for me to die?"

There were no charges to bring. He just wanted to look in her eyes.

It was a quarter of midnight when he pulled up to the back entrance on Coopersmith Road, a quarter mile from the main entrance. No trespassing and security signs warned that violators would be prosecuted, and that the wire carried ten thousand volts. Stashing his bike on a flat turn-off, he put the GPS in his backpack, vaulted the steel gate and entered the pasture, cutting straight for the wind break that divided the farm north and south.

From the windbreak he examined the main building through a pair of mini-binocs, its silhouette black against the lighter night sky. Faint light shone from the skylights at the top center of the main barn. Its silhouette resembled that of the Dane County Coliseum.

Some cattle grazed in the next pasture he crossed. He came to the rear of the barn and used his key card to slip inside. There was a security guard on duty in the administration building surrounded by monitors, and one who walked the perimeter. The monitor showed that Jane was in the building. If she were here to meet Hochrein, it was likely they had sent the security guards home. She wasn't meeting Hochrein at midnight to talk cattle.

Josh was in a corridor with stalls on either side, ending with the barn itself. Even from fifty feet he could feel its immensity, like a zeppelin hangar. The smell of hay, Pinesol, and cattle shit wafted through the air. Track lighting in the baseboard, like those at a theater, provided just enough light to see. A security camera pointed at him from above the inner entrance.

Carefully, with his back to the wall, Josh inched his way to the interior. A steel door with a window in it was open, latched to the wall. He hunkered at the entrance to the vast hexagonal barn and inhaled, listening carefully. Fitful snorts and the occasional brushing of a bovine body against the wood.

Josh was pretty sure she was going after Daddy's slush

fund. She'd tried everything else. Josh had seen cults in prison. The Muslims were a cult. So were the White Nationalists. A biker gang was sort of a cult. But the kind of control Hochrein exerted over his minions was on a whole other level. Jane had every advantage: wealth, looks, born in the greatest country in the world. She could have gone to the university and learned something useful, joined her father's firm. There was no shame in helping feed the world and this stuff about GMOs poisoning people was a crock of shit.

What a fucking waste.

He heard something, a half gasp. It came from inside the vast space and sounded human. Josh rose. Eyes fully adjusted he was able to discern the walls, the bleachers, the cat walks, illuminated by faint light through the skylights. He was about to step in when the soft sound of the outside door opening caused him to pause.

He looked back.

A massive shape stood framed in the entry.

"You motherfucker," Orlok rumbled.

CHAPTER 59

THAT'S GOTTA HURT

Josh wished he'd brought a gun. And the sad thing was, he liked the guy, and Orlok liked him. To a biker, betrayal was the greatest sin. In that enclosed space, he remembered what he'd felt like the first time he'd helped Willy milk that bull. He slipped into the barn and ran to the left. He sensed, rather than heard, Orlok follow.

Josh ran straight across the big open space to the hallway opposite and tried the door. Locked. He turned. Orlok stood in a crouch in the very center of the big barn.

"I trusted you," he said.

"I got no excuse," Josh said. He could leap the wall, run up the bleachers and hope for a way out, or he could circle around behind Orlok and exit the way he'd come in.

"Did you fuck her?" Orlok said.

"Yeah. She was rubbing her box up and down my leg. And then she saved the rubber. Did she ever save your rubbers?"

"Yeah, so what? That ain't gonna save your ass."

"She doesn't give a shit about you! It's all some half-assed plan to breed some kind of super man. Don't you get it? We're nothing but breeding stock to her!"

A ripple passed through Orlok. He slumped.

"I still gotta break your neck, Josh."

"You can try."

Orlok ran, surprisingly fast for such a big man. But Josh ran five miles every day, and quickly outpaced him, running around the perimeter of the barn, looking for a way out. Orlok was right behind him. Josh got about twenty feet on Orlok and leaped up to hurtle over the barricade. A massive shape appeared before him, a telekinetic mountain, and lightning flashed. The mountain ran into him.

Josh lay on his back looking up. The lights went on, illuminating a giant in XXXXL coveralls looking down at him from the bleachers, holding a cattle rod.

Axel.

A woman's laughter poured down like silver coins.

"Boys!" Jane sang. "Are you fighting over me? I am so flattered!"

Josh suddenly realized Orlok was standing right next to him, looking up.

"Jane! What the fuck are you doing?"

Josh lay, depleted. He worked on his breathing until he could get to his feet. Orlok had forgotten all about him. They stood side by side, past the mountain just above, to where Jane sat with Hochrein about ten rows up. Hochrein wore a white lab coat like some mad scientist. Jane looked stunning as usual, in a Lana Turner sweater, her blonde hair framing her heart-shaped face.

"That's Heinrich Hochrein," Josh said, "founder of Sustainable Protocols."

"What?" Orlok said.

"Yeah, baby. They've been working together this whole time. She's been tight with him since she went to Paraguay with the Peace Corps three years ago. When did she start writing you?"

"Motherfucker," Orlok said, drawing it out. "Let's get that motherfucker. You go right. I'll go left."

The springy hum of an electric stable gate sounded. Josh and Orlok turned to four o'clock to see a fur-covered meteor explode from the wall.

Dionysus.

Josh's legs turned to jelly. Orlok planted his palm in the small of Josh's back and shoved.

"Run!"

Josh sprinted to his left as Orlok advanced toward the bull, waving his arms. Dionysus lowered its massive head and ran straight at the Jugan. As Josh ran, Axel kept pace with him as far as one of the radial corridors. Just past the corridor, Josh stopped and looked back. Orlok stood in a horse stance, left hand raised in front of him, right balled in a fist. The meteor and the meteorite collided in a blur as Orlok struck the buffalo between its eyes.

"HITE!" he yelled.

Dionysus dropped to its knees, head at an angle. Orlok reeled back clutching his broken hand. Josh was mesmerized. He heard a low chuckle, looked up, and saw that Jane was filming the encounter while Hochrein smoked a pipe.

"Orlok!" Josh said. "Toss me your phone!"

Without looking, Orlok shoved his left hand into his right pants pocket and tossed Josh the iPhone, which sailed through the air like a Frisbee. Josh caught it in both hands and dialed nine-one-one.

"Axel!" Hochrein snapped.

The monster leaped the barricade and ran toward Josh clutching the cattle prod like a baton. Josh easily outran him but there was no place to go. In seconds they would round the perimeter and arrive at Dionysus, who had regained his feet and pawed the earth, trembling with rage, staring at Orlok.

"Thank you for calling emergency services," the phone said. "All our agents are occupied, but stay on the line..."

Josh whirled and hurled. The cell phone smacked Axel in the face causing him to pause momentarily, and grin.

"Good one," he said in a surprisingly high voice.

"It speaks!" Josh said.

"I can do a lot more than speak," Axel said, scooping up the cell phone and flipping it back, end over end like a shuriken. Josh dodged and took off. Within seconds he stood next to Orlok.

"How's your hand?"

"Fucked. It's gonna come at us. Kick out its front knee,

omma try to use my elbow."

A statistic flashed across Josh's brain. "Dionysus: 1000 kilograms or 2205 pounds."

Josh had no time to consider the physics or his fear. Dionysus slammed into them like an avalanche. Josh stomped his sidekick into the behemoth's leg and was instantly sent sprawling, piercing pain in his knee, as Orlok leaped forward and slammed his elbow down between the buffalo's eyes, the exact spot he'd struck before. Dionysus went down, taking Orlok with him, the weight of its head pinning Orlok to the ground even as the buffalo writhed in pain, a terrible bellowing coming from its mouth.

Axel emitted a banshee-like scream and ran holding the cattle prod like a club. Josh rolled over onto his right hip and hooked the giant's ankle with his left leg. Axel fell on his face, the cattle prod sailing through the air, landing near the creature's head.

"Axel!" Hochrein shouted, striding toward the arena on the bleacher seats. Jane grabbed his arm.

"Don't!"

Josh got his elbows under him and sat up. The buffalo lay on its side struggling futilely to right itself, its left front leg bent at an odd angle. Groaning, an arm the size of a boa constrictor reached out from beneath its massive head, seized one of the black curving horns, and pulled. Twisting and turning, Orlok struggled out, planting his right foot against the buffalo's head and freed his other leg.

Shaking off Jane's arm, Hochrein leaped over the abutment.

CHAPTER

60

TOUGH GUY

Hochrein reached inside his lab coat and pulled out a nine mm automatic, spreading his legs in a shooter's stance.

Axel got to his knees. "Don't shoot Dionysus!"

Orlok crawled over the buffalo's broken leg and crouched below the great hump, which lay between him and the geneticist.

Hochrein circled counter-clockwise keeping his pistol trained on the meat mash-up. "Get up. Come over here."

Axel crawled to the buffalo as Orlok backed away on his ass. Axel put his arms around the great beast's neck and sobbed.

"Father! Do something!"

Hochrein circled until he stood before the head, leveling his gun. But Axel lay between the geneticist and Orlok, who reached back and grabbed the cattle prod. Hochrein shifted his aim to Josh.

"How did you survive the jungle?" Hochrein said, his German accent more pronounced.

Josh thought it must be a relief for the Kraut to no longer have to pretend. "Some Indians saved me. What's it all about, Doc? Building the master race?"

"I don't expect someone like you to understand. My concerns are bigger than you can imagine. I embrace all of earth, all of life. You can't see beyond your own animal hungers."

"Well you musta fucked half the girls in your village, Doc, so don't preach to me about animal hungers."

"I don't expect you to understand."

"Then along comes Jane. She's perfect. Not only does her daddy have the ideal facility for you to test your theories, but she's highly fuckable. You sent her after Orlok. Did you send her after me?"

"That was Jane's idea."

"So me and Orlok, are we in test tubes in your fridge? Who else is in there? Who are the lucky girls?"

He looked up. No Jane. Josh craned his neck. She was nowhere to be seen.

"Looks like she left you in the lurch, Doc."

"You know nothing."

"What are you gonna do, Doc? Shoot us? They'll know who did it. NSA knows about you. They're gonna be all over your ass. You can run but you can't hide."

Dionysus released a terrible cry of pain. Tears streaming down his face, Axel looked up. "Do something!"

Hochrein stepped forward and fired between the buffalo's eyes. Its legs twitched and it died.

"NOOOOOO!" Axel cried, rising to his feet, lurching toward his father.

Hochrein fired five shots into the giant's chest, but Axel kept coming. He seized his father in both hands by the neck, raised him a foot off the ground and shook him like a rag doll. Josh heard Hochrein's neck snap like a bread stick.

Josh knew what it was like to hate your father. Axel wasn't finished. Tossing Hochrein aside like a piece of trash, he advanced on Orlok who stood in a crouch clutching the cattle prod in his left hand. As Axel ran at him, Orlok thrust like a fencer, loosing fifty thousand volts. The giant staggered, ripped the prod from Orlok's hands and snapped it in two. Orlok danced in working his jab, three battering rams to Axel's face. Axel ducked down and took Orlok to the ground, effortlessly passed the big man's guard and rained hell on Orlok's head, his fists the size of cantaloupes. Orlok reached for the giant's eyes, but Axel pulled back, his arm long enough to grip Orlok by the throat.

Both Orlok's hands went to the wrist, but Orlok's right hand was broken and couldn't get a grip. Axel leaned down, grimacing. His strangely elongated skull looked like a wolf.

Josh ran behind the giant, threw his right arm around Axel's neck and tried to close it in the crook of his elbow but the Brazilian was too big. Josh switched to a cable grip and tried to throttle Axel, who paid no attention to the flea on his back and continued to pummel Orlok with jackhammer blows. The Jugan leader's face resembled an eggplant, his left eye swollen shut, blood streaming from a gash on his forehead.

Josh doubled down, feeling the lactic acid building in his arms. Axel swallowed and noticed, reaching behind him for Josh's head, which he buried in his arm. Choking, Axel seized Josh's left forearm in both his hands and ripped it loose like a band-aid. Axel whirled with a concussion-causing elbow, but Josh abandoned his grip, rolled left, sprang to his feet and leaped over the buffalo. Axel jumped atop the four-foot carcass like a cat and sprang at Josh.

Josh ran. He felt Axel land through the wooden floor. Josh's ribs banged like a Tchaikovsky crescendo. He was faster than the giant, but he felt a cramp coming on. Josh ran like a wide receiver, zigged and zagged, the giant trying to cut off the enclosure.

Orlok hurtled at Axel, throwing himself down in front like the tackle he was. Axel went down, hard, rolled to his side and lashed out with a vicious ax kick. Orlok pulled back clutching his broken hand. As Axel got to his feet, Orlok danced in and threw a roundhouse, landing with the point of his boot, on Axel's liver.

Axel hissed, dropped his hand to his side and bent over. Josh came at him from behind, catching Orlok's eye.

Orlok winked.

Josh scooted like a water bug and kicked Axel in the crotch from behind, driving his instep up. Like kicking a sofa. Axel fell to his knees, hands over his groin. Josh gyroed and struck Axel with a spinning heel kick. Orlok juked in from the other side and whacked Axel in the face with a right roundhouse kick, striking with the leather inseam of his biker boot.

Axel uncoiled like a rattlesnake, seizing Orlok's left ankle in his right hand. He dragged Orlok to the ground and hauled him in like a big catfish. Josh leaped five feet in the air and came down with both heels between Axel's shoulder blades, shoving the big man to the ground.

Orlok pulled free, stood and wiped his forehead, flicking off sweat. "Phew!"

Josh ran to where Hochrein's automatic landed, scooped it up, gripped it in both hands and squeezed the trigger, aiming at Axel's center mass, until the slide jammed open.

Four shots.

Kneeling, Axel looked at the holes in his torso leaking blood. He dipped his finger

into his torn shirt and looked at it as if he'd never seen blood. Like he'd just woke up. Waiting for Daddy to tell him relax, it was just a bad dream. He toppled to the side.

"Timber," Orlok said.

Josh stood with hands on knees, panting. Separated by the corpse, they stood in companionable silence trying to catch their breaths.

"My ribs are killing me," Josh said.

"I think I broke my hand."

"You still want to kill me?" Josh said.

"I'm too tired. I'm just gonna go now."

"Okay. Later."

"Later," Orlok said, heading back the way he'd come in.

CHAPTER 61

DISH GIRL

Josh slumped on a pile of straw with his back against the wall. Hochrein's crumpled body lay to his left, the buffalo in the middle, Axel on the right. It looked like a bomb went off in a carnival.

Automatically he scanned the floor, bleachers, and catwalks. He felt alone.

"Anyone here?" he sang.

Nada.

Josh was dying for a drink. Using the wall for support, he hauled himself up and tried one of the doors leading to the administration building. Locked. He dragged ass across the floor, limping and went out the door he'd come in. Ten feet in was an alcove with water fountains. Josh bent over and swallowed. Faintly, he heard a Harley clear its throat and fade into the distance.

He thought he heard sirens. Holding onto the wall for

support Josh went back into the big room and boosted himself via steep stairs into the bleachers. He sat there breathing
slowly trying not to hurt. The room felt empty. He would
have called Franklin if he'd had a phone. Maybe Hochrein
had one, but Josh was too sore to go down and find out. He
just sat there until he heard the sirens. They got louder and
then they stopped. A few minutes later, the door to the administration building opened but no one came out. A pistol
poked around like a dog's snout, then a Monroe County
Deputy whirled in holding an automatic before him.

Josh put his hands on top of his head. "Officer."

The big cop whirled. He wore a Smokey hat. "Who are
you?"

"I'm Josh Pratt. I phoned it in."

Lowering the pistol, the deputy looked around. He took
out a little recorder, turned it on, and set it on top of the
retaining wall. "What happened?"

Josh told him.

"So you and some other guy killed the bull with your
bare hands."

"Sorta."

"And you broke in here."

"Yes, sir. I was concerned about Miss Franklin."

"I know who you are. Come down here, why don'tcha."

Josh wearily climbed down the steps and leaned against
the wall. "I think my ribs are broken."

"We got an ambulance on the way."

"What tipped you off?"

"That nine-one-one call. We traced it."

He heard a commotion and two more officers entered, one of them Monroe County Sheriff Bush Whitcomb. Bush was a bandy-legged little rooster with a handlebar mustache and a pearl-handled revolver. Deputy Bragg, the big one, filled him in while the other deputy checked the bodies.

The EMPs took Josh outside to an ambulance, examined him, taped up his ribs.

"That's some tattoo," said a tiny brunette as she wrapped the tape around his torso.

"Hides the bruises," Josh said.

She traced a long, diagonal scar across his abdomen. "What's this?"

"Mountain lion."

"Yeah, right."

Franklin steamed by, did a double-take and doubled back. "Where is she?"

"I don't know, boss. Last I saw her, she was up in the bleachers with Hochrein."

"Hochrein?"

"Hans Gruber. His real name is Heinrich Hochrein. He founded Sustainable Protocols, which is that cult that grabbed Jane in Paraguay. I think it was Jane's idea for him to come here, to use your facilities to advance their agenda."

"What agenda?"

Josh smiled. "Dat ol' ubermensch! If you can breed a superior bull, you can breed a superior man! I suspect they used your facilities for human gene mapping, and they were trying to get hold of a million bucks to buy some kind of fancy gene mapping machine. That's what the kidnapping was all about. Orlok didn't know boo about it."

Franklin was stunned. "But she told me..."

"Don't try to make sense of it, Mr. Franklin. It doesn't make sense."

Pointing a finger, Franklin headed for the facility. "We'll talk later."

Bush approached holding a cell phone. "Do you know a federal agent named Stoeckle?"

"Yes, sir."

Bush handed Josh the phone.

"Josh here."

"It's cover your ass time at the State Department and the NSA. Hochrein should never have been granted a visa. We are talking to Paraguayan National Security Forces."

"You're gonna raid the farm."

"How'd you guess? Where's Kuhn?"

"He split about ten minutes before the cops got here. I think he was on his bike. Did you raid Moore?"

"That's the Feeb's problem. I don't think they can find him. How are you doing?"

"Oh, you know. The usual cracked ribs. I'll survive."

"When can I expect a report?"

"I gotta crash. Next forty-eight hours."

"Is there any threat from these guys?"

"Not anymore. Bunch of crackpots, hoss. But mean. They tried to kill me. I'll tell you all about it in the report."

"Get a phone."

"Yes, sir."

They found Jane's backpack in the bleachers, empty, except for some used tissue and the tracking device. Franklin checked his slush fund. She'd never found the safe. It was three a.m. before they cleared Josh to leave, but he was too sore to ride his bike. Deputy Bragg ran him home in his cruiser. They heard Fig barking from inside the house.

Josh swallowed four ibuprofen and crashed. He woke with Fig beside him, on her back, four legs in the air, snoring. Light shone through the window. It was ten-thirty. When he tried to sit up it was like someone threw open the emergency exit only. Lights, sirens, and pain. He moved like a segmented worm into the bathroom, filled the tub and eased himself in. Josh toweled himself off, took more ibuprofen and went back to bed.

He woke to the doorbell ringing. It was two-thirty. Painfully he pulled on a pair of jeans and went to the front door using the wall for support. Detective Calloway stood on his stoop wearing a striped gray seersucker jacket over a black shirt with a purple tie, a gray fedora, aviator shades, holding a Rocky's pizza box.

Josh let him in. Calloway took the pizza into the kitchen and returned carrying two cans of ginger ale, handing one to Josh.

"You look like shit."

"A goddamn snake cracked my ribs and then that fucking buffalo finished me off."

"I hear that every day," the detective said, sinking into a Swedish modern chair. "I was on the west side, figured I'd stop in."

Josh carefully lowered himself onto the sofa as Fig laid her snout on the detective's seersucker pants. He gently pushed her away.

"Don't shed on the pants, Fig."

"What's up," Josh said.

"Still looking for Jane and Orlok. Ralph Symons was shot in Dubuque by a motorist with a concealed carry when he tried to boost the car.

"Who's Ralph Symons?" Josh said.

"His club name was Feral. He's the only one who surfaced. Law enforcement is questioning every Jugan they can find, which is about seventy. The rest are in the wind."

Fig leaped up next to Josh and curled up. "Jane and Hochrein were in cahoots. He was a bugfuck crazy neo-Nazi trying to engineer the perfect genetic specimen."

"Feds found a shitload of steroids at his house, plus several canisters of bull jizm, whatever you call 'em, in his refrigerator."

"They're called bells. But he wasn't the sperm thief. Jane talked some poor shmuck named Pat Murphy into stealing the sperm. He was in love with her. So she ran over him with that truck we found out at the farm."

"The department owes you. What snake?"

"A fucking anaconda. It tried to eat me."

Calloway took off his glasses, set them on the table,

leaned forward with his forearms on his thighs, and popped Josh with his high beams. Calloway's pupils were surrounded by white. One stared at Josh. The other stared at a corner of the ceiling.

"Dish, girl."

CHAPTER

62

Calloway grinned like a motherfucker as Josh told him about Paraguay.

"You should write this shit down. Nobody would believe it."

"I hardly believe it myself," Josh said. "Now I just want to hang here and catch up Game of Thrones."

Calloway stood. "Gotta go. Lunch is on me next time."

Josh watched Calloway walk to his plainclothes Dodge, as inconspicuous as a monitor lizard. Josh read his email, responding immediately to Kleiser.

"Still here," Kleiser wrote. "Will stop by after work with phone. Anything you need?"

"Could you get me some beef bones at the butcher?" Josh wrote.

"You gonna cook?"

"They're for Fig. I can hardly move."

Kleiser appeared at five-thirty with two bags full of groceries. He carried them into the kitchen, put them away, came back with two beers and handed Josh an iPhone. "That's my old phone. I reconfigured it with your number, but you lost all your contacts. You'll have to reenter them."

Josh took a slug of beer. "Where's Jane?"

"She's off the radar," Kleiser said, popping a Capital lager and sitting in the Swedish chair.

Josh sat on the sofa with his feet up on the coffee table. "She musta figured out I was tracking her at the farm. But she never got the money. On the other hand, she can take care of herself."

"The feds are charging her with espionage. They want Orlok for gun-running and stealing from the Army, plus federal charges for the marijuana farm."

"What about you, hoss? What are you gonna do?"

"I turned in my thirty-day notice. I'm outta here."

"Surprised you let 'em know."

"Dovetail's a good organization. They've treated me well. They asked if I'd stick around and train my replacement and I said sure, as long as he was here tomorrow."

"How'm I gonna replace you, Randall?"

"Fuck, man. It's been real. I'd hug ya but I don't want to hurt ya. I know a guy, black dude lives in St. Louis. His name is Ninja Preston. I'll put you in touch."

"I appreciate that, Randall. Will you stay in touch?"

Kleiser smiled and laid a finger on his nose. "I'm the Black Widower. I'll be in touch."

A week later Josh felt pretty good. His ribs healed faster every time he broke them. On a warm Tuesday in September, Peggy Albright phoned.

"The candidate would like to take you up on your offer. Can you meet her at her campaign headquarters tomorrow?"

"Sure. What time?"

"Come at one. Can you bring two helmets?"

"Sure."

Sheila Livermore-Epstein's Campaign Headquarters was a store front in a strip mall on the South Beltline, between an aquarium supply shop and a company that sold Venetian blinds. Josh pulled up and kicked out in front of the entrance wearing an open-face helmet and goggles, another helmet bungeed to the pillion.

The candidate herself came out with Peggy, a diminutive, smiling, silver-haired woman wearing Ray-Bans. She took Josh's hand in both of hers.

"Thank you so much for doing this, Mr. Pratt. Peggy has told me all about you."

"My pleasure, ma'am. How much time have you got?"

"A half hour."

The candidate wore jeans and sensible shoes. Josh handed her the helmet, got on the bike, and waited for her to mount behind him.

"Put your hands around my waist."

"Feels like you're taped up," she said. "I heard about your encounter with that bull."

"They're coming off tomorrow. Hang on."

Josh headed west on Schroeder Road, cut over to J, heading northwest of Mt. Horeb. A light breeze tossed leaves across the wooded rural roads.

"It's magnificent," Sheila said. "I can't believe I've never done this before!"

Josh rode smoothly with no sudden acceleration or deceleration. They ended up at Brigham Park with an expansive view of Blue Mounds State Park and the Baraboo Hills. Sheila got off, removed her helmet, and shook her short hair.

"I can't believe this. I'm actually thinking of getting a motorcycle. But they're so big!"

"They have little bikes, ma'am. My advice, spend a thousand dollars on a small displacement bike and enroll in some motorcycle riding courses."

"Could you teach me?"

"Sure, but I get two hundred dollars a day."

The candidate laughed. Her phone rang. She stepped away and spoke intensely for a few minutes, turning and slipping the phone into her pants pocket. "I'm running late. Can you take me back?"

"What about the helmet law? I know I speak for most bikers when we say let those who ride decide."

"The problem is, when somebody crashes and has expensive medical treatment, if they don't have insurance or resources, those expenses fall on everybody else."

"I'm aware of that, ma'am, but you must remember that bikers embody the virtues of the cowboy. We're self-sufficient and often successful. People have a right to take risks."

Sheila put a hand on his arm. "I'll tell you what. I will think about it. I will even meet with motorcycle executives and biker associations to discuss it. In the meantime, I'm removing it from my campaign platform. All it does is piss people off."

Josh laughed in delight. "I also provide security."

She patted his bicep. "I'll keep that in mind."

A half hour later, he dropped her off at campaign headquarters. There was a WMAD news van pulled up in front and Katy Varner, wearing a smart yellow sundress and a broad-brimmed straw hat, chatted with Peggy while her cameraman stood nearby smoking a cigarette. Katy's mouth opened when she saw Josh pull up. Josh waved and pulled out before she could talk to him.

Katy Varner had been dogging Josh ever since the Jesuit incident. She'd made no secret of her admiration, but the last thing Josh needed was to get involved with a careerist newscaster. He glanced in the rearview. Katy stood with hands on hips watching him go.

Josh wanted nothing more than to be left alone. Deliver summons for Fleiss because a man couldn't just sit around. He longed for the camaraderie of the Bedouins, but he was forbidden by law from joining a gang.

It was a short drive to his home on Ptarmigan Road. A weathered 2000 Camaro sat in his yard with mag wheels and mismatched tires. A horse needle penetrated Josh's heart, he didn't know why. The front door was open. Anybody could have gained entrance through the sliding glass patio door, which he'd left unlocked inside the fenced-in back yard.

Fig barked once as Josh let himself in, eyes adjusting to the relative gloom. He smelled graphite and Axe body wash. A man sat on his sofa with Fig's head in his lap, upside down, legs in the air.

"Hey there, boy! If I could get this dog off my lap, I'd get up and hug ya!"

"Huh?" Josh said.

"What's the matter? Don't you recognize your own father?"

IF YOU LIKED THE BIKER SERIES YOU MIGHT LIKE "RETRIBUTION: A TEAM REAPER THRILLER"

After he is betrayed and shoots the two most powerful men in the Irish Mob, John "Reaper" Kane is forced into hiding. He thinks Retribution, Arizona, is the perfect hiding place, but he is wrong. Underneath the old, crusty surface of the dying town, hides the Montoya Cartel, for they use it as a funnel to ship their drugs across the border.

Trying to lay low in a town gripped with lawlessness is impossible for the ex-recon marine, especially after the local sheriff is brutally murdered by the Montoya Cartel's sicario, leaving an old friend, Deputy Sheriff Cara Billings, the only person standing between them and the town.

Things go from bad to worse when Kane is arrested by Cleaver, the deputy in the cartel's pocket, for shooting a local gang member.

Enter DEA Agent Luis Ferrero who has expressed to his bosses for a long time the need for a task force to fight the cartels on their own ground. He's about to get his wish, and to head up his team, he wants the Reaper.

A thrill ride that doesn't let you go – Retribution is the first novel in the action-packed Reaper Series.

AVAILABLE NOW ON AMAZON

ABOUT THE AUTHOR

Mike Baron is the creator of Nexus (with artist Steve Rude) and Badger two of the longest lasting independent superhero comics. Nexus is about a cosmic avenger 500 years in the future. Badger, about a multiple personality one of whom is a costumed crime fighter. First/Devils Due is publishing all new Badger stories. Baron has won two Eisners and an Inkpot award and written The Punisher, Flash, Deadman and Star Wars among many other titles.

Baron has published ten novels that span a variety of topics. They have satanic rock bands, biker zombies, spontaneous human combustion, ghosts, and overall hard-boiled crimes.

Mike Baron has written for The Boston Phoenix, Boston Globe, Oui, Fusion, Creem, Isthmus, Front Page Mag, and Ellery Queen's Mystery Magazine.